Cooking For Life

Recipes for Health & Healing

Cherie Calbom
Vicki Rae Chelf

The health procedures in this book are based on the training, personal experiences, and research of the authors. Because each person and situation is unique, the publisher urges the reader to check with a qualified health professional before using any procedure where there is any question as to its appropriateness.

The publisher does not advocate the use of any particular diet program, but believes that the information presented in this book should be available to the public.

Because there is always some risk involved, the authors and publisher are not responsible for any adverse effects or consequences resulting from the use of any of the suggestions, preparations, or procedures in this book. Please do not use the book if you are unwilling to assume the risk. Feel free to consult a physician or other qualified health professional. It is a sign of wisdom, not cowardice, to seek a second or third opinion.

Cover Design: Whitney Pearce
Cover Photo: Michels Advertising Photography
Food Stylist: Amy Muzyka-McGuire
In-House Editor: Elaine Will Sparber
Typesetter: Bonnie Freid
Printer: Paragon Press, Honesdale, Pennsylvania

Library of Congress Cataloging-in-Publication Data

Calbom, Cherie
Cooking for life / Cherie Calbom, Vicki Rae Chelf.
p. cm.
Includes bibliographical references and index.
ISBN 0-89529-553-9
1. Fruit juices—Health aspects. 2. Vegetable juices—Health aspects. 3. Cookery (Fruit) 4. Cookery (Vegetables) I. Chelf, Vicki Rae. II. Title.
RA784.C225 1993
641.605'63—dc20 93-2737
CIP

Printed in the United States of America.

10 9 8 7 6 5 4 3 2 1

Contents

Preface

In April 1991, the Physicians Committee for Responsible Medicine (PCRM) proposed four new food groups as a replacement for the basic four food groups developed in 1956. The proposed four food groups were whole grains, vegetables, legumes, and fruits. A year later, in April 1992, the United States Department of Agriculture officially replaced the old four food groups—meat, poultry, and fish; dairy and eggs; fruits and vegetables; and breads and cereals—with the Food Guide Pyramid. Incorporating the PCRM's new four food groups, the pyramid features four levels and six groups of foods. The base group of the pyramid is formed by breads, cereals, rice, and pasta. Resting above it is the just slightly less important second level, composed of the (you guessed it!) vegetable group and fruit group. The less important third and fourth layers of the pyramid include the animal products, which should be used in small quantities. The fourth layer, at the very top, is composed of fats, oils, and sweets, to be used very sparingly.

Why the change? Mounting evidence supports the healthful effects of a diet rich in fresh, whole foods, low in fat and cholesterol, and as low as possible in processed and refined foods. Nutritionists and health professionals alike have hailed the new pyramid. Melissa Goldman, director of Public Affairs for the PCRM, notes, "We think it's beneficial to change the center of our diet to a plant base because of the overwhelming rates of heart disease, cancer, and stroke. People don't need to eat meat

Food Guide Pyramid

A Guide to Daily Food Choices

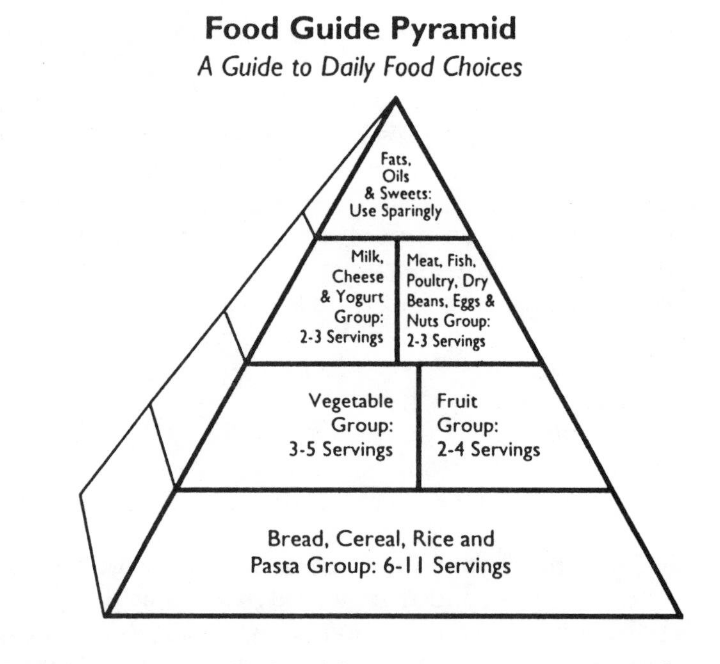

and dairy products to be healthy. You can get protein from other sources."

We agree with Ms. Goldman. That's why *Cooking for Life* reflects the new Food Guide Pyramid. Very few recipes have animal products among their ingredients. What you find instead is an abundance of tasty vegetables, whole grains, legumes, and fruits. We have also incorporated fresh juices and pulps in the recipes so that *Cooking for Life* can be used as a companion to *Juicing for Life*.

In addition to their healthful benefits, fresh juices and pulps will also add a whole new visual dimension to your cooking. As an artist, the first thing Vicki noticed when she started to cook with juices and pulps was the incredibly beautiful coloring of the finished dishes. Fruits and vegetables are so rich in natural pigments that their juices and pulps impart luscious, vibrant hues to all the foods with which they are combined. Cooking with juices and pulps allows you to push ordinary dishes into a realm of technicolor fantasy that is certain to delight everyone who tries them. Imagine bright green cornbread served with a steaming bowl of orange-colored soup!

Beautiful color is only the beginning. Fruit and vegetable juices are highly concentrated sources of vitamins and minerals.

Using juices in your daily food preparation is an easy way to naturally enrich everything you serve. The leftover pulp is a bonus. By using pulp in your recipes, you add valuable fiber to your diet. What's more, the recipes in this book are virtually cholesterol-free and low in fat, and contain no refined flours or refined sugars.

The concentrated nature of fresh fruit and vegetable juices gives you not only more vitamins and minerals but more flavor as well. Juices are light-tasting in addition to rich-tasting—a seeming contradition, yes, but a delicious truth—so the recipes made with juice are a superb mixture of lightness and richness. Wonderful textures also await you as you investigate the delights of cooking with juice and pulp.

You'll find *Cooking for Life* easy to use even if you're a novice cook. If you're just learning either natural-foods cooking or juicing, we suggest that you read Part One of this book for the basics, such as descriptions of the various fruits and vegetables used in the recipes, how to choose and prepare fruits and vegetables for juicing, how to store juice and pulp, and how to use pulp in recipes. Also included are a glossary describing in detail the other healthy ingredients used in the recipes, tips for selecting a juice extractor, and pointers on how to use the recipes, which are presented in Part Two.

To introduce your loved ones to healthier eating, try cooking one of their favorite recipes and accompanying it with a wonderful soup, salad, bread, or dessert made with juice or pulp. Check the menu suggestions offered in Part Three for ideas on how to create delicious balanced meals using juice and pulp recipes. We have included our favorite menus for entertaining, holiday dinners, and easy family meals, and we know you'll soon create your own special menus chosen from the delightful array of recipes provided in Part Two. We have also included a troubleshooting section that lists which recipes combat which health problems.

Cooking for Life is a complete cookbook, one that will become a basic resource in your kitchen. Fruits and vegetables are just two types of whole food, but they are important foods. Their juice and pulp can turn ordinary dishes into healthy, tasty, and beautiful gifts for your family. We hope you enjoy *Cooking for Life*. May our book become your trusted companion for many memorable, healthful meals!

Vicki Rae Chelf

Introduction

There is a revolution going on out there. People who have for years quietly questioned the types of commercial foods available to them are now taking things into their own hands. Instead of being swayed by terms such as "instant," "processed," "highly refined," "long lasting," and "enriched," people are now making a conscious effort to seek out foods that are labeled "fresh," "natural," "nutritious," and "whole." And why shouldn't they, since the latest scientific evidence clearly indicates that eating the right foods is directly related to the state of a person's health?

As a nutritionist, it is very gratifying to talk to someone who has rediscovered the wonderful tastes of wholesome foods that contain no additives, colorings, extenders, hydrogenated oils, artifical sweeteners, preservatives, etc. As an author, it is even more gratifying to see how my first book, *Juicing for Life*, has helped people take a little more control over their lives.

When the juicing craze began, I was fortunate enough to be in a position to speak to literally thousands of people throughout the United States about the power of fresh juices. As my nutrition workshops took me to almost every state in the Union, I was continously asked the same question: "How can I incorporate juicing into my daily diet?" With *Juicing for Life*, my coauthor and I were able to provide a basic resource for using juices effectively for various health disorders. With *Cooking for Life*, I can now present a unique cookbook that is an extension of my first book and, at the same time, provides new and exciting food ideas.

Working with my coauthor, natural food chef Vicki Rae Chelf, has enabled me to maximize both taste and presentation in all our recipes while sacrificing none of the nutritional values. In addition, our recipes allow the avid juicer to use the fruit and vegetable pulp created in the juicing process. The pulp now becomes an intregal and important part of a well-balanced diet.

Cooking with pulp is a new concept for most Americans. Quality nutrition is the best reason for using pulp in recipes. Though the majority of the nutrients found in fruits and vegetables are present in the juice, some remain in the pulp. Pulp also provides valuable fiber. Now you can use every part of the fresh fruits and vegetables you juice to pack exceptional nutrition into your daily diet. For example, replace milk with colorful juices in bread, muffin, and soup recipes. You'll decrease fat and cholesterol while increasing nutrients. Mix pulp into vegetarian burgers, salads, and muffins. You'll increase fiber. And discover delightful new desserts using pulp, juices, and small amounts of natural sweetener. You'll give your body valuable nutrients instead of the normal abundance of empty calories.

I am so excited about this *Juicing for Life* sequel, which I hope will help you to get the maximum nutritional benefits from the fruits and vegetables you juice. In *Cooking for Life*, you'll find over 100 great-tasting juice recipes plus more than 150 recipes using juice and/or pulp as ingredients. I know you'll be as pleased as I was to discover how delicious these recipes are. For example, when I made Spaghetti With Tomato Sauce (page 236) and Vegetarian Meatballs (page 237), a bit of the meatball mixture was left over. The next evening, I decided to form this mixture into hamburger-style patties, which I cooked and served on whole grain buns and accompanied with onion, lettuce, and mayonnaise. My husband, who has been a red-meat lover all his life, thought they were the best "hamburgers" he'd ever had. What a great surprise!

You, too, can use the recipes in this cookbook to hook the meat-and-potatoes or junk-food lovers in your house. Start by serving one of the nutritious desserts. Make a smoothie for breakfast or one of the pancake recipes for weekend brunch. Try Carrot-Cabbage Salad With Pink Yogurt Dressing (page 190)—it's a winner with everyone! Then get brave and try a main course recipe, such as Springtime Pasta (page 244) or Vegetable Quiche (page 252). Have fun in the kitchen. Enjoy eating all these fabulous low-fat foods. And get ready to feast your eyes on some of the most visually appealing dishes you'll ever see. You'll discover firsthand that juicing offers no waste at all; everything can be used. And most importantly, your health will reap the rewards.

Wishing you the best of health!

Cherie Calbom, M.S.
Nutritionist

PART ONE

The Basics

About the Fruits and Vegetables

To help you select the best fruits and vegetables for use in our recipes, we have assembled the following guide. It includes tips on selecting and preparing the fruit or vegetable; explains which part of the fruit or vegetable is the best part to use and what, if anything, should be discarded; and provides an estimate of how many pieces of the fruit or vegetable to use for what amount of juice. The entries additionally explain when the fruit or vegetable is available and how to store it, and provide information on how to use the juice or pulp in food preparation, noting which juices go well together. Sample recipes using the juice or pulp are also listed.

Apple

The apple is one of the world's oldest fruits, found in prehistoric Swiss lake dwellings. The fruit of a tree of the rose family, it is believed to have originated in western Asia but is now cultivated worldwide. The wild crabapple is parent to all of today's varieties. The most important temperate fruit commercially, the apple boasted 8,000 varieties in the United States alone at the beginning of the twentieth century. Only about 1,000 remain today, with a mere handful in common use. In the United States, the leading producer of apples is Washington, which calls the Red Delicious, the most popular variety, its native son. Other major producers are New York, California, Michigan, North Carolina, Pennsylvania, and Virginia. Other popular varieties are Winesap, McIntosh, Golden Delicious, Jonathan, Stayman, Cortland, Granny Smith, and Newton Pippins.

Season: Apples are available year-round because they come in summer, fall, and winter varieties. However, in the spring you take your chances since they probably have been pulled from cold storage. Most apple harvesting in the United States begins in late summer, around August or early September.

Selection: For juicing, choose crisp, firm apples; they contain the most juice. Mushy or mealy apples become too soupy when juiced. Cooking apples and immature apples do not have enough juice.

Preparation: Simply wash an apple if it's organic; peel it if it's non-organic or waxed. If juicing the apple, cut it into wedges that will fit through the hopper of the juice extractor. You can also juice the core, but first remove the seeds as they contain small amounts of cyanide. Many times you can simply flick the seeds out, but if they are hard to reach, cut out the core. If using the pulp, don't juice the core.

Juice yield: Three medium apples (approximately one pound) will yield about one cup of juice.

Storage: Keep apples cold, either in a refrigerator or root cellar.

Uses: Apple juice is a great mixer in almost any combination. When another juice is mixed with apple, the flavor of the other juice usually dominates. Apple juice goes very well with the juice of strawberries, cherries, cranberries, pineapples, peaches, pears, grapes, blueberries, mangoes, kiwis, carrots, celery, beets, all leafy greens, and even small amounts of rhubarb. Try running a small piece of ginger or approximately one-quarter of a lemon through the juice extractor along with the apples for a tasty change. For some delicious drinks, try Pink Lemonade on page 85, Ginger Hopper on page 91, and Beet-It Express on page 96. Apple juice and pulp also add something special to many cooked dishes, such as Apple-Strawberry Pancakes on page 125, Apple-Cinnamon Muffins on page 144, and Apple-Cinnamon Upside-Down Cake on page 285.

Apricot

Called Moon of the Faithful in Asian countries, the apricot is the fruit of a tree that belongs to the rose family. It is native to China, where it has been growing wild for 4,000 years. From China the apricot spread throughout Asia, then was brought to Greece and Italy by Alexander the Great. The Arabs carried it throughout the Mediterranean, and by the fifteenth century A.D., it was popular in Europe. Brought to North America in the seventeenth century, the apricot was found growing in abundance in Virginia in 1720. Later that century, Mission Fathers brought it to California, where it was discovered growing in Santa Clara in 1792. A summer fruit, the apricot today is grown in the western United States, with California producing around 97 percent of the crop. About six varieties are sold commercially, including the Blenheim, Tilton, Early Montgamet, and Wenatchee.

Season: Apricots are available from May through August, but especially during the peak months of June and July.

Selection: For juicing, try to find tree-ripened apricots, which are rare. Tree-ripened apricots are sweeter than fruits ripened after picking, which are more sour. Choose apricots that are golden yellow, nearly orange. Avoid light yellow or greenish fruits. Look for apricots that are plump, smooth, and slightly soft, yielding to gentle pressure.

Preparation: Wash apricots, cut them in half, and remove the stone. The kernels inside apricot stones should not be ingested since they contain the compound amygdalin.

Juice yield: Five apricots will yield approximately one-half cup of juice.

Storage: An apricot will ripen at room temperature. Refrigerate ripe apricots for up to three or five days.

Uses: Apricot juice is rather thick by itself and tastes best when combined with other juices such as apple. See Apricot Nectar on page 86. A recipe using whole apricots is Orange-Cinnamon Pancakes With Apricot-Orange Sauce on page 126. A recipe using apricot jam is Carrot Cake Icing on page 280.

Asparagus

Asparagus, a member of the lily family, is a perennial garden vegetable. Originally grown in the eastern Mediterranean, it is now cultivated worldwide, preferring fertile and sandy regions. Long in use, asparagus was described by the ancient Egyptians, Greeks, Romans, and Phoenicians. However, it seems to have disappeared during the Middle Ages everywhere but in the Arab countries. It finally surfaced in Europe again during the reign of Louis XIV of France. Cultivated asparagus is found in three colors: white, green, and purple. The white Argenteuil variety is considered the best, although green asparagus is the most nutritious. In the United States, where the Mary Washington variety is the most common, asparagus is grown in California, New Jersey, Washington, Michigan, Maryland, Delaware, Pennsylvania, Massachusetts, Illinois, and Iowa.

Season: Asparagus can be found from February through July, although its peak months are April, May, and June.

Selection: For juicing, choose asparagus spears that are either young and firm or large but tender. Avoid angular or flat stalks, which may be woody. The tips of asparagus spears should be closed; open tips indicate stringiness. Also watch for wilting and signs of decay, and avoid stalks that have been sitting in water for a while.

Preparation: Just wash asparagus thoroughly and break the stalks at the point where they snap easily. The tough bottom part of the spears, which is generally thrown away, is great for juicing. Save the tender tops for steaming.

Juice yield: The bottoms from one pound of asparagus spears will yield one-quarter to one-half cup of juice.

Storage: Wrap asparagus in either a damp cloth or wax paper and keep it refrigerated. Heat and dryness reduce asparagus's sugar content and increase its fiber content, making it almost inedible. If a stalk becomes limp, cut off a piece from the bottom on the diagonal and stand the stalk in water, but only for a short time.

Uses: Add asparagus juice to soups, stews, and sauces. It also works wonderfully in salads, such as Vegetable Terrine on page 185, and in main dishes, such as Spinach-Asparagus Quiche on page 254. It mixes well with any juice made from greens, sprouts, or vegetables. In any of the recipes in this book requiring a green juice, asparagus juice may be used to replace an equal amount of any other juice.

Beet and Beet Top

The beet, grown since pre-Christian times, is a root vegetable once used only for medicinal purposes. It originated in the Mediterranean, then spread to the Near East. In the fourth century A.D., beet recipes were recorded in England, and beginning in the nineteenth century, the plant was cultivated for sugar in France and Germany. At least one variety of beet was grown in the United States in 1806. Several varieties of beets are currently grown. They include the red beet, also known as the garden beet, and the sugar beet. Sugar beets, which are white, provide about one-third of the world's sugar supply. Garden beets range in color from dark reddish purple to bright vermillion to white, but the most common variety is red. Most commercial beets grown in the United States come from California, New Jersey, Ohio, and Texas.

Season: Beet roots are available all year, but especially from May through October. Beet tops are available from March through October.

Selection: For juicing, choose beet roots that are firm, well shaped, and medium to large in size. The color should be deep. Avoid beet roots that are spotted, scaly, or woody. Choose beet tops that are thin-ribbed. They are more tender.

Preparation: Both beet roots and tops are edible and excellent for juicing. If juicing a beet, first wash the top and scrub the root. If the root is large, trim the top from the root, then cut the root into chunks that will fit through the hopper of the juice extractor. Small beets can be juiced in one piece.

Juice yield: Two medium-size beets (approximately two inches in diameter) will yield about one-half cup of juice. One small bunch of beet tops will yield approximately 1 tablespoon of juice.

Storage: If the beet roots and tops are attached, cut them apart and use the tops as soon as possible. Keep the roots cold, either by wrapping them in plastic and storing them in a refrigerator for up to three weeks, or by keeping them in a root cellar for up to several months.

Uses: Beet-root juice is very strong, so use it in small quantities. One or two ounces of beet-root juice can be mixed with carrot, apple, lemon, lime, or cucumber juice. Beet-root juice is also an excellent food coloring. Just juice a one-inch or smaller cube of beet root and add the juice to whatever you wish to tint shocking pink! Try the recipe for Pink Potatoes on page 229. Also see the recipes for Pink Lemonade on page 85, Borscht on page 174, Carrot-Cabbage Salad With Pink Yogurt Dressing on page 190, and Beet Cake on page 281.

Beet tops are very nutrient-rich, being an excellent source of beta-carotene and the minerals calcium, magnesium, manganese, and iron. Although strong tasting, the juice of two or three beet tops mixes well with other juices. For example, beet tops are a nutritious and delicious addition to Chlorophyll Cocktail on page 95 and Beet-It Express on page 96. They can also easily be added to such combinations as Beet Surprise on page 95 or Red Sunset on page 96. In fact, if the beet as a whole is small enough, just wash it and push the entire vegetable—root, stems, and leaves—through the hopper of the juice extractor. There is no need to cut up the beet in this case.

Bell Pepper

Bell peppers, also known as sweet peppers, are annual or perennial herbaceous plants that belong to the nightshade family. They come in green or red, but the only difference between the two colors is age: red peppers are ripened green peppers. Yellow peppers can also be found occasionally. Bell peppers are cousins to the hotter peppers such as cayenne, chili, paprika, and pimiento peppers. They are native to the warm temperate and tropical regions of the Americas, originally Brazil. They were introduced to Europe after the discovery of the Americas. In the United States, the leading commercial varieties of bell peppers include Bellringer, Bell Boy, California Wonder, Merrimack Wonder, and Worldbeater. The leading producers of winter peppers are California, Florida, and Texas. Summer peppers come from southern, midwestern, and eastern growers.

Season: Bell peppers are available all year long, with a peak supply in markets in June through September.

Selection: For juicing, choose firm, shiny bell peppers that are heavy for their size and, preferably, unwaxed. The skin should be smooth and the flesh thick. The color, whether green, red, or yellow, should be medium to dark. Avoid peppers with soft spots.

Preparation: Wash bell peppers, then cut them in half and remove the seeds. If juicing the peppers, cut them into pieces that will fit through the hopper of the juice extractor.

Juice yield: One medium bell pepper will yield approximately one-quarter cup of juice.

Storage: Keep bell peppers in a plastic bag in the refrigerator at average humidity for up to one week.

Uses: Bell-pepper juice is surprisingly mild. It adds zest to tomato, cucumber, and carrot juices. Try Salad in a Glass on page 99 or Zippy Tomato Express on page 100. Use bell-pepper juice in soups, sauces, and stews. See the recipe for Sweet and Hot Pepper Sauce on page 206.

Blackberry

Blackberries grow on bramble bushes that belong to the rose family. Native to North America and Europe, the bushes grow wild along hedges, in woods, and in untilled fields in most of the northern hemisphere and South Africa. The blackberry is not really a berry but rather an aggregate of tiny stone-containing fruits. It is related to the raspberry, dewberry, loganberry, boysenberry, youngberry, and cloudberry. Historical findings show that the blackberry was one of man's first foods. It was mentioned by Aeschylus and Hippocrates around 400 to 500 B.C. Cultivation of the fruit was slow because of its wide availability, but several varieties have been grown since 1850, including a thornless variety for market. Cultivation of the blackberry is limited mainly to North America and Britain. In the United States, the leading producers are Texas and Oregon.

Season: Blackberries are available from May through August.

Selection: For juicing, choose blackberries that are bright, plump, and clean. Use berries that are a full black or blue color; avoid berries that are partly green or off-color. Blackberries should be fresh, solid, and dry. Avoid runny berries, and check the bottom of the container for wet or moldy spots.

Preparation: Immediately before using blackberries, rinse them under cold running water and drain them in a colander. Remove the stems and pick out any damaged berries.

Juice yield: One pint of blackberries will yield approximately one-half cup of juice.

Storage: Keep blackberries, unwashed and uncovered, in the refrigerator for one or two days. Blackberries must be kept dry.

Uses: Blackberries make an interesting addition to juice recipes such as Australian Surprise on page 88 and Sweet Magnesium Smoothie on page 108.

Blueberry

Blueberries grow wild on shrubs that belong to the heath family. Related to huckleberries and cranberries, they also resemble bilberries, or whortleberries, which are not as sweet. During World War II, British Royal Air Force pilots were given blueberry preserves before night missions because the berries supposedly improve night vision. After the war, studies showed that blueberry extracts do in fact improve nighttime sharpness, adjustment to darkness, and restoration of acuity after exposure to glare. Blueberries have been cultivated since 1909, but the wild varieties, while smaller than the commercial types, still taste superior. Both are popular, though. The favorite cultivated types are high-bush and low-bush blueberries. Leading production in the United States are New Jersey, Michigan, Maine, North Carolina, Washington, and Oregon.

Season: Blueberries are available for six to eight weeks sometime between May and September. The specific weeks vary with the area.

Selection: For juicing, choose clean, plump, well-rounded blueberries that are fairly uniform in size. They should be a bright, deep blue, black, or purple and appear slightly frosted. Look for fresh, firm, dry berries; check the carton for running juices and wet or moldy spots. Overripe blueberries will be dull, soft, and watery.

Preparation: Immediately before using blueberries, rinse them under cold running water and drain them in a colander. Leave the stems in, but pick out any damaged berries.

Juice yield: One pint of blueberries will yield approximately one-half cup of juice.

Storage: Keep blueberries, unwashed and uncovered, in the refrigerator for one or two days. Blueberries must be kept dry.

Uses: A great way to use those extra summer blueberries you can't eat is to make a blender smoothie such as Berry Smooth on page 111 or to juice the berries and add sparkling water as with Minty Blueberry Fizz on page 115.

Broccoli

Broccoli is a variety of cabbage, which belongs to the mustard family. Also known as Italian asparagus, it is related to cauliflower, kale, collards, turnips, rutabagas, Brussels sprouts, and Chinese cabbage. It is one of the cruciferous vegetables, known for their cancer-fighting properties, and is rich in vitamin C, beta-carotene, bioflavonoids, and calcium. Grown in Italy and France during the 1500s, broccoli was not well known in the United States until 1923, when the D'Arrigo Brothers Company planted a trial crop of Italian sprouting broccoli in California. After a few crates of the harvest were sent to Boston, the market was born. Since then, the demand for broccoli has been steadily increasing. Most of the domestic crop comes from California, with some from Arizona and Texas. Popular varieties are De Cicco, Calbrese, Waltham 29, and Green Comet.

Season: Broccoli is available year-round, with the least available during July and August, and the most from October through May.

Selection: For juicing, choose broccoli in a compact bunch, with florets that are small, closed, and dark or purplish green, depending on the variety. Avoid broccoli with yellow or wilted leaves. Also bypass broccoli with florets that have opened and show tiny yellow flowers. The size of the stalks is not important, but the stems and branches should be firm yet tender, not woody. The stems should be solid; check the bottoms of the stems to make sure they're solid throughout.

Preparation: Soak broccoli in cold water for ten minutes to remove any dirt and insects, then rinse it under running water. Remove the tough outer leaves and cut off the dried ends of the stalks. If juicing the broccoli, cut it into pieces small enough to fit through the hopper of the juice extractor.

Juice yield: Two to three stalks of broccoli will yield approximately one-half cup of juice.

Storage: Wrap broccoli in plastic and keep it in the refrigerator at high humidity for up to one week.

Uses: Broccoli makes a nutritious addition to any juice combination or recipe. For juice combinations, try Garden Cooler on page 91 and Hot Tomato on Ice on page 103. Broccoli can be added to soups such as Saint Patrick's Soup on page 162. Always an excellent side dish, it may steal the spotlight when served up as Broccoli in Cream Sauce, page 221.

Cabbage

A leafy biennial garden vegetable belonging to the mustard family, cabbage has been cultivated for over 4,000 years. It was one of man's first foods, although it isn't mentioned in the Bible. Native to western and central Europe and western Asia, cabbage was highly respected by the ancient Romans and Germans. It grows best in cool, moist climates, sprouting originally along rocky coastlines. The years of development have produced a diverse assortment of varieties. A head of cabbage can be red, white, or green; it can be round, oblong, or conical; it can have smooth or crinkled leaves. Family members include

Brussels sprouts, kohlrabi, cauliflower, collards, broccoli, and kale. In the United States, the largest producers of cabbage are Florida, Texas, California, New York, New Jersey, Colorado, Pennsylvania, and Wisconsin.

Season: Cabbage is grown throughout the year, although its peak months are October through May.

Selection: For juicing, choose heads of cabbage that are fresh, heavy, and firm, not soft, flabby, or split. Make sure the coarse outer leaves are in place, as this is a sign of freshness. Also look for leaves that are green and tender, not withered, puffy, or yellow. Avoid heads with soft rot, seed stems, or any kind of damage.

Preparation: Rinse cabbage under running water and remove any discolored outer leaves. If juicing the cabbage, cut it into wedges that will fit through the hopper of the juice extractor.

Juice yield: One pound of cabbage will yield three-quarters to one cup of juice.

Storage: Cabbage keeps best stored at high humidity in a refrigerator. In dry storage, it rapidly loses moisture. However, it does keep well in a root cellar.

Uses: Cabbage juice is surprisingly mild. It's delicious in mixed-vegetable drinks, such as Veggie Combo and Hot and Spicy Veggie Cocktail, both on page 98, and Three C's Medley on page 100. Try cabbage juice mixed with tomato or carrot juice. Use it in soups, such as Borscht on page 174, or in stews, such as Moroccan Stew on page 263.

Carrot

The carrot is an annual root vegetable, a member of the parsley family. It is probably derived from the wild carrot, also known as Queen Anne's lace, and has been cultivated as a food crop since the sixteenth century. Native to Europe, the carrot was a popular medicinal with the ancient Greeks and Romans. It came to the United States during the early colonization period and is today valued as the richest source of beta-carotene. Carrots are categorized according to color—red, yellow, or white—and size—short, medium, or long. The best are orange-yellow in color and short to medium in length. Organically grown carrots are especially sweet. Because carrots are an easy crop, they are grown in nearly every state. The major producers are Texas, Florida, and New York.

Season: Carrots are available all year.

Selection: For juicing, choose large, firm, smooth, well-shaped carrots with a good orange color. Healthy, green tops still attached indicate freshness. Avoid rough, cracked, or pale carrots, which often lack sweetness. A green tinge at the top indicates that the carrot was sunburned and has a bitter flavor. Also undesirable is a thick mass of leaf stems, a sign of a large, woody core. In addition, skip flabby or shriveled carrots, carrots with wilted greens, and trimmed carrots that are sprouting.

Preparation: Just scrub a carrot with a brush if it's organic; peel it if it's not organic. Always cut off the top; carrot greens contain toxic substances and are therefore inedible. If juicing the carrot, cut it in half lengthwise so that it will fit through the hopper of the juice extractor.

Juice yield: Five to seven medium carrots (approximately one pound) will yield about one cup of juice.

Storage: Keep carrots in a plastic bag in the refrigerator at high humidity. You can also keep them in a root cellar for several months.

Uses: Carrot juice is everybody's favorite vegetable juice. It's delicious alone or combined with the juice of celery, cabbages, tomatoes, beets, all leafy greens—really any vegetable. It adds great flavor to mixed-vegetable drinks, such as Ginger Hopper on page 91, Beet-It Express on page 96, and Veggie Combo and Hot and Spicy Veggie Cocktail, both on page 98. It also mixes well with apples and pineapples. Carrot juice is a delicious addition to breads, such as Carrot Cornbread on page 135; soups, such as Quick Carrot Soup on page 159; sauces, such as Fat-Free Mushroom Sauce on page 207; and stews, like Marinated Baked Tofu With Vegetables on page 257. In addition, carrot juice can be used to tint foods a lovely soft orange; see the recipe for Orange Potatoes on page 228. Real treats are Springtime Pasta on page 244 and Carrot Cake on page 278.

Cauliflower

Another member of the mustard family and a type of cabbage is the cauliflower. It is the same variety as broccoli and is related to kale, collards, turnips, rutabagas, Brussels sprouts, Chinese cabbage, and kohlrabi. Cauliflower is a leafy biennial garden vegetable whose name means "cabbage flower." It is one of the cruciferous vegetables, known for their cancer-fighting properties. It is, and always has been, extremely popular in Europe. Cultivated since Roman times, cauliflower is now available in more than thirty-five varieties, although only a handful are commercially grown. The popular varieties include Super Snowball, Snowball A, Dominant, Clou, White Horse, Igloo, Jet Snow, Purple Head, Burpeeana, and Self-Blanche. In the United States, California, Arizona, and New York are the main producers.

Season: Cauliflower is available year-round, with a peak from September through January and a slight dip during the summer months.

Selection: For juicing, choose cauliflower with a clean, firm, compact curd (edible portion) that is white to creamy white in color. The size of the curd is irrelevant, but the head should be heavy for its size. The outer leaves, if any, should be green, tender, and fresh. Avoid cauliflower with open flower clusters, a granular or speckled curd, yellowing leaves, or leaves dropping from the stalk. Also bypass cauliflower with a hollow core; turn the head upside-down and make sure the stalk is solid.

Preparation: Remove the outer leaves of the cauliflower and wash the head thoroughly. If juicing the cauliflower, cut it into pieces small enough to fit through the hopper of the juice extractor. The core can also be juiced.

Juice yield: One medium head of cauliflower will yield approximately one cup of juice.

Storage: Wrap cauliflower in plastic and keep it in the refrigerator at high humidity for up to three or five days.

Uses: Cauliflower can be juiced, but it is best to mix it with other juices, as in Bunny Hopper on page 99.

Celery

Celery is a biennial plant of the carrot family. Grown in temperate regions of the northern hemisphere, its forebear, wild celery, was valued by the ancient Orientals as a medicinal herb. Wild celery was also highly prized by the ancient Greeks, who not only used it as a medicament but awarded it to the winners of athletic contests and fashioned it into funeral wreaths. Cultivated first in the Middle Ages, celery today is used chiefly as a food. Two types are grown: common celery, which has a highly developed leaf stalk; and German celery, which is turnip-like with an extremely developed root. Common celery comes in green and white, but the former, especially the Pascal variety, is predominant. In the United States, the east and west coasts boast many celery producers, but the leaders are Florida and California.

Season: Celery can be found in markets all year long, but its peak season is from November through May.

Selection: For juicing, choose firm, crisp celery with a shiny luster. The best stalks are medium in length and thickness; thick stalks are often stringy. Avoid rubbery stalks, which are unpleasant to eat. Also forego celery that is developing a seed stem, an indication of poor taste.

Preparation: Just separate celery stalks from the bunch and wash them. Keep the leaves intact, if desired.

Juice yield: Three large (thirteen-inch-long) stalks of celery will yield approximately one-half cup of juice.

Storage: Keep celery wrapped in plastic in the refrigerator. Break off stalks as you need them.

Uses: Celery juice is good mixed with carrot, tomato, or apple juice or the juice of any leafy green. It's excellent in Veggie Combo on page 98. Use celery juice in any recipe that requires a green juice, such as Saint Patrick's Soup on page 162 or Green Sauce on page 204. An especially delicious recipe using celery juice is Pasta With Peas and Mushrooms in Cream Sauce on page 248.

Cherry

The fruit of trees and shrubs of the rose family, cherries have been cultivated since ancient times; the Egyptians, Romans, and Greeks all mentioned them in their writings. Cherry pits have even been found in prehistoric cave dwellings. Cherries can be classified into two species, sour and sweet, although some of the varieties sold today are a hybrid of the two. Native to eastern Europe and western Asia, sweet and sour cherries are grown everywhere between the Arctic Circle and Tropic of Cancer, with the United States ranking as one of the top four producers. Cherries are grown in every state, but Washington, Idaho, Oregon, and California are the major growers of sweet cherries, while Michigan, New York, and Wisconsin lead the pack for sour cherries. There are over 1,000 varieties of cherries, but the Bing, a sweet cherry, is by far the most popular.

Season: Sour cherries are available from June through August. Sweet cherries are available from April through August.

Selection: For juicing, choose dark-colored cherries that are shiny and full. These are the sweetest. They should be firm to the touch but not hard, just soft enough to be ripe. Avoid cherries with dark-colored stems.

Preparation: Pick through cherries and discard any mushy ones. Then rinse the remainder and remove their stems and pits.

Juice yield: One pound of cherries will yield three-quarters to one cup of juice.

Storage: Keep cherries in the refrigerator.

Uses: Pitting cherries can be time-consuming, but cherry juice is especially delicious. It's also very concentrated and can be diluted with water, sparkling water, or another fruit juice. Cherry juice is good with apple, peach, grape, or pineapple juice. Try mixing pear, apple, and cherry juices or peach, apple, and cherry juices. Also try Pineapple-Cherry Cocktail on page 83 and Cherry Cream on page 110.

Coconut

Coconuts are the fruit of the coco palm tree, the most important plant in the tropical and subtropical regions of the world. Cultivated for 3,000 years in southern Asia and on the East Indian islands, the tree can be traced back to the Malay Archipelago and tropical areas of the Americas. Now found along all tropical coasts, it is so highly valued because almost every part of it is utilized. The trunk is used as timber, the leaves for baskets and thatch, and the terminal buds as food. The fruit, really a single-seeded nut, is a major food item as well as the source of coconut milk; coconut oil; husk fibers, made into cordage and mats; and nutshells, made into containers. Some coconuts are grown along the Florida coast and sold to local tourists. The coconuts sold in markets are imported, mainly from Honduras, Panama, and the Dominican Republic.

Season: Coconuts can be found in markets throughout the year, but the peak months are October, November, and December.

Selection: For juicing, choose a coconut that seems heavy for its size. Shake it; you should hear liquid sloshing around inside. Avoid coconuts without liquid since this indicates the fruit has spoiled. Also bypass coconuts that have moldy or wet "eyes," the three dark, soft spots at the top of the shell.

Preparation: To begin, pierce the softest eye on a coconut shell with a knife or ice pick. Place the coconut over a glass or bowl and let the liquid drain out. The best way we know to crack a coconut shell is to place the drained coconut in a 375°F oven for five to ten minutes, then remove it and tap it forcefully with a hammer. Not only will the coconut easily break apart, but the flesh will already be loosened from the shell. Simply rinse the flesh and, if juicing it, break it into pieces small enough to fit through the hopper of the juice extractor.

Juice yield: One coconut will yield one-half to three-quarters cup of juice.

Storage: Keep coconut meat cold, in the refrigerator in a plastic bag. An unopened coconut does not need to be refrigerated.

Uses: Coconut juice, which is the consistency of cream, is good mixed with coconut milk (first strain the milk through a fine wire sieve to clean out any small pieces of shell). Combine one part coconut mixture with two to three parts pineapple juice for an absolutely divine, natural Piña Colada! Also, be certain to try the recipes for Summer on the Island on page 86, Fresh Coconut Cream Pie on page 289, and Coconut Sherbet on page 297. Coconut pulp can be used in any recipe that calls for unsweetened grated coconut.

Cranberry

Cranberries are one of the few fruits sold mostly in their wild form. Indigenous to the swampy regions of both the temperate and arctic zones of North America and Europe, cranberries were in common use by Native Americans before the Pilgrims landed. They are a member of the heath family, often classified in the blueberry genus. Cranberries grow on low, thick vines in bogs built in peat swamps. The bogs are cleared, drained, and leveled to facilitate the flooding and draining necessary for cranberry growth. A bog takes three to five years to come into full production. Most commercial cranberries are grown in the northeast, especially in Massachusetts, where cranberries were first cultivated in the early nineteenth century. Wisconsin, New Jersey, Washington, and Oregon are also major producers.

Season: Cranberries can be found in markets from September through March, although the peak season is from October through December.

Selection: For juicing, choose firm, round, plump cranberries that are brightly colored and lustrous. Avoid berries that are shriveled, soft, dull, or yellow.

Preparation: Just pick through cranberries and discard any bad ones, then rinse the remainder well.

Juice yield: Four to five cups (approximately one pound) of cranberries will yield about two-thirds cup of juice.

Storage: Keep cranberries for up to eight weeks in the refrigerator and longer in the freezer. Moisture makes cranberries spoil.

Uses: Cranberry juice is very sour and must be diluted with other juices. Try mixing two ounces of cranberry juice with six to eight ounces of apple juice. Also try Cranapple Cocktail on page 84, Pink Passion Potion on page 85, and Christmas Smoothie on page 106.

Cucumber

An annual herbaceous plant, the cucumber is a member of the gourd family. It is popular in Afghanistan, Iran, Pakistan, and Turkey, where fresh raw cucumbers, rich in water, are eaten all day long to cool off the body in the sweltering heat. They are even sold there by street vendors, who peel and quarter them for a nickel. The cucumber is believed to hail from India and tropical Asia, although botanists have not been able to discover its wild prototype. An ancient fruit, it was used by the Egyptians and was popular with the Greeks and Romans. It is one of the fruits mentioned in the Bible and has been used as a food by Oriental populations for over 3,000 years. In the United States, Florida supplies almost one-third of the cucumber crop. Other major producers are California, North and South Carolina, New Jersey, and New York.

Season: Cucumbers are marketed throughout the year, with a peak season from May through August.

Selection: For juicing, choose firm, bright, well-shaped cucumbers that are medium to dark green in color and five to seven inches in length. Avoid old cucumbers, which are dull green, yellowish, or large. Also skip puffy, withered, or shriveled cucumbers, which are rubbery and bitter tasting.

Preparation: Cucumbers that have been sprayed or waxed should be peeled; organic cucumbers just need to be rinsed. For juicing, cut cucumbers in half lengthwise so that they will fit through the hopper of the juice extractor.

Juice yield: One large, unpeeled cucumber (approximately eight ounces) will yield about one cup of juice.

Storage: Keep cucumbers refrigerated, in average humidity.

Uses: Cucumber juice is mild and refreshing. It combines well with tomato juice and carrot juice. Try it in mixed drinks, such as Beauty Spa Cocktail on page 90. Cucumber juice is also used in Cucumber Aspic on page 178 and Beet Aspic on page 179. It's delicious in Cold Cucumber Cream on page 172.

Fennel

Fennel is the common name for both a variety of herbs and a garden vegetable more specifically called sweet fennel. Sweet fennel was widely known in ancient Greece, where a region of the country was even named after it. The Greeks originally used fennel, a member of the carrot family, as a medicament. They thought it had slimming properties and, during the Middle Ages, often ate the seeds for their digestive qualities. First cultivated around the sixteenth century in Europe, especially in central and southern Italy, sweet fennel is now found throughout the Mediterranean. It is called "finocchio" in Italy and has a mild anise- or licorice-like flavor, fern-like leaves, and stems that swell into a thick bulb at the bottom. Fennel today can be found in most supermarkets and natural food stores. It is also commonly grown in home vegetable and herb gardens.

Season: The peak season for sweet fennel is October through January.

Selection: For juicing, choose sweet fennel that has firm, fresh stalks with green, feathery shoots. The bulb should be compact and greenish white.

Preparation: Just rinse fennel and, if desired, trim off the leaves, which can be used as an herb. If juicing the fennel, cut the bulb into chunks that will fit through the hopper of the juice extractor.

Juice yield: One medium bulb (approximately one pound) of sweet fennel will yield about one cup of juice.

Storage: Keep sweet fennel in a perforated bag in the refrigerator for up to a week.

Uses: Sweet fennel's hint of anise flavor adds an interesting touch to any recipe. Fennel mixes well with mild, sweet-tasting juices such as carrot, pineapple, and apple. Try Fennel Fresher on page 90. It's delicious! Also see Fennel-Apple Express on page 97.

Garlic

The king of vegetables in Latin countries because of the zip it adds to dishes, garlic, surprisingly, is a member of the aristocratic lily family. It is a perennial, a native of Asia now also found throughout the Mediterranean, and a cousin to the onion. Garlic was widely used by the ancient Egyptians, not only as a seasoning but also as an embalming aid. The Greeks and Romans, with whom it was immensely popular, used it as a seasoning and medicament. It was brought by the Spanish to the New World, where it was an immediate hit with the Native Americans. Known for its distinctive, pungent aroma, garlic comes in three varieties: the white Creole, or American, the strongest; the pink Italian, with its many cloves; and the Tahiti, the largest. All are equal in quality. In the United States, California supplies most cooks with garlic.

Season: Garlic is available throughout the year.

Selection: For juicing, choose garlic heads that are compact and well enclosed in the casing. Individual cloves should be plump and firm. Avoid heads that have shoots emerging from the crown, a sign that they have been stored for too long and under poor conditions.

Preparation: If juicing a garlic clove, just wash it. You don't even need to peel it! However, once you have juiced garlic, you may want to pour some water through the hopper of the juice extractor, or completely rinse out the juicer, before juicing anything else. Otherwise, any following juices may have a hint of garlic flavor.

Juice yield: Two cloves of garlic will yield approximately one-half teaspoon of juice.

Storage: Garlic can be stored indefinitely at a cool room temperature in a dry, well-ventilated place. Just keep it away from other foods, which may pick up its strong odor.

Uses: Yes, you can juice garlic! However, garlic juice is extremely strong and should be used in very small quantities. Garlic juice mixes well with vegetable-juice combinations. Try Gabby Gourmet's Cocktail on page 96.

Ginger Root

Ginger is the common name for a sturdy perennial herb that is cultivated for its root, which is candied or dried for medicine or spice. The gnarled light-brown root has a sweet, peppery taste that Orientals and Indians find a favorite in cooking. Native to Malabar, India, ginger root traveled from the Orient to southern Europe just ahead of the Romans. It then moved on to the West Indies, where its cultivation spread rapidly. Today ginger root is grown in many regions with warm climates. However, almost all of the ginger root used in the United States comes from Hawaii.

Season: Fresh ginger root is now available in most supermarkets year-round.

Selection: For juicing, choose ginger root that is firm, plump, and heavy. Ginger that is not fresh is light in weight and wrinkled in appearance. Also avoid roots with moldy or discolored ends. Small, greenish knobs growing on the main part of the root are new growth and usable.

Preparation: Just scrub ginger root well if it's organic; peel it if it's not organic. Cut off any damaged portions. If juicing the ginger root, you may want to pour some water through the hopper of the juice extractor, or completely rinse out the juicer, when you are finished. Ginger's strong flavor may affect whatever you juice next.

Juice yield: A half-inch slice of ginger root yields approximately one-half teaspoon of juice.

Storage: Ginger root will stay fresh for several months if kept in a cold and humid environment.

Uses: Ginger root can add zip to many juice recipes. But be careful! Ginger juice can be quite hot and spicy, so use it sparingly until you are accustomed to its strength. You may want to start with approximately a quarter-inch slice of fresh ginger root. Ginger mixes well with carrot juice, beet juice, and nearly every fruit juice. Try the recipes for Pineapple-Ginger Express on page 81, Ginger Hopper on page 91, and Beet-It Express on page 96.

Grape

Grapes are an *-est* fruit. They are one of the oldest, dating back to before man. They may have the greatest variety, with 6,000 to 8,000 named and described. And they are one of the most abundant, especially in the Mediterranean and western Asia, where they originated, and in North America, which the first Norse visitors wanted to call Vinland in honor of the grapes growing wild. Today 40 to 50 varieties of grapes are important commercially. They are divided into four classes: wine, table, raisin, and sweet juice. The most popular in the United States are varieties or hybrids of European stocks, including the blackish purple Concords and Ribiers, red Tokays and Emperors, and yellowish green Thompson Seedless. California is the leading producer of grapes, followed by New York and then Michigan and Washington.

Season: Domestic grapes can be found from late June or July through March, but the peak season is from September to November. Imported grapes can be found in the spring.

Selection: For juicing, choose grapes that are bright, plump, and firm. Select deep-colored red or purple grapes or green grapes that have turned slightly yellow. Look for stems that are green and firm. Avoid grapes that are dry, brown, or black, or that look as if they have been handled a lot.

Preparation: If juicing grapes, just pick through the bunch to remove any bad ones, then wash the remainder while still on the stems. They don't need to be seeded or removed from the stems.

Juice yield: One pound of grapes will yield approximately one cup of juice.

Storage: Grapes will keep for up to two weeks in the refrigerator, although the sooner they are eaten, the better they will taste.

Uses: Grape juice tastes wonderful combined with apple, pear, strawberry, lemon, or pineapple juice. Try Fruit Salad in a Glass on page 81, Pink Passion Potion on page 85, and Purple Monkey on page 111.

Grapefruit

The grapefruit is a citrus fruit, a cousin to the orange, lemon, lime, tangerine, and kumquat. It grows on a woody perennial tree with evergreen leaves that prefers the mild climates of the Mediterranean, Mexico, and southern United States. About 97 percent of the world's supply of grapefruits comes from the United States, with Florida and Texas producing 90 percent of the American supply. California and Arizona grow the rest. The grapefruit was originally cultivated more than 4,000 years ago in India and Malaysia. Experts believe that the pomelo, a popular Asian fruit, was introduced to the West Indies, where mutation produced the grapefruit. In the eighteenth century, the West Indians gave the fruit its name because it grows in grapelike bunches. Grapefruits come in three colors: white, pink, and red. Pink and red grapefruits are usually sweeter than white grapefruits.

Season: Grapefruits are available all year long, with a peak season between October and April.

Selection: For juicing, choose firm, heavy, well-rounded grapefruits with thin, smooth skins. These have the most juice and best flavor.

Preparation: If juicing grapefruit, peel the outer skin because it contains a toxic substance that should not be consumed in large quantities. However, leave plenty of the bioflavonoid-rich white rind. Cut the grapefruit into wedges that will fit through the hopper of the juice extractor. Grapefruit juice can be somewhat strong and can adversely affect the flavor of juices that follow. Therefore, once you have juiced enough grapefruits, you may want to pour some water through the hopper of the juice extractor, or completely rinse out the juicer, before juicing anything else.

Juice yield: One large grapefruit will yield approximately one cup of juice.

Storage: Keep grapefruits in the refrigerator for up to two weeks.

Uses: Grapefruit combines well with orange or pineapple juice. For a treat, mix all three. See the recipe for Pink Sunrise on page 80.

Green Bean

Don't call these beans "string beans" anymore. Hybridization has gotten rid of the strings! And in the market, ask for *fresh* green beans. They also come dried. Green beans are the seed of shrubs of the pulse family. Fresh green beans are marketed and used while still immature, which distinguishes them from their cousins that are shelled. There are over 150 varieties of green beans, including the French haricot, snap bean, pole bean, and wax bean. They can be yellow or green, and they come in many shapes and sizes. Native to South America, beans were introduced into Europe in the early 1500s. Fresh green beans were called "French beans" by the British, attesting to where they landed first. The French, however, called them "haricot." In the United States, local farmers supply the markets during the growing season, with Florida filling the off-season gaps.

Season: Fresh green beans are available year-round, with a peak season from May through October.

Selection: For juicing, choose fresh green beans that are young, long, slender, and well formed. They should be tender but crisp, snapping when broken. Look for pods that are bright green or yellow, depending on the variety, and that have a velvety look and feel. Avoid fresh green beans that are shriveled, wilted, or rusted. Also skip pods that are bulging, since the seeds should be less than half grown.

Preparation: If juicing fresh green beans, just rinse them. The ends can remain intact.

Juice yield: One cup of fresh green beans will yield approximately one-quarter cup of juice.

Storage: Keep fresh green beans in a plastic bag in the refrigerator for up to five days.

Uses: Fresh green-bean juice has been used as a traditional tonic for the pancreas and a natural remedy for diabetes and hypoglycemia. It does not taste good by itself, but it mixes well with other juices such as carrot or tomato, which disguise the taste. Good juice combinations to try are Three-Bean Juice and Jack and the Bean, both on page 104.

Green Pepper

See Bell Pepper.

Kale

Kale, a type of cabbage, is one of the oldest known members of the mustard family. Native to either the eastern Mediterranean region or Asia Minor, it has been eaten for more than 4,000 years. Use of kale in the United States was first recorded in 1669, although it was probably introduced here much earlier. The richest source of calcium, it is grown for both food and fodder in Europe, where it was named by the Scotch. Kale comes in several varieties, but the most popular are spring kale, which has smooth leaves, and green Scotch kale and Siberian blue kale, which have curly leaves. Scotch kale has leaves that are crinkled and finely divided, bright green to yellowish green in color. The leaves of Siberian kale have ruffled edges and flattened centers and are deep bluish green. In the United States, the major producers of kale are Virginia, Maryland, New York, and New Jersey.

Season: Kale can be found all year long, with a peak season from December through April.

Selection: For juicing, choose kale that is crisp, firm, and deep green. The color should be uniform.

Preparation: Just wash kale leaves. If juicing the kale, simply roll up the leaves lengthwise.

Juice yield: One pound of kale stems and leaves will yield approximately one cup of juice.

Storage: Keep kale refrigerated in high humidity.

Uses: Small amounts of kale juice can be mixed well with carrot, pineapple, or apple juice. Try Sweet Calcium Cocktail on page 91 or Green Surprise on page 92. Kale juice can also be used in non-beverage recipes. Try Green Cornbread on page 139 and Veggie Pâté on page 151. In any recipe that calls for a green juice, the juice from one or two leaves of kale can be substituted for some of the juice in the recipe.

Kiwi

The kiwi is a relatively new fruit, sold in Europe and the United States just since World War II. Native to eastern Asia, particularly China, it was until recently more commonly known as the Actinidia or Chinese gooseberry. It belongs to the Actinidia family, many species of which were introduced to Europe during the 1800s for use as ornamental plants. The Actinidia tree is small, up to twenty-five feet in height. Its new growth is marked by hair and it features round, velvety, dark green leaves and, at the end of spring, white flowers highlighted with touches of brownish yellow. The fruits, covered with down, are about the size of walnuts and have a pleasing, slightly sour taste. They ripen at the beginning of winter and can be stored till spring. In the United States, California has been the leading cultivator of the kiwi.

Season: The peak season for kiwis is June through December.

Selection: For juicing, choose kiwis that are firm but ripe, giving very slightly to pressure. The skin should be brown and fuzzy.

Preparation: Always peel kiwi. Tropical fruits like kiwi often come from foreign countries where the use of carcinogenic sprays is still legal. If juicing the kiwi, cut it in half.

Juice yield: One large or two medium kiwis will yield approximately one-half cup of juice.

Storage: Kiwis will ripen at room temperature. When ripe, they can be refrigerated for three to six weeks.

Uses: Kiwi juice is delicious mixed with apple, pear, strawberry, blackberry, or pineapple juice. See the recipes for Kiwi Cooler on page 82 and Australian Surprise on page 88.

Lemon

Lemons are a citrus fruit like the grapefruit, a member of the rue family that flourishes in mild climates, especially in the Mediterranean regions and southern United States. Native to tropical Asia, lemons have been cultivated for at least 2,500 years. The Arabs brought them to Spain and Africa in the twelfth century A.D., and Spanish adventurers brought them to the New World. In the United States, Florida was the first producer of lemons, cornering the market until 1895, when a big freeze killed all the lemon groves. California then took over, now growing 95 percent of the world's supply; the other 5 percent is produced by Italy. The most common American varieties of lemon are the Eureka and Lisbon. Other well-known varieties are the Meyer and Villa Franca. The better known Italian varieties include the Little Monk and Turk's Head.

Season: Since lemon trees bloom and ripen every month of the year, lemons are available all year long. However, the peak months are April through August.

Selection: For juicing, choose lemons that are deep yellow in color and firm but not hard. The skin should be oily to the touch and thin for the most juice and flavor. Look for fruits that are heavy for their size. Avoid lemons that are shriveled, have hard skin, or are soft or spongy to the touch. Look for signs of mechanical injury and decay, the latter of which shows as mold, softness, or discoloration at the stem end.

Preparation: Organic lemons just need to be washed. If the lemons are not organic, they should be peeled. If juicing the lemons, cut them into wedges so that they will fit through the hopper of the juice extractor.

Juice yield: One medium lemon yields approximately one-quarter cup of juice.

Storage: Keep lemons in the refrigerator for up to two weeks.

Uses: For an especially refreshing treat, try juicing one quarter of a lemon with three apples. Naturally sweet and invigorating! Also try the Pink Lemonade recipe on page 85 and the Strawberry Lemonade recipe on page 88. Lemon juice is used in Cucumber Aspic on page 178 and Tomato Aspic With Avocado Dressing on page 180. Dozens of other recipes also use lemon juice. Two not to miss are Cold Cucumber Cream on page 172 and the refreshing Lemon Sherbet on page 296.

Lettuce

When most people hear "salad," they think "lettuce." The two are almost synonymous. Lettuce is ancient, having been served to Persian kings in the sixth century B.C. The Romans grew a dozen varieties by the first century B.C., and the Chinese were cultivating it 200 years later. Columbus brought seeds to the New World, and sixteen varieties grew in American gardens by 1806. Today lettuce is the most valuable American truck crop. Botanists argue about its origin, although most feel it hails from Asia, descended from a weed called wild lettuce. Modern lettuce falls into three main categories: head or cabbage; romaine or cos; and curled or leaf. Over fifty varieties are now planted commercially. Popular varieties include iceberg, Boston, Bibb, green leaf, and red tipped. The coastal states, both east and west, are the primary domestic producers.

Season: Iceberg and romaine lettuce are available year-round. The growing season for the other varieties varies.

Selection: For juicing, choose lettuce that is fresh, tender, and crisp. The head should be heavy for its size and free of blemishes. The outer leaves should be dark and bright, and the veins and stems should be fine. Avoid lettuce that is wilted or discolored. Also avoid iceberg lettuce, which is so deficient in nutrients and so lacking in flavor that there seems to be no reason for its use.

Preparation: Rinse lettuce under cold running water; do not soak it. If juicing the lettuce, remove the desired number of leaves and bunch them up.

Juice yield: Four leaves of lettuce will yield approximately one-quarter cup of juice.

Storage: Keep all varieties of lettuce in a perforated bag in the refrigerator for up to five days. Make sure iceberg lettuce is completely dry before storing it or the leaves will rot.

Uses: Lettuce juice in combination with carrot, green pepper, and alfalfa-sprout juices has traditionally been used to help the growth of hair and to restore it to its natural color. Lettuce juice is not particularly tasty by itself, but it mixes well with carrot, tomato, or apple juice. Try the recipe for Hot Tomato on Ice on page 103 or Jack and the Bean on page 104.

Lime

Another member of the rue family is the lime, the most frost-sensitive of the citrus fruits. Native to southeastern Asia, limes have been cultivated for thousands of years, preferring rocky or sandy soil and tropical climates. Arabs may have brought limes from India around A.D. 570–900. In 1514, limes were found growing wild on Haiti, and from there they spread to Florida. In 1838, they were planted en masse by Henry Perrine in the Florida Keys after Congress granted him the land, and in 1895, after a frost that killed all their lemon groves, Florida citrus growers embraced the lime. Limes were also popular with British sailors, who carried rations of juice to prevent scurvy and were thus nicknamed "limeys." Florida today grows most of the American supply of limes, followed by California and Mexico. The principal variety grown in Florida is the Florida Persean.

Season: The peak months for limes are April through August.

Selection: For juicing, choose limes that are bright green in color and firm but not hard. They should be heavy for their size and have a glossy, thin skin for the most juice and best flavor.

Preparation: Organic limes don't need to be peeled, just washed well. Limes that are not organic, however, should be peeled. If juicing the limes, cut them into wedges that will fit through the hopper of the juice extractor.

Juice yield: One medium lime yields approximately two tablespoons of juice.

Storage: Keep limes refrigerated for up to two weeks.

Uses: Lime juice can be substituted for lemon juice in most recipes. It mixes well with most fruits and perks up vegetable juices superbly. Also try it in teas, such as Fruit Tea on page 117; salads, such as Gazpacho Salad With Tomato and Lime Juice Marinade on page 184 and Vegetable Terrine on page 185; and sauces, such as Ruby Red Sauce on page 212. Don't forget to try Southwestern Cocktail on page 99.

Mango

The mango is a member of the sumac family, believed to have originated in either Burma, Malaya, or the Himalayan region of India. Cultivated for over 4,000 years, it has been an important food in the tropics and was revered by the Hindus. Looking like a kidney-shaped peach, the mango comes in hundreds of varieties ranging in size from plums to melons. It is usually mottled orange but sometimes green, yellow, or red. Mango trees were successfully imported to the United States around 1900, although several attempts had been made earlier. The tree is extremely susceptible to frost, so even today it grows just in certain sections of Florida and California and then just during the summer. The most popular variety of mango in the United States is the Hayden from Florida. Other varieties sold here come from Haiti, the West Indies, and Mexico.

Season: Mangoes are available from May through September, with a peak in June.

Selection: For juicing, choose a mango that gives a little when pressed. Look for ripe mangoes, which are mottled with orange, gold, red, green, and black. Avoid mangoes that are all green; solid-green mangoes may never ripen. Also skip mangoes with black spots and extremely soft areas.

Preparation: Always peel a mango since it may have come from a foreign country where the use of carcinogenic sprays is still legal. Make several top-to-bottom incisions in the skin all around the fruit, then peel the skin away as you do with a banana. Also, remove the pit. You may want to slice the flesh away from the pit as you peel the fruit. If juicing the mango, cut it into chunks small enough to fit through the hopper of the juice extractor.

Juice yield: One medium mango (approximately one pound) will yield about one-half cup of juice.

Storage: A firm mango will ripen at room temperature in three to four days. Refrigerate ripe mangoes for up to three days.

Uses: Mango juice is very thick. It's wonderful diluted with apple, orange, or pineapple juice. Try Mango Cooler on page 83 as well as Exotic Tropical Smoothie on page 108.

Melon

Melons—commercially divided into cantaloupes and muskmelons, or winter melons—are another of the ancient fruits, with honeydews having been cultivated by the Egyptians at least 2,400 years ago. The cantaloupe, native to India and Guinea, has been grown for over 2,000 years. Belonging to the gourd family and related to watermelons and cucumbers, melons flourish in warm climates. Popular muskmelons include the Persian, casaba, cranshaw, and canary. Cantaloupes, widely cultivated in Asia, were brought to southern Spain by the Moors in the eighth century. However, they did not spread to the rest of Europe until the fifteenth century, when

Charles VIII carried seeds to France in 1495. Christopher Columbus had brought cantaloupes to the New World in 1492. In 1900, honeydews crossed the Atlantic. Today melons are grown in the southwest, especially in California and Arizona.

Season: Cantaloupes are available from May through September, with a peak in June and July. Honeydew melons are available year-round, with a peak from July through October. Cranshaw melons are also available from July through October, casabas can be found from July through November, and Persian melons are at a peak in August and September.

Selection: For juicing, choose melons that are firm, neither too soft nor too hard, and heavy for their size, which indicates juiciness. Cantaloupes should be cream colored and "netted." There should not be any smooth spots, but there should be a depressed scar, called a full slip, at the stem end. Persian melons also should have no smooth spots. A light grayish green color beneath the netting is normal, however. Honeydew melons should be green, not white or greenish white, which indicates immaturity. The skin should feel a little sticky and soft when pressed. Casaba melons should be golden yellow in color and should yield a little to pressure at the stem end. The cranshaw should be golden and sweet-smelling.

Preparation: Simply rinse, cut, and seed a melon. If juicing an organic melon, just cut it into wedges small enough to fit through the hopper of the juice extractor; the whole melon—skin, seeds, and all—can be juiced! Peel a melon that is non-organic.

Juice yield: One pound of melon will yield approximately one cup of juice.

Storage: Ripen melons at room temperature. Once ripe, wrap them tightly and refrigerate them for up to three days.

Uses: Melon juice is great all by itself, or try it with a little fresh mint. See the recipes for Watermelon Cooler on page 83, Mint Cooler on page 88, and Melon-Mint Sherbet on page 293.

Onion

The onion, probably the most popular vegetable ever, is believed to have originated in central Asia. One of the earliest known food medicines, it is a cultivated biennial no longer found in its wild form. It is, like garlic, a member of the dainty lily family and is known as a "kitchen lily." Its cousins include the leek, shallot, and chive. The onion made its appearance long before historians did. However, it is known to have been worshipped by the Egyptians and widely used by the Greeks and Romans. It was craved by the Israelites wandering in the desert with Moses. Onions are divided into two classes—strong and mild. The two classes are further divided into colors—red, brown, white, and yellow—which are then again divided into four sizes. Nearly a dozen varieties of onion are sold in the United States. The leading producers are Texas, California, and New York.

Season: Onions are available all year.

Selection: For juicing, choose clean, firm, well-shaped onions that are heavy for their size. The skin should be dry, paperery, and even in color. Avoid onions that are soft, moldy, or sprouting.

Preparation: Just slice off a piece of onion and peel it. You don't need a large piece because onions are so potent. In fact, once you have juiced the piece of onion, you may want to pour some water through the hopper of the juice extractor, or completely rinse out the juicer, before juicing anything else. Otherwise, any following juices may have a hint of onion flavor. To protect your eyes from the strong fumes, peel the onion under cold water.

Juice yield: A half-inch-thick slice of a large onion will yield approximately two tablespoons of juice.

Storage: Keep onions in a cool, dry, dark, well-ventilated place for up to one month. Do not refrigerate them.

Uses: Onion juice is quite strong and should be used in very small quantities, especially in mixed-vegetable drinks. See the recipes for Hot and Spicy Veggie Cocktail on page 98, Southwestern Cocktail on page 99, and Gazpacho Express on page 101. If the juice is to be cooked, as in Borscht on page 174, you can use larger quantities. Add onion juice to soups or stews, or even to the cooking water for rice or other grains.

Orange

Oranges are one of the oldest cultivated fruits. In 500 B.C., they were discussed in works edited by Confucius, and in A.D. 1178, a Chinese horticulturist mentioned 27 varieties. Perennials of the rue family and related to lemons, oranges are native to eastern Asia. They spread first to India, then slowly through the entire world. Spanish explorers brought them to Florida in the early 1500s, and Californians cultivated them in the late 1700s. Oranges prefer the milder climates of the Mediterranean, southern United States, Mexico, and Brazil. Today over 200 varieties grow in Florida and California. There are three kinds: sweet, sour, and a type that includes tangerines, mandarines, and Satsumas. Sweet oranges are classified as normal, blood, or navel. Among the popular sweet varieties are Washington Navel, Valencia, Hamlin, Indian River, and Jaffa.

Season: Oranges are available all year, but their peak months are in the winter and spring.

Selection: For juicing, choose oranges that are firm and heavy for their size. Some oranges are grown especially for juicing. The skin of the oranges should be thin, smooth, and bright.

Preparation: All oranges must be peeled because the outer skin contains a toxic substance that should not be consumed in large quantities. However, leave as much of the white pith as possible since it's rich in bioflavonoids and vitamin C. If juicing the oranges, cut them into wedges that will fit through the hopper of the juice extractor.

Juice yield: Two medium oranges (approximately one pound) will yield about one cup of juice.

Storage: Refrigerate oranges for up to two weeks.

Uses: Oranges produce more juice when put through a juice extractor than when pressed. The juice is also creamier. Both extracted and pressed orange juice tastes delicious combined with grapefruit or pineapple juice. Try Exotic Tropical Smoothie on page 108, Orange Cream on page 112, Pineapple-Orange Soda on page 116, and Orange-Amazake Sherbet on page 298.

Papaya

The papaya is another fruit considered exotic in the mainland United States, yet not only common but a food staple and economic lifeline in Hawaii. In fact, the papaya is considered second in importance only to the banana in Hawaii, as it is in Central and South America; Hawaii today is the commercial center for papayas. A member of the pawpaw family, the papaya resembles a melon, both in texture and appearance. It is four to twenty inches in diameter and up to twenty pounds or more in weight. It is yellow outside, and yellow or salmon inside. The papaya is native to Central America, particularly Mexico, and the West Indies. From these areas it spread to other tropical regions, mainly in Asia, Africa, and Polynesia. In the United States, it is grown successfully in Florida, Texas, and the southern part of California.

Season: Papayas are available year-round, but the peak months are May and June.

Selection: For juicing, choose a papaya that is golden orange or deep yellow, an indication of ripeness. The papaya should be somewhat soft but not mushy.

Preparation: Always peel a papaya. Tropical fruits like papaya often come from foreign countries where the use of carcinogenic sprays is still legal. First cut the papaya in half and scoop out the seeds. Then either remove the peel from the flesh or scoop the flesh from the peel. If juicing the papaya, make sure the pieces are small enough to fit through the hopper of the juice extractor.

Juice yield: One medium papaya will yield about one cup of juice.

Storage: Ripen papayas at room temperature. Once ripe, refrigerate papayas for up to two or three days.

Uses: Papaya juice is a real treat. Drink it plain or mix it with orange, mango, peach, pear, or pineapple juice. Papaya juice is also good with a little lemon, ginger, or lime juice added. Try Tropical Squeeze on page 82. Papaya juice makes delicious smoothies, such as Papaya-Pineapple Smoothie on page 109.

Parsley

If "only the wicked can grow parsley," as the old English saying goes, there must be a lot of wicked people in the world. Parsley is the most common herb today. Hailing from the Mediterranean and belonging to the carrot family, parsley was cultivated by the Romans, who fed it to their horses to make them speedy. It has been growing in European gardens since around the eighth century and was brought to the New World by the colonists. But in the Middle Ages, parsley was also considered the devil's herb, and many people believed that Good Friday was the only day on which it could be successfully sown. Parsley is a biennial plant and comes in three varieties in the United States: common, with small leaves; Naples, with large leaves and thick stalks; and curly. Florida is the major producer of parsley, followed by California, Texas, and Arizona.

Season: Fresh parsley is available all year, but the peak season is October through December.

Selection: For juicing, choose fresh, crisp, dark green parsley. Common and curly parsley should be springy. Avoid yellow parsley.

Preparation: Just wash parsley. If juicing the parsley, bunch it up; it doesn't need to be chopped.

Juice yield: Two cups of parsley will yield approximately one-quarter cup of juice.

Storage: Wrap parsley in plastic and keep it in the refrigerator for up to three weeks.

Uses: Parsley juice is very concentrated. Add a small amount of it to carrot or other vegetable juices. See Morning Energizer on page 94. Other juice recipes using parsley include Gabby Gourmet's Cocktail on page 96, Cucumber Cooler on page 97, and Salad in a Glass on page 99. Use one or two ounces of parsley juice in almost any recipe in this book that calls for a green juice, such as Saint Patrick's Soup on page 162 or Green Sauce on page 204. Parsley juice is also used in Green Cornbread on page 139 and Savory Rosemary-Onion Muffins on page 142.

Peach

Another extremely popular fruit is the peach. Chinese in origin, the peach has been cultivated since ancient times. From Asia, it traveled the world, coming to the Americas with the colonists. Today the United States, along with Italy, is considered the leader in peach production. A member of the rose family, the peach comes in two types: clingstone, in which the flesh clings to the pit; and freestone, in which the pit is loose. Clingstone peaches, grown mainly in California, are usually canned. In fact, California is the world's leader in fruit packing because of its peach canning. The Elberta is the leading freestone variety, first produced in 1870 in Marshallville, Georgia. Other freestone varieties, used for eating, are the Halehaven and Golden Jubilee. Georgia leads the production of freestones, followed by Michigan and the Carolinas.

Season: Peaches are available from May through October, but especially during the peak months of July and August.

Selection: Buy peaches only in season. For juicing, choose plump, slightly fuzzy peaches that are deep yellow or orange with a red blush. They should be firm but give slightly when pressed. Avoid overly green peaches, which will ripen after several days but will not be as sweet as tree-ripened fruits.

Preparation: Organic peaches just need to be washed; you may want to peel peaches that are not organic. If juicing the peaches, cut them in half and remove the pit. Cut the halves into wedges that are small enough to fit through the hopper of the juice extractor.

Juice yield: One pound of peaches will yield approximately three-quarters cup of juice.

Storage: Refrigerate ripe peaches for up to four days. Peaches can be ripened at room temperature, but this is not recommended (*see* Selection).

Uses: Peach juice is truly delicious combined with strawberry, apple, grape, cherry, raspberry, blackberry, or papaya juice. Try Peach-Apple Shake on page 85 or Peaches and Cream on page 109.

Pear

Like the peach, the pear is a member of the rose family. Native to western Asia and the Caspian Sea region, the pear was first cultivated about forty centuries ago and was prized by ancient Greeks and Romans as well as Chinese. Several Greek writers, including Homer in 1000 B.C., discussed pear trees, and Pliny the Elder, a Roman naturalist, listed 40 varieties in the first century A.D. In the early seventeenth century, settlers brought pear trees to the Colonies, where they thrived, with a nursery on Long Island listing 42 varieties in 1771. Over 5,000 varieties exist today, but commercially, less than a dozen are important. Bartlett, Anjou, Bosc, and Seckel are the main commercial varieties, and they come primarily from California, Oregon, Washington, New York, and Michigan. Most modern pears are hybrids of the European buttery pear and Asian sandy pear.

Season: Pears are available year-round, although the varieties differ. For example, Bartlett pears are a summer fruit, available from July through November. In early autumn, the Seckel is sold. The Anjou is in stores from October through May.

Selection: For juicing, choose a pear that is deep colored, plump, and firm but starting to soften. It should have a sweet fragrance when kept at room temperature and, although bruising is normal, as little damage as possible. Avoid mushy pears, which have little juice.

Preparation: Organic pears just need to be washed. If juicing the pear, cut it into pieces that will fit through the hopper of the juice extractor. Neither the core nor the seeds need to be removed.

Juice yield: Two and a half medium pears (approximately one pound) will yield about one and a half cups of juice.

Storage: Ripen pears at room temperature for two or three days. Refrigerate ripe pears for up to five days.

Uses: Pear juice is delicious alone or combined with apple, grape, cherry, peach, strawberry, blackberry, kiwi, or papaya juice. Try Tropical Squeeze on page 82. Pear juice also mixes well with carrot and fennel juices. See Fennel-Apple Express on page 97. Pear juice is wonderful in sauces, such as Pear and Fresh Mint Sauce on page 217, and in desserts, such as Strawberry Sherbet on page 295.

Pineapple

The Spanish say that Columbus discovered the pineapple along with America. The West Indians disagree—they had been cultivating it long before Columbus arrived. A member of the bromeliad family, the pineapple is native to South America. It was once a prized gift given to visitors to the tropics and was hung over doorways by Carib Indians as a sign of welcome. Still a symbol of hospitality, the pineapple today is grown around the world, even in European hothouses, although it does best in tropical regions. It is a major industry in Hawaii, where it was brought in 1901 by a young Bostonian who began commercial production on just 12 acres. That farm now comprises 25,000 acres. Hawaii supplies the major portion of the world's canned pineapple, with its Smooth Cayenne variety the biggest seller. Other varieties are Red Spanish, Queen, and Pernambuco.

Season: Pineapples are available year-round.

Selection: For juicing, choose a pineapple with a fresh, clean appearance; strong, sweet fragrance; and fresh, deep green crown leaves. The pineapple should be large, plump, and firm, and its color should be dark orange-yellow or golden. The eyes should be flat and almost hollow, with nearly all at the base yellow. Avoid watery or dark eyes, brown leaves, and discolored or soft spots. Some people feel that a pineapple can be tested for ripeness by pulling at its spikes—if the fruit is ripe, the spikes will pull out easily. Others feel this is an old wives' tale. To save time, buy pineapples that are already peeled and cored.

Preparation: If a pineapple is organic, simply wash it, cut off the top, slice the fruit open, and cut the flesh into cubes or rings. If the pineapple is not organic, peel it after cutting off the top. If juicing the pineapple, cut the flesh into spears that will fit through the hopper of the juice extractor. The core can also be juiced, as can the rind of an organic fruit.

Juice yield: Half of a pineapple with its core will yield approximately one cup of juice.

Storage: Keep a whole pineapple in the refrigerator for up to five days. Wrap pineapple pieces in plastic and keep them in the refrigerator in high humidity for up to three or five days.

Uses: Pineapple juice is delicious alone or combined with orange, papaya, grapefruit, or apple juice. It also mixes well with kale juice. Try Pineapple-Ginger Express on page 81, Spicy Delight on page 89, and Sweet Calcium Cocktail on page 91. Recipes using pineapple pulp include Pineapple Chutney on page 216, Tropical Squares on page 275, Piña Colada Cake on page 276, and Pineapple Sherbet on page 290.

Plum

Of all the fruits with one large stone, plums have the largest number and diversity of varieties. Some estimates place the figure at 2,000; some say there are more. The fruit of a tree of the rose family, plums are believed to have originated in western Asia over two millenia ago. Although the Pilgrims found them growing wild in the New World, native American plums are not commercially important today. The Pilgrims also planted European plum pits, and today both Japanese and European plums are cultivated for market in the United States. Plums come in all shades of blue, red, green, and yellow. The most popular commerical varieties are the Damson Beauty, Italian Prune, Burbank, Sugar, and Stanley. California is by far the leading domestic producer of plums for eating, for drying as prunes, and for preserving and candying.

Season: Plums are available from May through September.

Selection: For juicing, choose plums that yield to gentle pressure, are a good color for the variety, and have a slight glow to the skin.

Preparation: Wash plums, cut them in half, and remove the stones.

Juice yield: Six medium plums will yield about one cup of juice.

Storage: Ripen plums at room temperature (some varieties will not ripen off the tree). Keep fully ripe plums in the refrigerator for up to three or five days.

Uses: Plums make a tasty addition to any recipe when they're ripe and sweet. For a new treat, try Pink Plum Cooler on page 87.

Potato

Although generally held to be Irish in origin, the potato is actually a native of the Andes. It was widely cultivated in South America at the time of the Spanish Conquest and was popular with the Aztecs and Incas. The Spaniards brought the potato to Europe in the early 1500s, and Sir Walter Raleigh is credited with introducing it to Ireland later that century. It crossed the Atlantic again around 1600 and came to North America. A perennial and a member of the nightshade family, the potato today is one of the most important vegetable crops in the world. Its rise brought the decline of scurvy because of its vitamin C content, and it is considered a "complete food," containing most of the nutrients necessary for human survival. In the United States, the potato is grown mainly in California, Maine, and Idaho, and is classified according to shape and color.

Season: Potatoes are available all year long.

Selection: For juicing, choose potatoes that are firm, well shaped, and heavy for their size. New white round potatoes should have thin, glossy skin. Avoid potatoes that are wrinkled, cut, cracked, bruised, skinned, or decayed. Especially avoid potatoes with green areas or sprouting, both of which indicate the presence of solanin, an alkaloid substance that is sometimes toxic.

Preparation: Scrub potatoes and cut out any eyes or bad spots. If juicing the potatoes, cut them into chunks that will fit through the hopper of the juice extractor.

Juice yield: Two medium potatoes will yield approximately one cup of juice.

Storage: Keep potatoes in a cool, dry, dark, well-ventilated area for up to several weeks. Do not refrigerate them as the cold will change the starch into sugar. Do not keep them in a lighted area as light will cause them to turn green. Potatoes can also be kept in a root cellar for up to six months.

Uses: Potato juice may not be the best drink, but it's wonderful for cooking. It's a great thickener for sauces, soups, and stews. But be careful! If potato juice sits too long, the starch will settle to the bottom, so stir the juice before using it. See the recipes for Creamy Potato Soup on page 168, Borscht on page 174, Potato Sauce on page 203, and Fat-Free Mushroom Sauce on page 207. Potato juice also works well as a thickening agent in vegetable dishes. See the recipes for Creamy and Spicy Corn on page 223 and Oriental Broccoli on page 224.

Radish

The radish is a member of the mustard family and related to the cabbage, cauliflower, kale, and turnip. Its origin is a mystery, but it is known to have been used by the ancients. In fact, according to ancient Egyptian writings, it was common before the pyramids were built. And in ancient Greece, a physician wrote an entire book on the vegetable. It is believed the radish was brought to the Americas by Columbus. It was grown by the colonists and was found in Mexico in 1500 and in Haiti in 1565. It was popular in 1548 with the English, who ate it raw on bread. About half a dozen varieties of radish are grown in the United States, especially in California and Florida. They are loosely classified as either summer or winter variety; black, red, or white; and round or long-rooted. The most popular variety is the cherry-sized round red type.

Season: Radishes are available year-round, but the peak months are April, May, and June.

Selection: For juicing, choose fresh, small radishes that are smooth and well formed. They should be firm, tender, and crisp, not spongy or pithy. Avoid vegetables with blemishes, sprouting, black spots, or cracks. And remember: do not judge a radish by its leaves.

Preparation: Just cut the greens off radishes and wash the roots.

Juice yield: Five medium radishes will yield approximately two tablespoons of juice.

Storage: Refrigerate radishes in a plastic bag for up to two weeks.

Uses: Just a few radishes will make a mixed-vegetable drink hot and spicy. Don't overdo it, though, because radish juice is very strong. See the recipe for Hot and Spicy Veggie Cocktail on page 98. It's delicious! Also try Cherie's Spring Tonic on page 100.

Raspberry

The raspberry, sister of the blackberry, is the fruit of thorny shrubs of the rose family. Not a berry at all (*see* Blackberry), it is also related to the loganberry, boysenberry, and dewberry. Raspberries grow wild in most of Europe, eastern Asia, and North America. Red raspberries are native to the northern United States, black raspberries to the southern states. Raspberries were first cultivated in the mid-1500s in England, where they were called hindberries, and in 1845 in the United States. By 1870, they were an important crop in the States. Raspberries are available in many varieties and colors. Yellow berries grow in Maryland, pink in Alabama and Oregon, and lavender in North Carolina. White berries grow wild. Purple berries are a hybrid of the black and the red. And in the western United States, wild black raspberries are often a deep wine color.

Season: Raspberries, both black and red, are available from mid-April through July, with July the peak month.

Selection: For juicing, choose raspberries that are bright, plump, and clean. The color should be full and solid. Raspberries should be fresh, solid, and dry. Avoid berries that are dull, soft, or runny; check the bottom of the container for wet or moldy spots. Also skip berries that still have their caps attached, a sign of immaturity.

Preparation: Immediately before using raspberries, rinse them under cold running water and drain them in a colander. Pick out any damaged berries.

Juice yield: One pint of raspberries will yield approximately one-half cup of juice.

Storage: Keep raspberries, unwashed and uncovered, in the refrigerator for one or two days. Raspberries must be kept dry.

Uses: For a delicious way to use those extra summertime raspberries, enjoy Summertime Raspberry Cocktail on page 87.

Red Pepper

See Bell Pepper.

Rhubarb

Rhubarb resembles large, red celery. A perennial herbaceous plant, rhubarb grows in northern temperate areas. It is the best known of the aromatic plants, with leaves containing a pungent juice that includes oxalic acid, a poison used as a cleansing agent. Rhubarb's cousins include the knotweeds, smartweeds, some sorrels, and buckwheat. Native to Tibet and northern Asia, rhubarb came to Europe around the fourteenth century. It is still a popular and inexpensive vegetable there, especially in Zurich, Switzerland, where it is grown in every family garden. It is usually stewed or baked, with plenty of sugar, and very rarely eaten raw. In the United States, rhubarb is usually cooked as a side dish or dessert, and in France, it is used chiefly in jams and compotes.

Season: Rhubarb is available from January through June.

Selection: Look for rhubarb with crisp, reddish green stalks.

Preparation: Wash rhubarb stalks under cold running water. Trim off the leaves, which contain a substance that is poisonous.

Juice yield: One large or two medium stalks of rhubarb will yield approximately one-half cup of juice.

Storage: Refrigerate rhubarb for up to five days.

Uses: Rhubarb juice is quite sour but makes a very refreshing drink when mixed with apple and/or strawberry juice. See the recipe for Sweet and Sour Springtime on page 87.

Scallion

Scallions are immature white onions, pulled from the ground before the bulb has had a chance to develop. They can also be young shallots. Other names for scallions are "green onion" and "spring onion." Both the scallion's bulb and leaves are used. They are excellent as a garnish, in relishes, and in salads. In the United States, Florida and Texas are the main producers of green onions. For more information about scallions, see Onion on page 34.

Season: Scallions are available all year long, with a peak season from May through August.

Selection: For juicing, choose scallions with firm, crisp, straight stems; tender white bulbs; and crisp, bright green tops.

Preparation: Cut off a scallion's roots, remove any loose skin, and wash the stem, bulb, and top.

Juice yield: One scallion will yield approximately one teaspoon of juice.

Storage: Keep scallions in a plastic bag in the refrigerator for up to four days.

Uses: The juice of just one small scallion can liven up a one- or two-serving batch of vegetable juice. Try Salad in a Glass on page 99. Don't add too much scallion juice to a recipe, though, because it's very strong. In fact, once you have juiced the scallion, you may want to pour some water through the hopper of the juice extractor, or completely rinse out the juicer, before juicing anything else. Otherwise, any following juices may have a hint of scallion flavor. When making juice to use in a soup, aspic, or stew, or for soaking couscous, add just one to three scallions, as desired. A teaspoon or two of scallion juice can also be added to salad dressings.

Spinach

What child (or adult) of the last fifty years hasn't cheered the appearance of spinach in Popeye's hand—yet secretly cursed the green fleshy leaves for all the times Mom made him or her eat it? But spinach survives the dislike—it's a hardy winter vegetable native to Iran and grown all over Europe and the eastern and southern United States, especially Texas. A member of the goosefoot family, spinach did not leave the Mideast until the Christian Era, then spread like wildfire. It moved into China and Nepal in A.D. 647, reached Spain around 1100, and took over Germany by the end of the 1200s. By the 1300s, it was commonly grown in European monastery gardens, and in 1390, a British cookbook included recipes for "spynoches." Spinach came to the Colonies early on, and today, several varieties, both flat and curly, are cultivated.

Season: Spinach is available all year, but especially during the peak months of April and May.

Selection: For juicing, choose spinach with crisp, deep green leaves. The stalks should be firm and not overgrown. Loose spinach is better than packaged spinach.

Preparation: Wash spinach well (but don't soak it) in cold water, then place it in a colander or salad spinner to drain off the excess water. If juicing the spinach, just bunch it up; it doesn't need to be chopped.

Juice yield: One pound (four bunches) of spinach will yield approximately one cup of juice.

Storage: Keep spinach in a perforated plastic bag in the refrigerator for up to three or five days.

Uses: Spinach juice is too strong to drink alone. For drinking, mix a small quantity of spinach juice with carrot, celery, parsley, apple, or tomato juice. Try Popeye's Favorite on page 92 and Bunny Hopper on page 99. In recipes, spinach juice can be very versatile. It adds color, flavor, and valuable nutrients. Just a few of the many recipes in this book using spinach juice are Veggie Pâté on page 151, Saint Patrick's Soup on page 162, Brightly Colored Couscous on page 232, Green Polenta on page 233, and Spinach Loaf on page 246.

Squash

See Summer Squash; Winter Squash.

Strawberry

Widely loved for their taste and aroma are strawberries. Perennials of the rose family, strawberries are an international fruit, growing wild in many parts of the world. Also known as wood strawberries, the original five or six wild species prefer temperate climates and are believed to be native to Chile and western North America. Strawberries were first grown in gardens in the thirteenth century after a French sailor brought them home from his travels. They were hybridized in Europe within the last sixty years to improve their hardiness and size for market. The popular varieties grown commericially in the United States include the Scarlet Virginia and Pocahontas. Others are the Blakemore, Klondike, Howard 17, and Marshall. In the United States, strawberries are grown in every state, even Alaska, but California, Oregon, and Washington are the leaders.

Season: Strawberries are available from January through July, with a peak season from April through June.

Selection: For juicing, choose firm, ripe, dry strawberries that are fresh, clean, and shiny. They should be solid red in color. The caps should be attached and bright green in color. Size is unimportant. Avoid berries with missing caps, which indicates rough handling or overmaturity. Also avoid moldy berries. The best strawberries are locally grown, in season, and organic.

Preparation: Simply wash strawberries. You can juice the green caps, but you may want to remove them if using the pulp since they will cause the pulp to taste bitter and look speckled.

Juice yield: One pint of strawberries will yield approximately one cup of juice.

Storage: Keep strawberries in the refrigerator, uncovered, for one or two days. Frozen strawberries will keep much longer.

Uses: Strawberry juice by itself is a little thick, so try diluting it with some apple juice. Try Strawberry-Apple Swinger on page 113. Strawberry juice can also be mixed with peach, pear, pineapple, grape, or another berry juice. See Fruit Salad in a Glass on page 81. Be sure to try the recipes for Strawberry Lemonade on page 88, Strawberry Pie on page 291, and Strawberry Sherbet on page 295.

String Bean

See Green Bean.

Summer Squash

What home gardener doesn't have a file full of zucchini recipes to use up the crop that always overflows? All the summer squashes are popular home-garden vegetables, and they also take up a good share of the produce section of the supermarket. Annual herbaceous plants of the gourd family, the summer squashes are related to the winter squashes, pumpkins, melons, cucumbers, and watermelons. They are native to the western hemisphere and grown throughout the United States. They were known to native Americans before the colonists arrived, although today's varieties are different. Zucchini is the most popular summer squash. The other two varieties are the yellow squashes, such as the crookneck and straightneck, and the patty pan, including the scallop gourd and white squash. In the United States, the seasonal supply is local; Florida is the leading off-season producer.

Season: Summer squashes are available all year, with a peak from April through August.

Selection: For juicing, choose firm, fresh, shiny summer squashes that are heavy for their size. The rind should be tender and easily punctured with a thumbnail. Patty pan squashes should have white skin and be no more than four inches in diameter. Yellow squashes should have light yellow skin, zucchini should have dark green skin, and both should be about six to ten inches in length. Avoid summer squashes with a hard rind, soft spots, or mildew.

Preparation: Summer squashes that have been sprayed should be peeled. Organic summer squashes just need to be rinsed. If juicing the squash, remove the stem and cut the flesh into pieces small enough to fit through the hopper of the juice extractor.

Juice yield: One medium yellow or zucchini squash will yield approximately one-half cup of juice.

Storage: Keep summer squashes in a plastic bag in the refrigerator for up to one week.

Uses: Zucchini can be juiced, but by itself it does not offer much flavor. It's best mixed with other vegetables in soups, sauces, and similar dishes. Try adding it to Garden Gazpacho on page 173.

Tomato

Generally considered a vegetable because of its uses, the tomato is a fruit that can be classified as a berry. It is a member of the nightshade family, native to the Andean region of South America. Originally cultivated in Peru, it was brought to England and the Netherlands in the sixteenth century by Portuguese and Spanish conquerors. It was originally prized as an ornamental plant and token of affection, and has been recognized as nonpoisonous and a food only within the last century. Today it is the third most important commercial vegetable crop in the United States, the leading imported vegetable from Mexico, and the leading greenhouse and hydroponic vegetable. Numerous varieties are cultivated including the small cherry tomato, yellow pear tomato, and large red beefsteak tomato. The leading producers are Texas, California, Florida, Ohio, and Tennessee.

Season: Tomatoes are available year-round, but the peak season is May through September.

Selection: For juicing, use only vine-ripened, in-season tomatoes from your garden or a local grower. Vine-ripened tomatoes cannot be bought in a supermarket, and greenhouse and cold-storage tomatoes have the opposite qualities and effects on the body from fresh tomatoes. When selecting tomatoes, choose firm, plump, smooth tomatoes that are free of decay, cracks, and bruises. The color, shape, and size will vary with the variety, but the tomato should be heavy for its size, well developed, and uniform in color. Avoid tomatoes with ridges at the stem end since this is a sign of mealiness.

Preparation: Just wash tomatoes. If juicing the tomatoes, cut them into chunks that will fit through the hopper of the juice extractor. You don't need to remove the stem.

Juice yield: Two large tomatoes will yield one to one and one-quarter cups of juice.

Storage: Keep ripe tomatoes in the refrigerator for up to one week.

Uses: The juice from fresh, ripe tomatoes is wonderful alone or combined with carrot, celery, cucumber, sweet-pepper, or cabbage juice. Try Veggie Combo or Hot and Spicy Veggie Cocktail, both on page 98, Southwestern Cocktail on page 99, or Zippy Tomato Express on page 100. In cooking, tomato juice is very versatile. Some other recipes in this book using tomato juice include Tomato Cream Supreme on page 161, Tomato-Vegetable-Rice Soup on page 165, Tomato Aspic With Avocado Dressing on page 180, Dominique's Tomato Sauce on page 210, and Tomato Couscous on page 231. Add tomato juice to soups, stews, sauces, and even muffins. See Blue Cornmeal Muffins on page 143.

Turnip Top

The turnip is a garden vegetable grown for both its root and top. It is a biennial of the mustard family and related to cabbage. Native to Europe, the turnip has been cultivated since prehistoric times. Two varieties were grown in A.D. 42 in what is now France, and Pliny spoke of five types used by the Romans. In northern and central Europe, the turnip was a staple food until the introduction of the potato in the 1500s. In the Colonies, it was first cultivated in Virginia in 1609 but was grown in abundance in Philadelphia by 1707. Turnips come in several varieties that all have the same flavor. In general, they are classified by color (yellow or white) and shape of root. A fifth type, such as the Seven-Top and Shogoin, is grown just for the top. In the United States, California is the leading producer of turnips.

Season: Turnip tops are available from March through September.

Selection: For juicing, choose turnip tops that are fresh, bright, and deep colored. Bypass tops that are wilted or spotted.

Preparation: Turnip tops should be rinsed under cold running water. If juicing the top, just bunch it up to fit through the hopper of the juice extractor.

Juice yield: One small bunch of turnip tops will yield approximately one tablespoon of juice.

Storage: Keep turnip tops in plastic bags in the refrigerator for up to one week.

Uses: Turnip tops are chock-full of beta-carotene and a good selection of minerals. Adding the juice of a few leaves to a recipe can greatly increase the nutritional value. Try Garden Cooler on page 91, Sunshine Salad Cocktail on page 102, and Mineral Medley on page 103.

Watercress

"Pungent," "peppery," and "tangy" are the words used most often to describe watercress. It looks like a delicate herb but packs a punch tastewise, making it popular as a garnish and salad ingredient. A hardy perennial of the mustard family, watercress is related to cabbage, kale, broccoli, cauliflower, Brussels sprouts, and collards. Along with its cousins, it is believed to have originated in the eastern Mediterranean and Asia Minor areas. It is common in North America, Europe, and southern South America, and was cultivated in

France as far back as the twelfth century A.D. Watercress grows in and around water. It prefers areas that have small streams and lots of limestone, and thrives when submerged in fresh running water. Botanists are now cultivating improved varieties in special fields. In the United States, Florida is the leading producer.

Season: Watercress is available all year, with a peak during the summer.

Selection: For juicing, choose watercress that is fresh, crisp, bright, and deep green. If it has flowered, it will be peppery hot. Avoid watercress that is wilted, yellowed, or bruised.

Preparation: Wash watercress. If juicing the watercress, just bunch it up; it doesn't need to be chopped.

Juice yield: One small bunch of watercress will yield approximately one tablespoon of juice.

Storage: Keep watercress in the refrigerator for up to one week. The best way to store it is to stand it upright in a glass or bowl of water. However, it can also be stored like other greens, in a perforated plastic bag. Avoid crushing watercress because it bruises and decays easily.

Uses: Watercress makes a nutritious addition to any recipe. It can be juiced, although it does not taste great alone because of its very strong flavor. Try adding it to mild-tasting juices, such as tomato or carrot. See Watercress Express on page 101 and Very Veggie Cocktail on page 102.

Watermelon

Watermelons are probably the most aptly named fruit, containing 92 percent water and eaten more for thirst than hunger. An annual herbaceous plant, the watermelon belongs to the gourd family but is botanically unrelated to muskmelons. It is believed to hail from Africa, where it still grows wild. Over the years, the watermelon has changed with efforts to improve yield and resistance to disease. As a result, the fruits of the pre-1960s no longer exist. Today, the flesh is usually red but can be pink, yellow, or white. The seeds, which many people eat, can be black, brown, or mixed. The rind, which can be pickled, is generally green. The most popular variety is large and oval with a variegated or striped rind, such as the Charleston Gray, Klondike Striped, Blue Ribbon, and Dixie Queen. In the United States, watermelons are grown in the South and in California.

Season: Watermelons are available from May through September, with a peak season from June through August.

Selection: For juicing, choose a well-shaped watermelon with smooth, velvety, hard skin. The flesh should be firm, juicy, and a good color, and the seeds should be shiny. Look for a ripe watermelon, which will sound hollow when you thump it with your finger. Avoid watermelons with greenish or white "ground spots"—the spots that touched the ground—which should be yellow, amber, or creamy. Also skip shiny melons.

Preparation: If a watermelon is organic, just wash it. If juicing the watermelon, cut it into pieces that will fit through the hopper of the juice extractor. The rind of organic watermelons provides lots of health-promoting chlorophyll but won't alter the delicious flavor of the juice. Juice the whole thing—rind, seeds, and all! However, if the watermelon is not organic, remove the most exterior portion of the rind to avoid the pesticides.

Juice yield: One pound of watermelon will yield approximately one cup of juice.

Storage: Keep watermelons in the refrigerator for up to a week, with any exposed surfaces covered.

Uses: Drink watermelon juice alone or with the juice of other melons. See Watermelon Cooler on page 83.

Winter Squash

When you think of autumn, what comes to mind? Falling leaves, ghosts and goblins, Thanksgiving—and winter squash, in all its shapes and sizes and colors. Winter squash, like summer squash, melons, and pumpkins, is a member of the gourd family. An annual herbaceous plant, it can reach, depending on the variety, three feet in length and fifteen pounds in weight. Found in green, gold, orange, and other fall colors, the different varieties of winter squash can create a beautiful autumn tapestry. They can be round, oval, or pear-shaped; straight or curved; large or small. Some popular varieties are acorn, buttercup, butternut, chayote, hubbard, and spaghetti. Winter squash is native to the Americas and grown all over the United States. During the growing season, local farmers supply most of the vegetable. In the off-season, Florida is the leading producer.

Season: Winter squash is available year-round, with a peak season from October through February.

Selection: For juicing, choose winter squash that has a hard rind. The rind of all varieties except acorn squash should resist being dented by a fingernail, which shows that the squash has been cured (*see* Preparation, below). Acorn, buttercup, and hubbard squash should have a dark green rind; butternut squash should have a beige rind; chayote squash should be pale green; and spaghetti squash should be yellow. Avoid winter squashes with soft spots or mold, which may indicate internal deterioration.

Preparation: If a winter squash has been cured (except for acorn squash, which doesn't need to be cured), simply wash it. If juicing the squash, cut it into strips that will fit through the hopper of the juice extractor and juice the rind, seeds, and all. If you're going to use the pulp, however, remove the peel and seeds. If the squash hasn't been cured, set it in a warm place for a couple of days to further harden the skin and remove moisture. If curing it outside in the sun, keep it up off the ground and cover it at night to protect it against frost. When the skin of the squash resists denting by fingernail, the curing is complete.

Juice yield: One medium butternut squash will yield approximately two cups of juice. Two acorn squashes will yield approximately one cup of juice.

Storage: Store winter squashes in a cool, dry place for up to several months.

Uses: Cherie has been told that banana squash is a good substitute for carrots in many recipes. You may want to try it when it's in season. Recipes using butternut-squash juice are Butternut Pâté on page 153 and Butternut Squash Loaf on page 247. Butternut-squash juice can also be added to soups, stews, and sauces.

Zucchini

See Summer Squash.

Ingredient Glossary

If you are not familiar with an ingredient used in one of our recipes, or if you have a question about it, just look it up in the following glossary. The glossary also provides basic cooking information for some of the ingredients.

All of the ingredients used in this book can be purchased in most large natural food (health food) stores or co-ops.

Agar-agar. A jelling agent. Tasteless, odorless, and colorless, agar-agar is made from a sea-vegetable species known as red algae. It can be used in place of gelatin to make wonderful desserts, aspics, jams, kantens, and so forth. Agar-agar is available in powder, flakes, and feather-light bars. In this book, we always use agar flakes. Agar-agar is preferable to gelatin, which is a very low quality protein extracted from bones, because agar is a strictly vegetarian jelling agent.

Amazake. A sweetener or refreshing drink. Literally translated as "sweet sake," amazake is made from rice that has been inoculated with koji (a special type of bacteria) and allowed to ferment in a warm place for several hours. As the rice ferments, it becomes delectably sweet and soft. Amazake is a magic ingredient for cakes, making them light and moist, and a delicious replacement for milk in smoothies, on fresh fruit, or as a drink by itself. It is also known as amasake.

Arrowroot. A thickening agent. A white powder made from the tuberous root of a tropical plant, arrowroot is used mainly as a thickening agent for sauces and puddings. It can be evenly substituted for cornstarch, or vice versa. Arrowroot is preferable to cornstarch because it is a natural food that is processed using a simple, traditional method, whereas cornstarch is chemically bleached and treated.

Baking powder. A leavening agent. Baking powder is usually used in quick breads and other baked goods not using yeast. A homemade version can be made from sodium bicarbonate (baking soda), cream of tartar, and arrowroot, cornstarch, or salt. When you buy baking powder, be sure to get one that does not contain aluminum.

Barley flour. A flour made from barley, which is a cereal grass. Barley flour is worth getting to know. It is as high in fiber as whole wheat flour, but it makes cakes, muffins, and cookies that are much lighter and more tender than baked goods made from whole wheat flour.

Black bean. A dried legume. Really dark purple in color, the black bean is considered one of the finest tasting of the dried legumes. It is native to the Americas but is also used extensively by the Chinese. Black beans are also known as turtle beans.

For the recipes in this book, you can either use canned black beans or cook your own from dried beans. To cook dried black beans: Wash one cup of black beans, culling any bad ones. Place the good beans in a bowl, cover them with water, and let them soak for eight to ten hours. Drain and rinse the beans. Put the beans in a large kettle with water to cover. Bring the water to a boil, then reduce the heat and simmer, covered, until the beans are tender, about one and a half hours. Stir the beans occasionally as they cook and add more water if necessary to keep them from sticking to the bottom of the pot. Do not add salt to the beans until they are done, as adding salt during cooking will toughen the beans.

Brown rice. Whole rice that contains the bran and the germ of the grain. Organically grown brown rice has a superior flavor. Many varieties of brown rice are available in natural food stores. The recipes in this book call for brown rice as a bed for stews or vegetables. For this purpose, try a long grain brown rice or a brown basmati rice. Basmati rice is an especially flavorful rice that is sometimes called scented or aromatic rice.

To cook brown rice: Place one cup of rice in a heavy pan. Cover the rice with water and swish it around with your hand to wash it. Drain the rice using a fine wire strainer. Return the rice to the pan, add two cups of water, cover the pan, and bring the water to a boil. Reduce the heat to low and simmer for about forty-five minutes or until the water is absorbed. Avoid removing the lid or stirring the rice during cooking.

Brown rice flour. A flour made from finely ground brown rice. Brown rice flour combines well with other flours in cookies, pancakes, and tempura batters. It also makes a thick, creamy base for soups.

Brown rice syrup. A sweetener made from brown rice. Brown rice syrup is less sweet than honey and is especially recommended, along with malt barley syrup, for anyone with a sugar-metabolism disorder, such as hypoglycemia. It is delicious and can be evenly substituted for any other sweetener. Brown rice syrup is produced when malt enzymes convert the starch in brown rice to a sweet syrup. Some malted sweeteners make the mixtures to which they are added more liquid due to their starch-splitting enzymes. Eggs can counteract this.

Chick pea. A dried legume. The chick pea has been an important food for thousands of years in the Mediterranean region. It is a favorite with Greeks, Italians, Latin Americans, and Arabs. It is also known as the garbanzo or ceci bean.

The chick peas used in the recipes in this book can be either canned or cooked from dried beans. To cook dried chick peas: Wash one cup of chick peas, culling any bad ones. Place the good chick peas in a bowl, cover them with water, and let them soak for eight to ten hours. Drain and rinse the chick peas. Put the chick peas in a large kettle with water to cover. Bring the water to a boil, then reduce the heat and simmer, covered, until the chick peas are tender, about three hours. Stir the chick peas occasionally as they cook and add more water if necessary to keep them from sticking to the bottom of the pot. Do not add salt to the chick peas until they are done, as adding salt during cooking will toughen the chick peas.

Cornmeal. A flour made from coarsely ground corn. The corn flour sold in many American markets is simply finely ground cornmeal. When buying cornmeal, select one that is made from whole corn and that does not contain added ingredients. You may also want to try blue cornmeal, which was a staple in the Native American diet. Blue corn is higher in protein than yellow corn and is sweeter, making it desirable for baked goods.

Couscous. A precooked wheat that has been dried. Couscous is a staple of Tunisian and Moroccan cuisine. It is used like rice as a bed for vegetables, beans, and stews. Until recently, the only couscous available was made from refined wheat. Now, however, a more nutritious whole wheat couscous is available. The recipes in this book call for whole wheat couscous.

Dehydrated cane juice. A sweetener. Dehydrated cane juice is made from organically grown sugar cane. Although it looks and tastes like brown sugar, it is not quite as sweet as brown sugar and is much more nutritious. One popular brand of dehydrated cane juice is Sucanat.

Dry active yeast. A leavening agent. Made from living microorganisms that are in a dormant state, dry active yeast is used to leaven breads. Do not confuse it with brewer's yeast or nutritional yeast, which have no leavening power.

Fruit concentrate. A sweetener. Fruit concentrate describes various forms of fruit-juice concentrates, including frozen juice concentrate and refrigerated or shelf-stable juice concentrate. Fruit concentrates are made from fruit juices that were mixed and then cooked down to a syrup. The most common are made of white grape juice or blends of pineapple, peach, and pear juices. Since processing is minimal, the fruit flavor may carry over into your product—a plus or minus depending upon your recipe. Although fruit concentrates are not as sweet as honey, they can be substituted for honey in most recipes, and vice versa. They can also replace white, brown, or turbinado sugar at a rate of one-half to three-quarters cup fruit concentrate for one cup sugar. When substituting fruit concentrate for honey, you may need to use slightly more concentrate than honey, depending on the concentrate. Let your tastebuds be your guide.

Fruit-sweetened jam. A jam that contains only concentrated fruit. Fruit-sweetened jams add both sweetness and flavor to recipes without adding refined sugar.

Gluten flour. A type of wheat flour. Gluten is the protein of wheat. Gluten flour is wheat flour that has had some of its starch removed and its proteins concentrated, producing a flour that is 70 percent pure gluten. Adding gluten flour to a yeast-bread recipe makes the bread light and spongy.

Miso. A savory fermented paste made from soybeans, sea salt, koji (a special bacteria), and sometimes a grain such as barley or rice. Miso is used as a soup base or versatile seasoning ingredient. Unpasteurized miso, like yogurt, contains bacteria that aid the circulation and digestion. To preserve the benefits of the bacteria, add the miso at the end of cooking whenever possible. White and yellow misos, made from white rice, are sweet and mild as well as salty. Mugi miso, made from barley, is darker and richer flavored. Red miso, made with more salt, less koji, and more soybeans, is darker and saltier flavored.

Nutritional yeast. A food supplement that is very rich in the B vitamins and protein but low in calories. Nutritional yeast gives a pleasant nutty taste to spreads, sauces, dinner loaves, and veggie burgers. Do not confuse nutritional yeast with torula yeast or brewer's yeast, which are also food supplements but which many people feel have a disagreeable taste.

Oat flour. A flour made from ground whole oats. Oat flour makes baked goods that are tender and moist. If you do not have oat flour on hand, just grind some rolled oats in a blender. Measure the oats after grinding to get the amount called for in the recipe.

Rolled oats. Whole grains of oats that have simply been run through heavy metal rollers to flatten them out and enable them to cook faster. In our recipes, we use the old-fashioned type of rolled oats, which is higher in nutrients than the quick-cooking variety.

Silken tofu. An especially mild and custard-like type of tofu (*see* Tofu). The difference in texture between tofu and silken tofu is due to a different production process. The soy milk from which silken tofu is made is much thicker, and the coagulant is added when the hot soy milk is already in the mold, which has no draining holes. When the coagulant is added, the milk does not separate into curds and whey, as regular tofu does, but instead forms into an extra-soft cake. Because no whey is drained off, silken tofu has more water and less protein than regular tofu.

Silken tofu comes packaged in a little hermetically sealed

rectangular container. It does not need refrigeration until the container is opened.

Do not confuse silken tofu with regular tofu, which is simply called tofu in this book.

Soy cheese. A cheese-like product made mostly from soybeans. Soy cheese comes in many of the same flavors as cow's-milk cheese, including cheddar, mozzarella, Monterey jack, American, and Parmesan. It can be found as a solid chunk or sliced, grated, or creamed. Soy cheese can be used any way and anywhere you use cow's-milk cheese. It is found in the dairy section of natural food stores.

Soy milk. The milk made from soybeans that are soaked, ground, and pressed through a fine cloth. The varieties of soy milk sold in quart containers in natural food stores also contain ingredients to improve their flavor and texture. For use in recipes, be sure to buy plain, or original, soy milk because the flavored milks, such as chocolate and vanilla milk, will not taste good. Soy milk can be substituted for dairy milk in any recipe. It is delicious on breakfast cereal.

Sprouts. Seeds that have begun to germinate. Sprouts can be made from most nuts, grains, and legumes, which are all seeds. The seeds are first soaked for eight to twelve hours, then drained and allowed to germinate for one to six days. Popular sprouts include adzuki bean, mung bean, alfalfa, wheat, chick-pea, soybean, sunflower, and lentil sprouts. Sprouts can be purchased in most natural food stores or grown at home at any time of the year.

Tahini. A paste made from ground hulled sesame seeds. Do not confuse tahini with sesame butter, which is made from toasted and ground unhulled sesame seeds. A staple in Mideastern cuisine, tahini is lighter in taste and appearance than sesame butter and is a good source of calcium. It can be used as a spread for bread and crackers or as an ingredient in dips, sauces, desserts, veggie burgers, and smoothies.

Tamari. A natural Japanese soy sauce. Tamari is made from cultured soybeans, water, and sea salt, which are fermented for up to two years in a wooden keg. It should not be confused with shoyu, which is often labeled as tamari in North America but which also contains wheat. Avoid the cheap commercial soy sauces on the American market since they contain wheat and additional salt and have an inferior flavor.

Tempeh. A fermented soybean product. A traditional food of Indonesia, tempeh is made from partially cooked, split, and hulled soybeans that are inoculated with a special bacteria and incubated for about twenty-four hours. During incubation, a white fluffy mold develops around the beans, holding them together to form a slab. Tempeh has a firm but tender texture and a likeable flavor.

Before being used, tempeh must be cooked. In addition, it is very perishable and should be kept frozen until needed. Unfrozen, tempeh will keep for just a few days.

Tofu. A fermented soybean product. A staple of both Chinese and Japanese cuisines, tofu has become popular with Westerners who want an easy-to-prepare protein that does not contain cholesterol or saturated fat. It is made from soybeans that have been soaked for eight to ten hours and then ground to a puree. The puree is pressed through a cloth to extract the soy milk from the pulp. The milk is cooked, and a coagulant (traditionally nigari, which is extracted from sea salt) is added to cause the milk to curdle. The curds are then carefully ladled from the whey and placed in a mold where they are pressed until firm.

Tofu is available in soft, medium, firm, and extra firm consistencies. Do not confuse tofu with silken tofu, which is made by a different process (*see* Silken tofu). Tofu can be found in the refrigerator section of natural food stores and some supermarkets. After opening the package, transfer the tofu to a container and cover it with fresh water. Store tofu in the refrigerator; it does not need to be frozen. Tofu can be sliced and eaten as is or used as a cooked or uncooked ingredient in recipes. It is extremely versatile.

Tofu cream cheese. *See* Soy cheese.

TVP. Textured vegetable protein. TVP is a convenience food made from soybeans. It adds texture along with protein to veggie burgers, meatless loaves, chili, and other dishes in which a ground beef-like texture is desirable. It comes in the form of granules, which are then hydrated. Look for it in natural food stores.

Vinegar. A condiment or preservative. Vinegar is made from several sources and in many flavors. Among the most common are white or distilled vinegar, made from alcohol; wine vinegar, made from red, rosé, or white wine; cider vinegar, made from apple cider; malt vinegar, made from barley malt or another cereal grain; and rice vinegar, made from white or brown rice. Herbs, such as tarragon, can be added, usually to cider or wine vinegar. Balsamic vinegar, a very rich tasting and aromatic red vinegar made from sweet wine, is especially popular.

Wakame. A mild-flavored sea vegetable. Wakame comes from the cold waters off Japan's northern island of Hokkaido. During the spring, it is sold fresh in the Orient, but during the rest of the year in the Orient and all year in North America, it is available only in dried form. Traditionally used in miso soup, wakame can be found in most natural food stores. It comes in a regular and a quick-cooking variety. Like all sea vegetables, wakame is very high in iron and other minerals.

Wheat germ. The embryo of a grain of wheat. Wheat germ is a rich source of all the B vitamins and several minerals. However, because it also contains fat, it spoils very quickly and is therefore removed in modern wheat processing. Wheat germ can be purchased separately in most supermarkets and natural food stores. It comes raw or toasted, and can be stored in the refrigerator or freezer. It can be eaten alone as a cereal, sprinkled on top of salads and desserts, blended with yogurt and fruit, and added to pancakes and any baked goods.

Wheatgrass. Wheat sprouts. *See also* Sprouts.

Whole wheat flour. Flour made from whole wheat berries and without chemical whiteners. Whole wheat flour is made from hard red spring wheat. It is higher in gluten (protein) than soft wheat and is thus used to make breads, which need to rise well. It also gives breads their uniform consistency. Because of its use in bread baking, whole wheat flour is also known as whole wheat bread flour.

Whole wheat pastry flour. A whole wheat flour made from soft winter wheat (*see* Whole wheat flour). Pastry flour is lower in gluten than bread flour, which makes it better for pastries, cakes, crackers, and other baked goods that should be finer and lighter than bread.

Preparing and Using Juice and Pulp

Adding fruit and vegetable juices and pulps to your recipes is one of the best gifts you can give to yourself and your family. Juice and pulp are concentrated sources of nutrients, those life-sustaining, life-enhancing substances so vital for every living creature. Juice and pulp naturally enrich everything to which they're added, including even the most ordinary dishes. And they make these dishes so beautiful to look at that you'll devour them with your eyes before you even sit down at the dinner table. Juices and pulps add the natural, refreshing flavors of nature's fruits and vegetables along with beautiful colors. And pulp adds fiber without loading on calories.

Juicing fruits and vegetables is easy, but as with anything new, until you get used to what you're doing, it can be a little confusing. To help you gain confidence at the farm stand or supermarket, we've prepared the following guide to help you choose and prepare produce for juicing, store the juice you don't use immediately, and use the pulp. Combined with all the information in About the Fruits and Vegetables, this guide should help you become an expert in the produce aisle very quickly.

Purchasing a Juicer

If you don't own a juice extractor, or if you have one but want to replace it, we'd like to point out some important features to keep in mind when shopping for a good juicer. (Please note that a blender cannot be substituted for a juicer because it doesn't separate the pulp from the juice.) First, however, you should be aware that there are three basic types of juicers:

1. *Masticating juicers have blades that tear apart the plant cells to produce a paste, which is then squeezed through a screen to be separated into pulp and juice. Example: Champion.*
2. *Masticating juicers with a hydraulic press deposit the paste in a cotton bag to be pressed and separated. Example: Norwalk Press.*
3. *Centrifugal juicers produce a paste and then spin it at a high rate of speed to separate it into juice and pulp, the latter of which is either ejected into a separate receptacle or deposited in an internal receptacle. Examples: Braun, Oster, Phoenix, Acme, Salton, AEG, and Juiceman.*

Many juicers look similar on the exterior, and sometimes, the only visible difference is the price. But what you can't see is what matters. Look for a juicer with a strong motor—.4 horsepower (hp) or more. (Many of the well-advertised brands have .25 hp or less.) A juicer with a small motor tends to stop in the middle of juicing, to vibrate, to smoke, or to quit permanently. It also can't juice rinds, tough skins such as pineapple, or stems. Cherie has spoken with many seminar participants who have discovered this to their dismay, including one woman who had "blown up" six juicers in a year and a half because they all had small motors. Vicki has heard similar stories.

Speed and efficiency are necessary features when juicing is part of your daily routine. Some juicers take two or three times longer than others to make juice. Also, a juicer that ejects the pulp rather than depositing it in an inner basket helps save time. (And if you have to stop and empty an inner basket after every glass or two of juice, you may lose interest in juicing.) The size of the pulp receptacle is another consideration—the larger the receptacle is, the more pulp you can collect before you need to empty it. Finally, some juicer receptacles are designed so that a plastic bag from the produce section of the grocery store will fit in nicely as a liner, saving you from needing to constantly wash the receptacle. You simply lift out the plastic bag when you're done, with the receptacle itself remaining pulp-free.

Make sure the juicer you buy is easy to clean; the fewer the parts you have to wash, the better it is—unless you enjoy doing dishes! One of the first juicers Cherie owned had six parts to wash, and she found herself on many an evening deciding not to use the juicer because it was such a bother to clean. Cherie and Vicki both agree that the best juicer they have found, and one that meets all the criteria noted above, is the Juiceman™ juicer. With its powerful .485-horsepower motor, twist-together components, and separate pulp receptacle, it allows nonstop juicing and quick, easy clean-up.

With an efficient juicer, you'll be able to quickly and easily enjoy the energizing, healthy benefits of fresh juice every day. And the recipes in this cookbook hopefully will help you discover a variety of exciting ways in which to use the juice and juice pulp.

Choosing Produce

The highest quality produce available is that which is grown locally and organically. Fruits and vegetables grown in your area and without insecticides or chemical fertilizers are the best. Local produce is likely to be more flavorful as well as more healthful because it doesn't have to be picked before it's ripe. In addition, it's more likely to be fresh because it's not shipped halfway around the world. Anyone who has ever eaten garden-fresh, organic fruits and vegetables knows that the commercial counterparts cannot even come close in flavor, texture, or sweetness.

If better taste and freshness are not enough, there are other reasons for buying organic. Organically grown produce, grown in rich soil, has been shown to be higher in nutrients than chemically fertilized produce. Even more important, it doesn't contain insecticide residues. Furthermore, when you buy organic, you are helping to promote and encourage organic agriculture and the dedicated individuals who are working to protect and enrich our precious farmland.

When it comes to non-organically grown produce, be aware that chemical dips are often applied to certain vegetables and fruits after harvest to inhibit decay. Many of the dipping compounds are controversial and have been shown to penetrate the flesh of the vegetable or fruit. Therefore, if you cannot buy organic produce, be sure to peel it. Waxes are also something to watch. They are often used to slow moisture loss. They may be applied alone or mixed with a fungicide, bactericide, ripening inhibitor, or coloring agent. Waxed produce also should always be peeled.

Avoid buying produce from South American countries. Fruits and vegetables from South America are often higher in insecticide residues than produce from the United States, and some of the insecticides used are banned in the United States. The laws concerning these chemicals are stricter in the United States than in South American countries.

Also be wary of irradiated produce. Irradiation is a technique in which food is treated with ionizing radiation to kill insects and other organisms and to inhibit ripening. The goal is to prolong shelf life. However, irradiation has been found in some cases to actually increase a food's susceptibility to fungal attacks. Nevertheless, it was approved in 1986 for the treatment of fresh fruits and vegetables. When the process is used, the fruit or vegetable is supposed to carry a label showing a stylized flower inside a circle, a symbol similar to the "Radura" label developed in South Africa and the Netherlands.

Irradiation processing, we feel, should be avoided for several reasons. First, irradiation is very destructive to nutrients, such as vitamin C, certain B vitamins (especially folic acid and thiamine), and beta-carotene. Second, it also breaks down complex carbohydrates, such as cellulose and pectin, which are valuable fibers. Third, when studies were conducted testing the use of irradiated food with animals, concerns arose regarding the creation of mutagen and radiolytic particles in the food. And fourth, irradiation treatment makes it very difficult to determine the freshness of produce. For all these reasons, we feel it is

Giving Pets the Benefits of Fresh Produce

People are not the only ones who benefit from fresh fruits and vegetables. In fact, they are not the only ones who need the nutrients from produce.

Two friends told Vicki that they add vegetable pulp (mostly carrot pulp) to their dogs' food. Both of the dogs are healthy and energetic, with beautiful shiny coats. This was an interesting idea to Vicki but one she didn't know anything about, so she contacted Dr. Martin Neher at the Palmer Ranch Animal Hospital in Sarasota, Florida. Dr. Neher assured Vicki that as long as a dog's diet is balanced, supplementing it with vegetable pulp is just fine. In fact, he said that some dogs need supplementary fiber in their diet. According to Vicki's friends, dogs love carrot pulp and, when it is mixed with their regular food or some meat broth, they enthusiastically eat every last morsel.

Cherie has also been using pulp as a pet-food supplement. She has been mixing one or two teaspoons of carrot and other vegetable pulps in her cat's food for several years. The cat doesn't even know that the pulp is in his food. However, it's obvious that he's eating well because he has a very thick, shiny black coat, his eyes sparkle, and he is very healthy. Best of all, Cherie hasn't had a vet bill in three years.

During the writing of "Cooking for Life," Cherie's sister-in-law's dog, McKenzie, a nine-month-old schnauzer, made a permanent move to Cherie's home. Cherie immediately decided to see if the dog would eat a little carrot-cabbage pulp. The dog lapped it up in seconds. Since that first day, McKenzie has had many kinds of pulp. He loves it! Cherie mixes it with his wet food or gives it to him straight. She also rolls up carrot pulp into little balls, which she calls "treats"! McKenzie dances for the treats. Cherie has decided that McKenzie is a very smart dog!

In addition, Cherie has noticed that McKenzie no longer constantly scratches, as he did when he first arrived. Cherie recently learned that many small dogs develop a number of skin problems, such as flaking skin, itching, and hair loss, because they lack certain nutrients or get too much protein in their pet food. She also found out that dogs need some vegetables in addition to their meat- and grain-based food. Adding pulp to their diet is one very easy and economical way to get them to eat vegetables.

One of the best pet stories we've heard yet came from a woman in one of the groups Cherie lectured on juicing. The woman stood up and said that for years her dog had had a degenerative hip condition that was getting progressively worse. When someone suggested she feed him carrot pulp with his other dog food, she eagerly tried it. Within a short period of time, the dog began to improve.

Ask your veterinarian about feeding vegetable pulp to your pet. The chances are good that your pet will love it and his health will benefit.

advisable to avoid the purchase of irradiated produce. You may also want to boycott the sale of any other foods subjected to this treatment.

Also of questionable safety is the genetic engineering of produce. Genetically engineered foods have been altered via gene splicing, the recombination of DNA. Again, the produce industry's motives are pest resistance and longer shelf life. According to current Food and Drug Administration (FDA) policy, most transgenic foods will not be subjected to premarket testing. In addition, the FDA has given the companies selling these products the responsibility for labeling them. Without FDA directives, the companies will probably provide consumers with little or no information about the alterations.

Until now, scientists have mixed genes only within a plant genus, for example, wheat genes with wheat genes, or corn genes with corn genes. Today, however, any genes can be mixed. Supermarkets will soon stock such new foods as potatoes that had silkworm genes added to increase the tuber's resistance to disease, or tomatoes that had flounder genes added to reduce the fruit's susceptibility to frost damage. Knowing what genes are present in foods is important for allergic or food-sensitive individuals, who need to avoid foods with potentially harmful allergens. For example, peanut genes are to be inserted into tomatoes even though peanut allergies are fairly common and often cause severe adverse reactions. A consumer allergic to peanuts may purchase a genetically altered tomato and experience very unpleasant effects.

Biotechnology also may accelerate the loss of many of the plant species that have been a part of our food supply for centuries as foods genetically engineered for longer shelf life replace our traditional foods. With this loss will come the disappearance of certain nutrients, causing a drop in health. It's the variety of foods we eat that supplies the range of vitamins, minerals, trace elements, and accessory food components we need for good health. No one food—or food type—supplies all the necessary nutrients. We do not need more technology. Rather, we need less manipulated and more nurtured produce and farmland. You may want to voice your opinion regarding genetically engineered food and avoid purchasing it whenever possible.

As far as what to look for or avoid when purchasing a specific type of fruit or vegetable, refer to About the Fruits and Vegetables on page 7. This listing includes all the fruits and vegetables that we juice in our recipes, and each description provides guidelines for selection.

Preparing Produce for Juicing

As soon as possible after purchasing a fruit or vegetable, remove all visible dirt from it and place the fruit or vegetable in the refrigerator. When you are ready to juice the produce, cut out any discolored, bruised, or moldy spots. Remove and discard the peel and outer leaves if the fruit or vegetable is non-organic. Also peel it if it is waxed. Then cut the produce into pieces that will fit through the hopper of the juice extractor.

For further tips regarding the preparation of a specific fruit or vegetable, see About the Fruits and Vegetables, page 7.

Washing Produce

All produce should be washed before being juiced. Organic produce can simply be rinsed with fresh, pure water. Non-organic produce, however, should be thoroughly washed with a nontoxic, biodegradable cleanser. Trillium Health Products, the natural health products company that developed the Juiceman™ juice extractor, offers an economical product called Nature's Wash™. Your local health food store or co-op should also be a good resource for suggestions of brands. Whichever cleanser you choose, it should be able to remove surface pesticides, soil, and microorganisms that may have contaminated the produce. Scrub your fruits and vegetables well with a natural-bristle vegetable brush. And don't forget to rinse.

Storing Juice and Pulp

The fresher juice is, the more nutrients it has. To preserve the nutrients in a juice, store the juice in an air-tight, opaque container in the refrigerator. Heat, light, oxidation, and aging all destroy nutrients. (Just think about all the nutrients you don't get from commercially bottled or canned juices!) The best container for storing juice is a stainless steel thermal container. Put the container in the refrigerator or freezer and chill it well, then fill it to the brim with your juice and screw on the cap, allowing a little bit of the juice to splash over. Filling the thermal container to the very top ensures that no air is left in.

People often ask if juice can be frozen. It definitely can. Freezing juice is an efficient way to preserve excess garden produce. Or use "juice cubes" as a delightful addition to a cool, refreshing drink. You'll probably lose some nutrients, but you'll also preserve a lot. However, don't plan to store frozen juice any longer than you would store fresh vegetables that you freeze. And remember, the same is true for frozen juice as for fresh: the sooner you drink it once it thaws, the more nutrients you'll get.

As far as storing pulp is concerned, the same principles apply. Just put it in a covered container in the refrigerator. The only difference is that the maximum length of time pulp will keep is one to two days, depending on the pulp.

Using Pulp in Recipes

Cooking with pulp is very easy. If you glance through the recipes in this cookbook, you'll see that it is just another ingredient. Once you've run the fruit or vegetable through the juice extractor

Using Pulp as Compost

Another wonderful use for fruit and vegetable pulp is as compost for your garden.

Vicki has found that composting gives her a sense of kinship with the earth because, rather than creating garbage with her food scraps, she is feeding and enriching the soil on her tiny piece of land. Mother Nature rewards those who take the trouble to compost by returning beautiful fruits, vegetables, flowers, and shrubs that grow and flourish without the use of chemical fertilizers. Because of the seeds sometimes present in pulp, composting also has a surprise benefit. Every summer, you will find vegetables that you did not plant growing out of the compost. Imagine going out in your garden and discovering a watermelon!

Vicki has not had any problems with odor or animals in her compost. Odor is easily controlled by lightly dusting the compost pile with powdered lime, which can be purchased at any garden center. The only animals Vicki has noticed are little insects that never go beyond the confines of the compost bin and the birds and lizards that feed on them.

Composting is not much trouble either. Rather than throwing fruit and vegetable scraps into the garbage pail or down the garbage disposal, just throw them into the compost bin. Leaves and grass clippings can also be added. Every week or so, turn the compost with a pitchfork (or find someone to do it for you) and, once in a while, sprinkle it with special enzymes, available in gardening stores, which help break it down more quickly.

Vicki's compost bin is made of concrete blocks stacked four rows high, one block on top of another, forming a large rectangle measuring about three feet by six feet. An opening at the front allows easy access for turning or removing compost. Compost bins can also be purchased at many garden and home centers. When Vicki lived in the country, she did not use a compost bin. She just threw her vegetable scraps in a pile at the back of her garden. In the fall, she would rake the compost into the garden and turn it into the soil. As you can see, there is nothing complicated or mysterious about making compost.

If you have never tried composting, maybe it's time to start. You'll save money on your garbage-collection bills and on fertilizer. Composting is really easy and is one way in which people with a backyard can do something good for the earth.

and have the pulp prepared, there isn't anything really special you'll need to do. Just make sure that the pulp doesn't have any large pieces of flesh or skin that didn't get ground up. And when measuring pulp for a recipe, fill the measuring cup with the pulp but don't pack the pulp down.

If you wish to add fruit or vegetable pulp to your own recipes, the best suggestion we can give you is to use it sparingly at first. Too much pulp tends to make baked goods overly moist and gives vegetable loaves and patties an unappealing texture. Here's a hint: when creating your own recipes using pulp, don't use more than a half cup. If the half cup of pulp works well, you can increase the amount the next time.

The kinds of recipes in which fruit or vegetable pulp works well are muffins, quick breads, cakes, cookies, veggie burgers, meatless loaves, pâtés, and sandwich spreads. In addition, tomato pulp can be added to soups, sauces, and stews, and fruit pulp can be added to sherbets and pies. As you become adept at cooking with pulp, you'll probably think of many other delicious uses for it. Be creative and see what kind of gourmet masterpieces you can come up with!

How to Use This Cookbook

Except for a juice extractor, no special equipment is required to prepare the recipes in this cookbook. Nor is any specialized knowledge necessary. If you have a question concerning the selection or preparation of a certain fruit or vegetable, check About the Fruits and Vegetables on page 7. If another ingredient leaves you wondering, look it up in the Ingredient Glossary on page 55. We don't ask you to use any unusual techniques to make our recipes. We've tried to keep the recipes easy, even though the results are fantastic.

The following list provides some tips for using the recipes in this cookbook. The tips, like the recipes, are simple and straightforward.

☐ Always preheat the oven. The only times you shouldn't are when you make Dill Bread on page 130 and Carrot Bread on page 133, two yeast breads that should be placed in a cold oven.

☐ All ovens are different. If baked dishes seem to rarely turn out correctly, you should consider investing in a good oven thermometer. Also, use your common sense as well as a watch or oven timer to determine when a dish is done.

☐ Be careful when measuring ingredients, especially agar-agar. If a heaping spoonful is indicated, fill the spoon as full as possible.

If a slightly rounded spoonful is specified, make sure the ingredient is neither heaping nor flat but slightly rounded. If a level spoonful is called for, level off the ingredient.

☐ When a recipe calls for a certain number of fruits or vegetables to be juiced, remember that the amount listed is an approximation. Fruits and vegetables can vary dramatically in size and no definite number can be given. Juice as much of the fruit or vegetable as necessary to yield the amount of juice or pulp required by the recipe.

☐ When a recipe calls for ground nuts or seeds, measure the whole nuts or seeds before grinding them. Then grind them in a blender or food processor, running the machine on high until the ground nuts or seeds are of the desired consistency. A blender is fine for a coarse grind, but a fine grind will probably require a food processor. A nut grinder or coffee grinder will also provide a fine consistency.

☐ When a recipe calls for flour, make sure you use the exact type of flour specified. Use the flour straight from the bag—do not sift or stir it before measuring.

☐ While not as healthful, dairy milk and cheese can be substituted for soy milk and cheese in any recipe.

☐ To lower cholesterol in recipes using eggs, substitute two egg whites for each whole egg or use an egg replacer, which is a packaged product that can be purchased in a health food store.

☐ When a recipe calls for oil, use a cold-pressed (mechanically or expeller pressed) oil that does not contain any additives. For sautéing vegetables, as a seasoning, and on salads, extra virgin olive oil is good. For desserts and any recipe calling for a light-flavored oil, try canola, sunflower, or safflower oil.

☐ When a recipe calls for tofu, make sure you use the type of tofu specified. Silken tofu is always called silken tofu. Regular tofu is just called tofu.

☐ When a recipe calls for sun-dried tomatoes, do not use oil-packed tomatoes unless marinated sun-dried tomatoes are specified.

☐ Always use dried herbs unless fresh herbs are specifically indicated. The only exception is parsley, which is always available fresh and should always be used in fresh form.

☐ When a recipe calls for nuts, use raw, unsalted nuts. Try to purchase nuts still in their shells and shell them immediately before use. If you decide to buy shelled nuts, look for them in a vacuum-packed container or in the refrigerator case at your health food store since they can quickly become rancid. Store shelled nuts in the refrigerator or freezer.

☐ When a recipe calls for sunflower seeds, use raw, unsalted seeds that have been removed from their hulls. Look for seeds in the refrigerator case at your natural food store and either refrigerate or freeze those that you don't immediately use.

☐ When a recipe calls for something like sun-dried tomato halves to be cut into small pieces, use a scissors instead of a knife. A scissors can also be used to "chop" parsley.

☐ After removing a cornbread or meatless loaf from the oven, allow it to sit for ten to fifteen minutes before slicing. Otherwise, it will crumble.

☐ Remember that all recipe yields and times are estimates. Use them as guides, not rules.

PART TWO

The Recipes

Beverages

We've developed over one hundred recipes for the Beverages section. These recipes are divided into six groups: Fruit Juices, Fruit-and-Vegetable Juices, Vegetable Juices, Smoothies, Fizzes, and Teas. Each group includes some of Cherie's old favorites, plus many new recipes. If you've never tried fresh juice, the fruit-juice recipes as well as the fruit-and-vegetable-juice combinations are a great place to start. Fruit makes everything taste better. But, be aware that, particularly if you're sensitive to sugar, too much fruit sugar can cause a hypoglycemic reaction. It's a good idea, therefore, to drink more vegetable-juice combinations than pure fruit juices.

Many vegetable-juice recipes are very tasty because the addition of a small amount of lemon, lime, ginger, or hot-pepper sauce can spark up a drink or change its flavor completely. To see what we mean, try Southwestern Cocktail on page 99 or Peppy Tomato on page 104. If you have hypoglycemia, diabetes, or Candida, these delicious vegetable-juice recipes will be especially healthful for you. As a nutritionist, Cherie recommends that people with these conditions have little or no fruit juice. Be warned, however, that some combinations contain a variety of vegetables for which you may need to acquire a taste.

The remaining recipes are for the drinks nearly everyone likes best: the smoothies, fizzes, and fruit-juice teas. Drink the fruit-rich combinations sparingly, though, as you would fruit juices. When you do drink them, however, you'll enjoy them. Some of the smoothie combinations are simply fabulous, such as Green Velvet on page 106 and Peaches and Cream on page 109. Some of the delicious teas, such as Ginger Tea on page 118, are also therapeutic. And some of the fizzes, like Lemon Spritzer on page 114, can be enjoyed every day without guilt because they are so low in calories. The fizzes are also free of the unhealthy ingredients present in soft drinks, while at the same time offering you a bubbly, delicious taste.

FRUIT JUICES

Strawberry-Cantaloupe Shake

A delicious, creamy drink that truly tastes like a shake.

½ cantaloupe
½ pint strawberries

Yield: 2 servings

Cut the cantaloupe into wedges. Juice the cantaloupe wedges with the strawberries. Stir the combined juice, pour it into 2 glasses, and serve.

Pink Sunrise

A perfect drink for a festive brunch!

1 orange
½ pink grapefruit
1 strawberry or slice lemon, as garnish

Yield: 1 serving

Peel the orange and grapefruit, and cut them into wedges. Juice the orange wedges with the grapefruit wedges. Stir the combined juice, pour it into a glass, and serve it garnished with the strawberry or lemon slice.

Fruit Salad in a Glass

The special flavors of these delicious fruits combine to make an outstanding drink.

½ apple
1 bunch grapes on stems (approximately 1 cup)
6 strawberries
¼ lemon

Yield: 1 serving

Cut the apple into wedges and remove the seeds. Juice the apple wedges with the grapes, strawberries, and lemon. Stir the combined juice, pour it into a glass, and serve.

Pineapple-Ginger Express

Not only is this drink delicious, but it soothes sore throats.

¼ pineapple
¼-inch slice ginger root

Yield: 1 serving

Cut the pineapple into strips. Juice the pineapple strips with the ginger root. Stir the combined juice, pour it into a glass, and serve.

Orange Delight

Frothy homemade orange juice combines with sweet apple juice for a double delight.

2–3 oranges
½ Golden Delicious or other sweet apple

Yield: 2 servings

Peel the oranges and cut them into wedges. Cut the apple into wedges and remove the seeds. Juice the orange wedges with the apple wedges. Stir the combined juice, pour it into 2 glasses, and serve.

Tropical Squeeze

Ginger for zest, papaya for creamy richness, and pear for sweetness—yummy!

1 firm papaya
1 pear
¼-inch slice ginger root

Yield: 1–2 servings

Peel the papaya, cut it into strips, and remove the seeds. Cut the pear into wedges. Juice the papaya strips and pear wedges with the ginger root. Stir the combined juice, pour it into 1 large or 2 small glasses, and serve.

Kiwi Cooler

An especially refreshing drink on a hot summer day.

1 firm kiwi
1 green apple
1 bunch grapes on stems (approximately 1 cup)
1 slice kiwi, as garnish

Yield: 1 serving

Peel the kiwi and cut it in half. Cut the apple into wedges and remove the seeds. Juice the kiwi halves and apple wedges with the grapes. Stir the combined juice, pour it into a tall ice-filled glass, and serve it garnished with the kiwi slice.

Mint Medley

An after-dinner mint!

1 firm kiwi
1 green apple
3–4 sprigs mint
1 sprig mint, as garnish

Yield: 1 serving

Peel the kiwi and cut it in half. Cut the apple into wedges and remove the seeds. Bunch up the 3–4 mint sprigs and juice them with the kiwi halves and apple wedges. Stir the combined juice, pour it into an ice-filled glass, and serve it garnished with the 1 mint sprig.

Mango Cooler

The tartness of lemon enlivens this rich, sweet drink.

1 mango
½ apple
¼ lemon
1 slice lemon, as garnish

Yield: 1 serving

Peel the mango and cut it into wedges. Cut the apple into wedges and remove the seeds. Juice the mango and apple wedges with the lemon quarter. Stir the combined juice, pour it into an ice-filled glass, and serve it garnished with the lemon slice.

Watermelon Cooler

A summertime favorite, this is a fantastic thirst quencher.

¼ cantaloupe
2-inch slice watermelon
1 sprig mint or slice lemon, as garnish

Yield: 1 serving

Cut the cantaloupe and watermelon into wedges and juice them. Stir the combined juice, pour it into an ice-filled glass, and serve it garnished with the mint sprig or lemon slice.

Pineapple-Cherry Cocktail

Sweet, with just a hint of tartness.

4–6 cherries
3 one-inch slices pineapple
½ lime

Yield: 2 servings

Remove the pits from the cherries. Cut the pineapple slices into strips and the lime into wedges. Juice the cherries with the pineapple strips and lime wedges. Stir the combined juice, pour it into 2 glasses, and serve.

Cranapple Cocktail

Once you've tried homemade cranapple, you'll never want to drink store-bought again.

2 Red Delicious or other sweet apples
¼ cup cranberries, unfrozen
1 thin wedge lemon

Yield: 1 serving

Cut the apples into wedges and remove the seeds. Juice the apple wedges with the cranberries and lemon. Stir the combined juice, pour it into a glass, and serve.

Grape-Pineapple Party

Sweet, frothy, and so delicious!

2 one-inch slices pineapple
½ lemon
1 bunch green grapes on stems (approximately 1 cup)

Yield: 1 serving

Cut the pineapple slices into strips and the lemon into wedges. Juice the pineapple strips and lemon wedges with the grapes. Stir the combined juice, pour it into a glass, and serve.

Pool Party Cooler

A zesty, refreshing drink that will be the life of your party.

1 medium orange
3 one-inch slices pineapple
⅛ lemon
2 slices lemon, as garnish

Yield: 2 servings

Peel the orange and cut it into wedges. Cut the pineapple slices into strips. Juice the orange wedges and pineapple strips with the ⅛ lemon. Stir the combined juice, pour it into 2 ice-filled glasses, and serve each drink garnished with a lemon slice.

Peach-Apple Shake

This drink is so creamy and delicious that it's hard to believe it's just juice—so we call it a shake.

2 peaches
1 Golden Delicious or other sweet apple

Yield: 1 serving

Remove the stones from the peaches and cut the flesh into wedges. Cut the apple into wedges and remove the seeds. Juice the peach wedges with the apple wedges. Stir the combined juice, pour it into an ice-filled glass, and serve.

Pink Lemonade

The best lemonade in the world!

2 Red or Golden Delicious apples
1 small wedge lemon
1 very small piece beet, for color
1 slice lemon, as garnish

Yield: 1 serving

Cut the apples into wedges and remove the seeds. Juice the apple wedges with the lemon wedge and beet. Stir the combined juice, pour it into an ice-filled glass, and serve it garnished with the lemon slice.

Pink Passion Potion

One sip and you'll be passionate for this drink!

1 apple
1 bunch grapes with stems (approximately 1 cup)
½ cup cranberries, unfrozen
1 small wedge lemon

Yield: 1 serving

Cut the apple into wedges and remove the seeds. Juice the apple wedges with the grapes, cranberries, and lemon. Stir the combined juice, pour it into a glass, and serve.

Strawberry Cooler

The apples and strawberries make this drink cool even without the ice.

1 Golden Delicious or other sweet apple
1 pint strawberries
⅛ lemon
1 slice lemon, as garnish

Yield: 1 serving

Cut the apple into wedges and remove the seeds. Juice the apple wedges with the strawberries and ⅛ lemon. Stir the combined juice, pour it into an ice-filled glass, and serve it garnished with the lemon slice.

Summer on the Island

You'll feel like you're on vacation when you sip this Piña Colada.

3 one-inch slices pineapple
¼ lime
½ cup coconut milk (or coconut juice)

Yield: 2 servings

Cut the pineapple slices into strips. Juice the pineapple strips with the lime. Add the coconut milk to the combined juice and stir. Pour the drink into 2 ice-filled glasses and serve.

Apricot Nectar

Truly the nectar of the gods.

3 apricots
1 sweet apple

Yield: 1 serving

Cut the apricots in half and remove the stones. Cut the apple into wedges and remove the seeds. Juice the apricot halves with the apple wedges. Stir the combined juice, pour it into a glass, and serve.

Pink Plum Cooler

Pretty as a picture and good for you, too!

3 plums
1 bunch purple grapes with stems (approximately 1 cup)
8 strawberries
1 very small piece beet, for color (optional)
2 slices lemon, as garnish

Yield: 2 servings

Cut the plums in half and remove the stones. Juice the plum halves with the grapes, strawberries, and beet. Stir the combined juice, pour it into 2 ice-filled glasses, and serve each drink garnished with a lemon slice.

Summertime Raspberry Cocktail

Delectable, light, and delicious!

1 sweet apple
1 pint raspberries
1 sprig mint, as garnish

Yield: 1 serving

Cut the apple into wedges and remove the seeds. Juice the apple wedges with the raspberries. Stir the combined juice, pour it into an ice-filled glass, and serve it garnished with the mint sprig.

Sweet and Sour Springtime

Easier to make than rhubarb pie and every bit as delicious!

3 medium apples
1 large or 2 medium stalks rhubarb
½ cup strawberries

Yield: 2 servings

Cut the apples into wedges and remove the seeds. Cut the leaves off the rhubarb stalks. Juice the apple wedges and rhubarb stalks with the strawberries. Stir the combined juice, pour it into 2 glasses, and serve.

Australian Surprise

This elegant drink is worth every cent you spend on the blackberries!

1–2 kiwis
3–4 apples
½ pint blackberries
¼ cup water

Yield: 1–2 servings

Peel the kiwis and cut them in half. Cut the apples into wedges and remove the seeds. Juice the kiwi halves and apple wedges with the blackberries. Pour the water through the hopper of the juice extractor to rinse out any remaining drops of juice. Stir the juice mixture, pour it into 1 large or 2 small glasses, and serve.

Mint Cooler

This drink is very refreshing and has a beautiful pale green color.

1 honeydew melon, chilled
1 bunch fresh mint (approximately 1 cup, tightly packed)

Yield: 2 servings

Cut the melon into wedges. Bunch up the mint and juice it with the melon wedges. Stir the combined juice, pour it into 2 glasses, and serve.

Strawberry Lemonade

An unusual and beautiful lemonade.

4 large apples
1 lemon
1½ cups strawberries

Yield: 3 servings

Cut the apples into wedges and remove the seeds. Cut the lemon into wedges. Juice the apple and lemon wedges with the strawberries. Stir the combined juice, pour it into 3 glasses, and serve.

Spicy Delight

Ginger adds just the right touch of spice to this great combination.

½ pineapple
1 large apple
¼-inch slice ginger root

Yield: 1 serving

Cut the pineapple into strips. Cut the apple into wedges and remove the seeds. Juice the pineapple strips and apple wedges with the ginger root. Stir the combined juice, pour it into a glass, and serve.

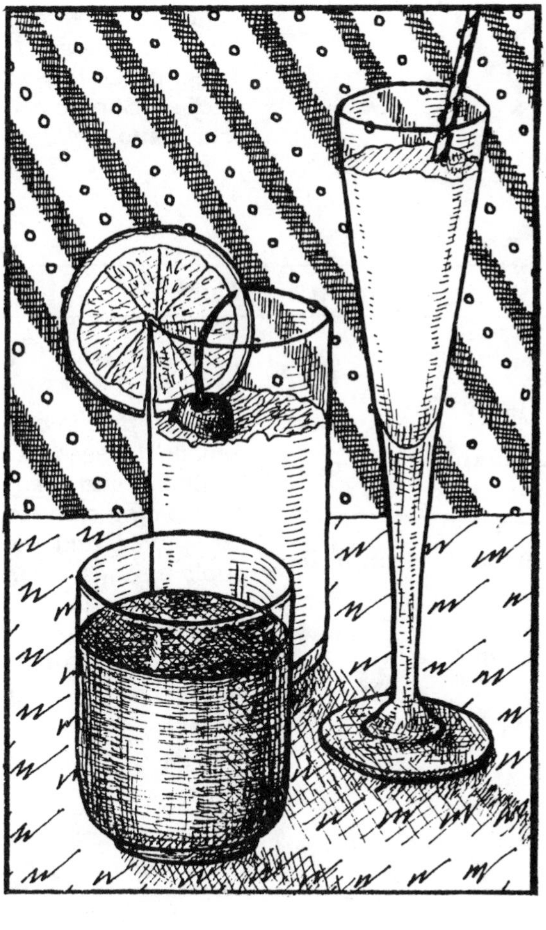

FRUIT-AND-VEGETABLE JUICES

Fennel Fresher

If you like the anise-like taste of fennel, you will love this sweet, mild drink.

1 pineapple
1 bulb fennel
3 apples

Yield: 3 servings

Cut the pineapple into strips. Cut the leaves off the fennel and cut the bulb and stalks into chunks. Cut the apples into wedges and remove the seeds. Juice the pineapple strips with the fennel chunks and apple wedges. Stir the combined juice, pour it into 3 glasses, and serve.

Beauty Spa Cocktail

This is a great salad in a glass!

½ apple
½ medium cucumber
4 medium carrots
Handful spinach (approximately ½ cup)
2 stalks celery

Yield: 1–2 servings

Cut the apple into wedges and remove the seeds. Cut the cucumber into spears. Cut the greens off the carrots. Bunch up the spinach and juice it with the apple wedges, cucumber spears, carrots, and celery. Stir the combined juice, pour it into 1 large or 2 small glasses, and serve.

Sweet Calcium Cocktail

A drink rich in calcium that tastes fantastic and, unlike dairy products, has no cholesterol!

3 one-inch slices pineapple
1 medium leaf kale

Yield: 1 serving

Cut the pineapple slices into strips. Bunch up the kale leaf and juice it with the pineapple strips. Stir the combined juice, pour it into a glass, and serve.

Garden Cooler

Both carrots and broccoli have been shown to exert a protective effect against cancer.

1 Red Delicious or other sweet apple
4 medium carrots
1 turnip top
1 stalk broccoli

Yield: 1 serving

Cut the apple into wedges and remove the seeds. Cut the greens off the carrots. Bunch up the turnip top and juice it with the apple wedges, carrots, and broccoli. Stir the combined juice, pour it into a glass, and serve.

Ginger Hopper

The delightful spicy-sweet flavor of this drink makes it a favorite with many people!

½ apple
4–5 medium carrots
¼-inch slice ginger root

Yield: 1 serving

Cut the apple into wedges and remove the seeds. Cut the greens off the carrots. Juice the apple wedges and carrots with the ginger root. Stir the combined juice, pour it into a glass, and serve.

Green Surprise

The surprise is that you don't taste the calcium-rich kale.

2–3 green apples
2 medium leaves kale

Yield: 1 serving

Cut the apples into wedges and remove the seeds. Bunch up the kale leaves and juice them with the apple wedges. Stir the combined juice, pour it into a glass, and serve.

Garden Salad Special

Even the kids will love this garden salad.

½ apple
½ medium beet
4–5 medium carrots
¼ cup parsley
2 stalks celery

Yield: 1 serving

Cut the apple into wedges and remove the seeds. Cut the beet into chunks. Cut the greens off the carrots. Bunch up the parsley and juice it with the apple wedges, beet chunks, carrots, and celery. Stir the combined juice, pour it into a glass, and serve.

Popeye's Favorite

Not only healthier than Popeye's canned spinach, but a lot tastier, too!

½ apple
4–5 medium carrots
½ cup spinach

Yield: 1 serving

Cut the apple into wedges and remove the seeds. Cut the greens off the carrots. Bunch up the spinach and juice it with the apple wedges and carrots. Stir the combined juice, pour it into a glass, and serve.

Calcium Express

Rich in calcium, this drink is a tasty way to boost your daily calcium intake!

1 apple
4–5 medium carrots
1 medium leaf kale
1/4 cup parsley

Yield: 1 serving

Cut the apple into wedges and remove the seeds. Cut the greens off the carrots. Bunch up the kale leaf and parsley, and juice them with the apple wedges and carrots. Stir the combined juice, pour it into a glass, and serve.

Carotene Cocktail

A delicious way to protect yourself against cancer.

1/2 Red Delicious or other sweet apple
4–5 medium carrots
1/2 cup spinach
1/4 cup parsley

Yield: 1 serving

Cut the apple into wedges and remove the seeds. Cut the greens off the carrots. Bunch up the spinach and parsley, and juice them with the apple wedges and carrots. Stir the combined juice, pour it into a glass, and serve.

Refreshing Summer Cocktail

Cucumber does wonders for the complexion.

1/2 apple
2 one-inch slices pineapple
1/2 medium cucumber

Yield: 2 servings

Cut the apple into wedges and remove the seeds. Cut the pineapple slices into strips and the cucumber into spears. Juice the apple wedges with the pineapple strips and cucumber spears. Stir the combined juice, pour it into 2 glasses, and serve.

Morning Energizer

Start your day with this drink for exuberant health.

½ apple
5 medium carrots
¼ cup parsley

Yield: 1 serving

Cut the apple into wedges and remove the seeds. Cut the greens off the carrots. Bunch up the parsley and juice it with the apple wedges and carrots. Stir the combined juice, pour it into a glass, and serve.

Wheatgrass Express

If you've never liked wheatgrass, try this. It's certain to improve your opinion . . . and your health!

2 one-inch slices pineapple
Handful wheatgrass (approximately ½ cup)
2 sprigs mint
1 sprig mint, as garnish

Yield: 1 serving

Cut the pineapple slices into strips. Bunch up the wheatgrass and 2 mint sprigs, and juice them with the pineapple strips. Stir the combined juice, pour it into a glass, and serve it garnished with the 1 mint sprig.

Wheatgrass Light

The apple and lemon add a sweet zest to this drink.

1 apple
Handful wheatgrass (approximately ½ cup)
⅛ lemon

Yield: 1 serving

Cut the apple into wedges and remove the seeds. Bunch up the wheatgrass and juice it with the apple wedges and lemon. Stir the combined juice, pour it into a glass, and serve.

Chlorophyll Cocktail

You just have to try this to find out how delicious, as well as health promoting, it is.

½ apple
4 medium carrots
3 beet tops
Handful spinach (approximately ½ cup)
Small handful parsley (approximately ¼ cup)

Cut the apple into wedges and remove the seeds. Cut the greens off the carrots. Bunch up the beet tops, spinach, and parsley, and juice them with the apple wedges and carrots. Stir the combined juice, pour it into a glass, and serve.

Yield: 1 serving

John's Zombie

A drink so delicious, who would believe it's a liver cleanser?

½ apple
½ medium beet
5 medium carrots
Handful spinach (approximately ½ cup)
2 stalks celery
⅛ lemon

Cut the apple into wedges and remove the seeds. Cut the beet into chunks. Cut the greens off the carrots. Bunch up the spinach and juice it with the apple wedges, beet chunks, carrots, celery, and lemon. Stir the combined juice, pour it into 2 glasses, and serve.

Yield: 2 servings

Beet Surprise

Do you dislike beets but want their nutritional benefits? Try this drink—you won't taste the beet!

2 Red Delicious or other sweet apples
½ medium beet
⅛ lemon

Cut the apples into wedges and remove the seeds. Cut the beet into chunks. Juice the apple wedges and beet chunks with the lemon. Stir the combined juice, pour it into a glass, and serve.

Yield: 1 serving

Beet-It Express

The great taste of this refreshing spicy-sweet drink will surprise you.

½ medium or 1 small beet
½ lime
5 medium carrots
2 beet tops
¼-inch slice ginger root

Yield: 1 serving

Cut the beet into chunks and the lime into wedges. Cut the greens off the carrots. Bunch up the beet tops and juice them with the beet chunks, lime wedges, carrots, and ginger root. Stir the combined juice, pour it into a glass, and serve.

Red Sunset

A delightful drink for sailors and landlubbers.

½ apple
1 medium beet
4 medium carrots
¼-inch slice ginger root

Yield: 1 serving

Cut the apple into wedges and remove the seeds. Cut the beet into chunks. Cut the greens off the carrots. Juice the apple wedges, beet chunks, and carrots with the ginger root. Stir the combined juice, pour it into a glass, and serve.

Gabby Gourmet's Cocktail

Cherie tasted this "cocktail" for the first time on the Gabby Gourmet's noon show in Salt Lake City and was pleasantly surprised. You'll barely detect the garlic.

2 apples
7 medium carrots
Small handful parsley
(approximately ¼ cup)
1 large or 2 small cloves garlic

Yield: 2 servings

Cut the apples into wedges and remove the seeds. Cut the greens off the carrots. Bunch up the parsley and juice it with the apple wedges, carrots, and garlic. Stir the combined juice, pour it into 2 glasses, and serve.

Cucumber Cooler

Guaranteed to refresh you!

¼ apple
2 one-inch slices pineapple
½ medium cucumber
Small handful parsley
(approximately ¼ cup)
2 sprigs parsley, as garnish

Yield: 2 servings

Cut the apple into wedges and remove the seeds. Cut the pineapple slices into strips and the cucumber into spears. Bunch up the parsley and juice it with the apple wedges, pineapple strips, and cucumber spears. Stir the combined juice, pour it into 2 ice-filled glasses, and serve each drink garnished with a parsley sprig.

Fennel-Apple Express

The unusual light anise flavor of this drink is simply wonderful.

½ apple
½ pear
4 medium carrots
¼ cup fennel chunks
1 stalk celery

Yield: 1–2 servings

Cut the apple into wedges and remove the seeds. Cut the pear into wedges. Cut the greens off the carrots. Juice the apple wedges, pear wedges, and carrots with the fennel and celery. Stir the combined juice, pour it into 1 large or 2 small glasses, and serve.

VEGETABLE JUICES

Veggie Combo

Here is a mixed-vegetable drink that tastes as good as it is good for you.

1 large or 2 medium tomatoes
1- to 2-inch wedge cabbage
1 medium cucumber
2 large or 5 medium carrots
1–2 stalks celery

Yield: 3 servings

Cut the tomatoes into wedges, the cabbage into chunks, and the cucumber into spears. Cut the greens off the carrots. Juice the tomato wedges, cabbage chunks, cucumber spears, and carrots with the celery. Stir the combined juice, pour it into 3 glasses, and serve.

Hot and Spicy Veggie Cocktail

Lightly piquant but very delicious.

1 large or 2 medium tomatoes
1- to 2-inch wedge of cabbage
2 large or 5 medium carrots
5 medium radishes
½-inch slice sweet onion
2 teaspoons tamari

Yield: 2 servings

Cut the tomatoes into wedges and the cabbage into chunks. Cut the greens off the carrots and radishes. Juice the tomato wedges, cabbage chunks, carrots, and radishes with the onion. Add the tamari to the combined juice and stir. Pour the juice mixture into 2 glasses and serve.

Bunny Hopper

Garlic has natural antibiotic properties.

4–5 medium carrots
Handful spinach
(approximately ½ cup)
4 buds cauliflower
1 clove garlic

Yield: 1 serving

Cut the greens off the carrots. Bunch up the spinach and juice it with the carrots, cauliflower, and garlic. Stir the combined juice, pour it into a glass, and serve.

Southwestern Cocktail

This gazpacho-in-a-glass is an all-time favorite.

2 medium tomatoes
½ medium cucumber
Small handful cilantro
(approximately ¼ cup)
¼ lime
Small piece purple onion

Yield: 2 servings

Cut the tomatoes into wedges and the cucumber into spears. Bunch up the cilantro and juice it with the tomato wedges, cucumber spears, lime, and onion. Stir the combined juice, pour it into 2 glasses, and serve.

Salad in a Glass

A wonderful combination of salad veggies.

3 tomatoes
½ medium cucumber
1 slice medium green bell
pepper
4 sprigs parsley
1 scallion
⅛ lemon

Yield: 2 servings

Cut the tomatoes into wedges and the cucumber into spears. Clean the seeds off the green pepper. Bunch up the parsley and juice it with the tomato wedges, cucumber spears, green pepper, scallion, and lemon. Stir the combined juice, pour it into 2 glasses, and serve.

Zippy Tomato Express

If you like mixed-vegetable juices, you'll love this drink!

2 tomatoes
¼ medium green bell pepper
Handful spinach
(approximately ½ cup)
Small handful parsley
(approximately ¼ cup)
Dash Tabasco sauce

Yield: 1 serving

Cut the tomatoes into wedges. Clean the seeds from the green pepper. Bunch up the spinach and parsley, and juice them with the tomato wedges and green pepper. Add the Tabasco to the combined juice and stir. Pour the juice mixture into a glass and serve.

Cherie's Spring Tonic

Great in the summer, fall, and winter, too!

5 carrots
2 radishes
1 stalk celery
1 scallion

Yield: 1 serving

Cut the greens off the carrots and radishes. Juice the carrots and radishes with the celery and scallion. Stir the combined juice, pour it into a glass, and serve.

Three C's Medley

This drink is surprisingly delicious and has a slightly "nutty" flavor.

¼ head green cabbage
5 medium carrots
3 stalks celery

Yield: 1 serving

Cut the cabbage into chunks. Cut the greens off the carrots. Juice the cabbage chunks and carrots with the celery. Stir the combined juice, pour it into a glass, and serve.

Gazpacho Express

The perfect accompaniment to a Southwestern meal.

4 medium tomatoes
½ medium cucumber
¼ medium green bell pepper
1 stalk celery
Small piece purple onion
1 clove garlic
Dash Tabasco sauce

Yield: 2 servings

Cut the tomatoes into wedges and the cucumber into spears. Clean the seeds from the green pepper. Juice the tomato wedges, cucumber spears, and green pepper with the celery, onion, and garlic. Add the Tabasco to the combined juice and stir. Pour the juice mixture into 2 glasses and serve.

Green Garden Cocktail

Rich in chlorophyll, this drink is a wonderful blood purifier.

4–5 medium carrots
¼ green bell pepper
Handful spinach
(approximately ½ cup)
1 medium leaf kale
¼ lemon

Yield: 1 serving

Cut the greens off the carrots. Clean the seeds from the green pepper. Bunch up the spinach and kale leaf, and juice them with the carrots, green pepper, and lemon. Stir the combined juice, pour it into a glass, and serve.

Watercress Express

First stop—your taste buds, which will savor every drop.

4–5 medium carrots
3 radishes
Small handful watercress
(approximately ¼ cup)

Yield: 1 serving

Cut the greens off the carrots and radishes. Bunch up the watercress and juice it with the carrots and radishes. Stir the combined juice, pour it into a glass, and serve.

Very Veggie Cocktail

This energizing drink will delight true vegetable lovers.

4 medium carrots
Small handful parsley (approximately ¼ cup)
Small handful watercress (approximately ¼ cup)
Small handful wheatgrass (approximately ¼ cup)
½ cup fennel chunks
2 stalks celery

Cut the greens off the carrots. Bunch up the parsley and watercress, and juice them with one of the carrots. Bunch up the wheatgrass and juice it with the fennel, celery, and remaining carrots. Stir the combined juice, pour it into a glass, and serve.

Yield: 1 serving

Grasshopper

This spritely drink is a wonderful combination of just two simple ingredients.

4–5 medium carrots
Handful wheatgrass (approximately ½ cup)

Cut the greens off the carrots. Bunch up the wheatgrass and juice it with the carrots. Stir the combined juice, pour it into a glass, and serve.

Yield: 1 serving

Sunshine Salad Cocktail

This drink is high in iron and vitamin C, which are important building blocks for red blood cells.

4–5 medium carrots
1 turnip top
½ leaf kale
Small handful parsley (approximately ¼ cup)

Cut the greens off the carrots. Bunch up the turnip top, kale leaf, and parsley, and juice them with the carrots. Stir the combined juice, pour it into a glass, and serve.

Yield: 1 serving

Hot Tomato on Ice

You have to freeze the cubes ahead of time, but the result is a spectacular company drink!

2 medium tomatoes
½ medium red bell pepper
Dash Tabasco sauce
4 dark green leaves lettuce
1 small stalk broccoli
1 sprig parsley or slice lemon, as garnish

Yield: 1 serving

Cut 1 tomato into wedges. Halve the red bell pepper half and remove the seeds. Juice the tomato wedges with the red bell pepper pieces. Add the Tabasco and stir. Pour the juice mixture into an ice cube tray and place the tray in the freezer.

When the tomato cubes are frozen, cut the second tomato into wedges. Bunch up the lettuce leaves and juice them with the broccoli and the wedges from the second tomato. Stir the combined juice, pour it into a tall glass, add a few tomato cubes, and serve the drink garnished with the parsley sprig or lemon slice.

Mineral Medley

This drink is rich in many minerals, including calcium, magnesium, potassium, iron, and selenium.

4–5 medium carrots
2 turnip tops
1 leaf kale
Small handful parsley (approximately ¼ cup)
⅛ lemon

Yield: 1 serving

Cut the greens off the carrots. Bunch up the turnip tops, kale leaf, and parsley, and juice them with the carrots and lemon. Stir the combined juice, pour it into a glass, and serve.

Three-Bean Juice

*Bean sprouts are delicious, nutritious . . .
and luscious in this drink.*

1 tomato
2 medium carrots
¼ cup mung bean sprouts
¼ cup adzuki bean sprouts
½ cup green beans
1 slice lime, as garnish

Yield: 1 serving

Cut the tomato into wedges. Cut the greens off the carrots. Juice the mung bean and adzuki bean sprouts, then the tomato wedges, carrots, and green beans. Stir the combined juice, pour it into a glass, and serve it garnished with the lime slice.

Peppy Tomato

A spicy, festive cocktail.

1 tomato
½ medium cucumber
1 stalk celery
Dash Tabasco sauce
1 stalk celery, as garnish

Yield: 1 serving

Cut the tomato into wedges and the cucumber into spears. Juice the tomato wedges and cucumber spears with the first celery stalk. Add the Tabasco to the combined juice and stir. Pour the juice mixture into an ice-filled glass and serve it garnished with the second celery stalk.

Jack and the Bean

You'll even climb a stalk for this one.

4–5 carrots
3 dark green leaves lettuce
Handful green beans
(approximately ½ cup)

Yield: 1 serving

Cut the greens off the carrots. Bunch up the lettuce leaves and juice them with the carrots and green beans. Stir the combined juice, pour it into a glass, and serve.

Popeye's Garden Favorites

Mother always said that Popeye has good taste.

1 large tomato
Handful spinach
(approximately ½ cup)
3 stalks celery
2 stalks asparagus
1 stalk celery, as garnish

Cut the tomato into wedges. Bunch up the spinach and juice it with the tomato wedges, 3 celery stalks, and asparagus. Stir the combined juice, pour it into a glass, and serve it garnished with the 1 celery stalk.

Yield: 1 serving

Seven-Vegetable Cocktail

This hearty drink will soon be another mixed-vegetable favorite.

Small wedge cabbage
(approximately ½ cup)
3–4 medium carrots
3 beet leaves
1 medium leaf kale
Handful spinach
(approximately ½ cup)
1 stalk celery
1 scallion
1 clove garlic

Cut the cabbage into chunks. Cut the greens off the carrots. Bunch up the beet leaves, kale leaf, and spinach, and juice them with the cabbage chunks, carrots, celery, scallion, and garlic. Stir the combined juice, pour it into 2 ice-filled glasses, and serve.

Yield: 2 servings

SMOOTHIES

Green Velvet

Incredibly nutritious, absolutely delicious, and a beautiful mint green color!

½ Red or Golden Delicious apple
Handful spinach (approximately ½ cup)
1 medium banana
1 tablespoon tahini
6 ice cubes
1 sprig mint, as garnish

Yield: 1 serving

Cut the apple into wedges and remove the seeds. Bunch up the spinach and juice it with the apple wedges. Pour the combined juice into a blender or food processor and add the banana, tahini, and ice cubes; blend until smooth. Pour the mixture into a glass and serve it garnished with the mint sprig.

Christmas Smoothie

1 Red Delicious or other sweet apple
¼ cup cranberries, unfrozen
1 very small piece beet, for color
1 medium banana
½ cup low-fat dairy yogurt or soy yogurt
6 ice cubes
1 sprig mint, as garnish

Yield: 1 serving

Cut the apple into wedges and remove the seeds. Juice the apple wedges with the cranberries and beet. Pour the combined juice into a blender or food processor and add the banana, yogurt, and ice cubes; blend until smooth. Pour the mixture into a tall glass and serve it garnished with the mint sprig.

Note: You can make this smoothie as bright red as you wish by adding a little more beet.

Sweet Potassium Shake

It'll shake up your taste buds, too!

½ cantaloupe
1 medium banana
6 ice cubes

Yield: 1 serving

Cut the cantaloupe into wedges and juice it. Pour the juice into a blender or food processor and add the banana and ice cubes; blend until smooth. Pour the juice mixture into a glass and serve.

Tropical Smoothie

This drink brings Hawaii to your kitchen.

1 orange
½ pineapple
1 medium banana
2 pitted dried dates
Pinch nutmeg
6 ice cubes

Yield: 1 serving

Peel the orange and cut it into wedges. Cut the pineapple into strips. Juice the orange wedges with the pineapple strips. Pour the combined juice into a blender or food processor and add the banana, dates, nutmeg, and ice cubes; blend until smooth. Pour the mixture into a glass and serve.

Tropical Shake

A great drink for mornings in Hawaii—
or for mornings when you wish you were in Hawaii!

½ medium papaya
½ orange
1 medium banana
6 ice cubes
1 orange twist, as garnish

Yield: 1 serving

Peel the papaya, cut it into strips, and remove the seeds. Peel the orange and cut it into wedges. Juice the papaya strips with the orange wedges. Pour the combined juice into a blender or food processor and add the banana and ice cubes; blend until smooth. Pour the mixture into a glass and serve it garnished with the orange twist.

Exotic Tropical Smoothie

One sip and you'll imagine you're in the Caribbean.

1 mango
1 one-inch slice pineapple
1 medium banana
6 ice cubes

Yield: 1–2 servings

Peel the mango and cut it into wedges. Cut the pineapple slice into strips. Juice the mango wedges with the pineapple strips. Pour the combined juice into a blender or food processor and add the banana and ice cubes; blend until smooth. Pour the mixture into 1 large or 2 small glasses and serve.

Pineapple Protein Smoothie

Energize your morning with this delectable, nutrient-dense smoothie.

3 one-inch slices pineapple
1 medium banana
3 tablespoons protein powder
½ cup soy milk
6 ice cubes

Yield: 2 servings

Cut the pineapple slices into strips and juice them. Pour the juice into a blender or food processor and add the banana, protein powder, soy milk, and ice cubes; blend until smooth. Pour the mixture into 2 glasses and serve.

Sweet Magnesium Smoothie

Rich in calcium and magnesium, this drink's great after a hard day.

1 pint blackberries
1 medium banana
2 ounces silken tofu
1 tablespoon nutritional yeast (optional)
6 ice cubes
3–4 blackberries, as garnish

Yield: 1 serving

Juice the pint of blackberries. Pour the juice into a blender or food processor and add the banana, silken tofu, nutritional yeast, and ice cubes; blend until smooth. Pour the mixture into a glass and serve it garnished with the 3–4 blackberries.

Peaches and Cream

The ambrosial taste of peaches makes this protein-rich smoothie a real favorite.

1 apple
2 peaches
½ cup silken tofu
6 ice cubes
Dash cinnamon, as garnish

Yield: 1 serving

Cut the apple into wedges and remove the seeds. Remove the stones from the peaches and cut the flesh into wedges. Juice the apple wedges with the peach wedges. Pour the combined juice into a blender or food processor and add the silken tofu and ice cubes; blend until smooth. Pour the mixture into a tall glass and serve it garnished with the cinnamon.

Papaya-Pineapple Smoothie

The perfect blend for a hot summer afternoon.

½ medium papaya
½ orange
1 one-inch slice pineapple
1 medium banana
6 ice cubes

Yield: 2 servings

Peel the papaya, cut it into strips, and remove the seeds. Peel the orange and cut it into wedges. Cut the pineapple slice into strips. Juice the papaya strips with the orange wedges and pineapple strips. Pour the combined juice into a blender or food processor and add the banana and ice cubes; blend until smooth. Pour the mixture into 2 glasses and serve.

Strawberry-Almond Smoothie

A hint of almond renders this nutritious smoothie exotic as well as delicious.

½ pint strawberries
1 medium banana
½ cup blanched almonds
½ cup water (add more, if necessary)
1 teaspoon vanilla extract
2–3 drops almond extract (optional)
6 ice cubes
Dash nutmeg, as garnish

Yield: 1 serving

Juice the strawberries. Pour the juice into a blender or food processor and add the banana, almonds, water, vanilla extract, almond extract, and ice cubes; blend on high until the almonds are no longer gritty and the mixture is smooth. Pour the mixture into a tall glass and serve it garnished with the nutmeg.

Note: If you omit the strawberry juice, banana, and nutmeg, you'll have a recipe for almond milk. Almond milk is a wonderful alternative to dairy milk. It's perfect over cereal, in white sauce, or as a delicious drink all by itself.

Cherry Cream

This creamy smoothie will rival the rich taste of any milk shake, yet it's so nutritious.

1 cup cherries
½ Red Delicious or other sweet apple
½ cup low-fat dairy yogurt or soy yogurt
½ teaspoon vanilla extract
6 ice cubes

Yield: 1 serving

Remove the pits from the cherries. Cut the apple into wedges and remove the seeds. Juice the cherries with the apple wedges. Pour the combined juice into a blender or food processor and add the yogurt, vanilla extract, and ice cubes; blend until smooth. Pour the mixture into a glass and serve.

Purple Monkey

Grapes and bananas make such a great couple.

2 cups red or purple grapes
1 medium banana
6 ice cubes

Yield: 1 serving

Juice the grapes. Pour the juice into a blender or food processor and add the banana and ice cubes; blend until smooth. Pour the mixture into a glass and serve.

Berry Smooth

And berry cool, too!

3 medium apples
1 medium banana
1 heaping cup strawberries or blueberries
½ teaspoon vanilla extract (optional)
6 ice cubes

Yield: 2 servings

Cut the apples into wedges, remove the seeds, and juice the wedges. Pour the juice into a blender or food processor and add the banana, berries, vanilla extract, and ice cubes; blend until smooth. Pour the mixture into 2 glasses and serve.

Strawberry-Cashew Milk Shake

The cashews add a wonderful flavor.

1 large Yellow Delicious apple
1 large Red Delicious apple
1 cup whole strawberries
⅓ cup raw cashews
½ teaspoon vanilla extract
6 ice cubes

Yield: 1 serving

Cut the apples into wedges and remove the seeds. Juice the apple wedges with the strawberries. Pour the combined juice into a blender or food processor and add the cashews, vanilla extract, and ice cubes; blend on high until the cashews are no longer gritty and the mixture is smooth. Pour the mixture into a glass and serve.

Orange Cream

Another drink for cashew fans.

2 medium oranges
1 medium banana
¼ cup raw cashews
1 teaspoon vanilla extract
6 ice cubes

Yield: 1 serving

Peel the oranges, cut them into wedges, and juice them. Pour the juice into a blender or food processor and add the banana, cashews, vanilla extract, and ice cubes; blend on high until the cashews are no longer gritty and the mixture is smooth. Pour the mixture into a glass and serve.

Pink Panther

A creamy, rich smoothie that's as nutritious as it's delicious.

1 pint strawberries
1 medium banana
½ package (5¼ ounces) silken tofu
6 ice cubes
1 strawberry, as garnish

Yield: 1 serving

Juice the pint of strawberries. Pour the juice into a blender or food processor and add the banana, silken tofu, and ice cubes; blend until smooth. Pour the mixture into a glass and serve it garnished with the 1 strawberry.

Strawberry-Pineapple Smoothie

Three delicious fruits make one nutritious drink.

½ pineapple
1½ cups strawberries
1 medium banana
6 ice cubes

Yield: 1 serving

Cut the pineapple into strips. Juice the pineapple strips with the strawberries. Pour the combined juice into a blender or food processor and add the banana and ice cubes; blend until smooth. Pour the mixture into a glass and serve.

FIZZES

Strawberry-Apple Swinger

Why drink commercial soda with its refined sugars and chemicals when you can enjoy this?

½ Golden Delicious or other sweet apple
6 strawberries
½ cup sparkling water
1 strawberry, as garnish

Yield: 1 serving

Cut the apple into wedges and remove the seeds. Juice the apple wedges with the 6 strawberries. Pour the combined juice into a glass, add the sparkling water, and stir. Serve the drink garnished with the 1 strawberry.

Apple-Mint Fizz

A sweet, bubbly drink with a hint of mint.

1 orange
2 green apples
4 sprigs mint
¼ lemon
Sparkling water
2 sprigs mint, as garnish

Yield: 2 servings

Peel the orange and cut it into wedges. Cut the apples into wedges and remove the seeds. Bunch up the mint and juice it with the orange wedges, apple wedges, and lemon. Pour the combined juice into 2 ice-filled glasses, fill the glasses with the sparkling water, and stir. Serve the drinks garnished with the remaining mint sprigs.

Lime Pop

A wonderful, bubbly limeade.

½ Golden or Red Delicious apple
½ lime
Sparkling water

Yield: 1 serving

Cut the apple into wedges and remove the seeds. Cut the lime into wedges. Juice the apple wedges with the lime wedges. Pour the combined juice into a tall, ice-filled glass, fill the glass with sparkling water, stir, and serve.

Grape-Ginger Ale

This drink is delicious with or without the sparkling water.

1½ pounds grapes
¼- to ½-inch slice ginger root
1 cup sparkling water

Yield: 2 servings

Juice the grapes with the ginger root and reserve 1½ cups of the combined juice. Pour the combined juice into 2 ice-filled glasses, add ½ cup sparkling water to each glass, stir, and serve.

Note: If you prefer a stronger ginger flavor, use more ginger root the next time.

Lemon Spritzer

With only about 5 calories to a glass, enjoy as much of this refreshing drink as you like.

½ lemon
Sparkling water

Yield: 1 serving

Cut the lemon into wedges and juice it. Pour the juice into an ice-filled glass, fill the glass with sparkling water, stir, and serve.

Cherry Cooler

A great sweet and sour sparkling drink.

1 pint cherries
¼ lemon
Sparkling water

Yield: 1 serving

Remove the pits from the cherries. Juice the cherries with the lemon. Pour the combined juice into an ice-filled glass and stir, fill the glass with sparkling water and stir again, and serve.

Ginger Ale

Now you can make your own ginger ale, and you won't believe how good it tastes.

2 sweet apples
¼-inch slice ginger root
½ cup sparkling water

Yield: 1 serving

Cut the apples into wedges and remove the seeds. Juice the apple wedges with the ginger root. Stir the combined juice and pour it into an ice-filled glass, add the sparkling water and stir again, and serve.

Minty Blueberry Fizz

Sweet and minty!

4 sprigs mint
1 pint blueberries
Sparkling water

Yield: 1 serving

Bunch up the mint and juice it with the blueberries. Pour the combined juice into a tall, ice-filled glass, fill the glass with sparkling water, stir, and serve.

Apple-Mint Soda

Very refreshing! With the sparkling water it's like a soda, but without the water it's also delicious.

3 large apples
½ cup fresh mint, lightly packed
½ cup sparkling water
Mint leaves, as garnish

Yield: 2 servings

Cut the apples into wedges and remove the seeds. Bunch up the mint and juice it with the apple wedges. Pour the combined juice into 2 ice-filled glasses, add ¼ cup sparkling water to each glass, and stir. Serve the drinks garnished with the mint leaves.

Pineapple-Orange Soda

This drink adds some tropical sparkle to your day.

1 large orange
½ pineapple
½ cup sparkling water

Yield: 1 serving

Peel the orange and cut it into wedges. Cut the pineapple into strips. Juice the orange wedges with the pineapple strips. Add the sparkling water to the combined juice, pour the drink into a glass filled with crushed ice, stir, and serve.

TEAS

Fruit Tea

On a cold winter's day, this will warm you up with great flavor!

1 orange
1 Red Delicious or other sweet apple
1/4 lime
2 cups water
3 cinnamon sticks

Yield: 3 servings

Peel the orange and cut it into wedges. Cut the apple into wedges and remove the seeds. Juice the orange and apple wedges with the lime. Pour the combined juice into a medium-size saucepan, add the water and cinnamon sticks, and stir; heat gently. Pour the tea into 3 mugs and serve each drink garnished with a cinnamon stick.

Hot Apple Pie

If you're hungry for apple pie but want to avoid the refined sugar and calories, this is the drink for you.

1 tart apple
1/2 cup water
1/4 teaspoon pumpkin pie spice
1 cinnamon stick

Yield: 1 serving

Cut the apple into wedges, remove the seeds, and juice the wedges. Pour the juice into a small saucepan and add the water, pumpkin pie spice, and cinnamon stick. Bring the mixture to a boil, cover the saucepan, reduce the heat, and simmer for about 10 minutes. Pour the tea into a teacup and serve it garnished with the cinnamon stick.

Ginger Tea

This is an excellent drink on any day but is therapeutic when you have a cold, the flu, or a sore throat. Ginger has been shown in scientific studies to have anti-inflammatory properties.

1-inch slice ginger root
¼ lemon
2 cups water
1 tablespoon loose licorice tea (optional)
1 stick cinnamon, broken
4–5 cloves
Dash nutmeg or cardamom
2 sticks cinnamon, as garnish

Yield: 2 servings

Juice the ginger root with the lemon. Pour the combined juice into a small saucepan and add the water, licorice tea, cinnamon pieces, cloves, and nutmeg. Bring the mixture to a boil, then reduce the heat and simmer for 10–15 minutes. Pour the tea into 2 teacups or mugs and serve each drink garnished with a whole cinnamon stick.

Note: Look for licorice tea at your health food store. It's well worth the search because it naturally sweetens this drink and adds great flavor and nutritional value.

Orange Spice Tea

A spicy-sweet drink perfect for a cold winter's night.

1 orange
½-inch slice ginger root
1 cup water
1 cinnamon stick

Yield: 1 serving

Peel the orange and cut it into wedges. Juice the orange wedges with the ginger root. Pour the combined juice into a small saucepan and add the water and cinnamon stick. Bring the mixture to a boil, then reduce the heat and simmer until warm. Pour the tea into a teacup and serve.

Spicy Mint Tea

The mint and ginger can give you a lift in the late afternoon.

1 orange
4 sprigs mint
½-inch slice ginger root
1 cup hot water

Yield: 2 servings

Peel the orange and cut it into wedges. Bunch up the mint and juice it with the orange wedges and ginger root. Pour the combined juice into 2 teacups or mugs, add ½ cup hot water to each cup, stir, and serve.

Lemon-Apple Iced Tea

Refreshingly sweet without added sugar.

2 bags lemon grass tea
2 cups boiling water
1 apple
1 thin slice lemon
2 slices lemon, as garnish

Yield: 2 servings

Steep the lemon grass tea in the boiling water. Meanwhile, cut the apple into wedges and remove the seeds. Juice the apple wedges with the thin lemon slice. Strain the lemon grass tea, add the combined juice, and stir. Pour the tea mixture into 2 ice-filled glasses and serve the drinks garnished with the remaining lemon slices.

Breakfasts

It's so easy to incorporate juicing into a healthy breakfast. A glass of fresh fruit juice before your morning meal is an excellent way to start the day. Or try substituting fruit juice for milk in your favorite muffin or pancake recipe. The juice will add both flavor and sweetness without changing the texture. Also try the Orange-Spice Granola recipe on page 122 and the Muesli recipe on page 123; they contain both pulp and juice. You can also add juice and pulp to your own muesli recipe.

Don't forget about smoothies. There are several deliciously satisfying recipes in the Beverages section of this book. A fresh fruit smoothie and some whole grain toast spread with nut butter make a quick yet very nourishing breakfast.

Orange-Spice Granola

Your store-bought cereal will shrivel in shame next to this wonderful, healthy granola.

1 orange
2 apples
1 lemon
8 cups rolled oats
1 cup bran
1 cup raw wheat germ
½ cup raw almonds or hazelnuts, chopped
¼ cup raw sunflower seeds
¼ cup sesame seeds
2 tablespoons cinnamon
1 teaspoon cardamom
1 teaspoon ginger
½ teaspoon coriander
½ teaspoon nutmeg
¼ cup honey or brown rice syrup
¼ cup canola or safflower oil
1 tablespoon vanilla extract
1 teaspoon almond extract

Preheat the oven to 300°F.

Peel the orange and cut it into wedges. Cut the apples into wedges and remove the seeds. Cut the lemon into wedges. Juice the orange, apple, and lemon wedges, and reserve all of the combined juice.

In a large bowl, mix together the oats, bran, wheat germ, nuts, sunflower seeds, sesame seeds, cinnamon, cardamom, ginger, coriander, and nutmeg.

In a medium-size saucepan over low heat, stir together the combined juice, honey or brown rice syrup, oil, vanilla extract, and almond extract; blend well and heat thoroughly.

Pour the hot liquid ingredients over the dry ingredients and toss them together until well mixed. Spread the mixture in a thin layer on a lightly greased baking sheet.

Bake the mixture until it's well toasted and golden, about 20–25 minutes. Stir it often, especially when the granola along the edges of the baking sheet starts to brown. Remove the granola from the oven and let it cool on the baking sheet. Store it in a covered container.

Yield: 11 cups Preparation time: 20 minutes
Baking time: 20–25 minutes

Muesli

7 medium apples
1 cup rolled oats
¼ cup raisins
¼ cup almonds (optional)
½ teaspoon cinnamon

Cut the apples into wedges and remove the cores. Juice the apple wedges and reserve 2¼ cups of the juice and ½ cup of the pulp.

In a medium-size bowl, combine the apple juice and pulp with the oats, raisins, almonds, and cinnamon; mix well. Cover the bowl and place it in the refrigerator. Allow the muesli to soak overnight.

To serve, pour some of the muesli into a bowl and add fresh berries and a dollop of either low-fat dairy yogurt or soy yogurt.

Yield: 3½ cups Preparation time: 10 minutes
Chilling time: Overnight

Top-of-the-Morning Muesli

This is a delicious muesli variation.

4½ medium apples
½ small or ¼ medium lemon
1 cup rolled oats
¼ cup rye flakes
¼ cup pitted prunes
¼ cup nuts or sunflower seeds (optional)
2 Medjool dates or 3–4 regular soft dates, pitted

Cut the apples into wedges and remove the cores. Juice the apple wedges and reserve 1½ cups of the juice and all of the pulp. Juice the lemon and reserve all of the juice.

In a food processor, combine the rolled oats, rye flakes, prunes, nuts or seeds, and dates; process until coarsely ground. Transfer the ground mixture to a large bowl.

Pick through the apple pulp and remove any large pieces of skin, then add the pulp to the ground mixture in the bowl. Add the apple juice and lemon juice, and mix well. Let the mixture sit for about 10 minutes.

Serve the muesli with fresh fruit, such as strawberries or peaches, and soy milk.

Yield: *3–3½ cups*
Preparation time: *15 minutes*
Soaking time: *10 minutes*

Apple-Strawberry Pancakes

Apples, strawberries, and pancakes—
what a great combination to start off the day!

1 large apple
1 cup strawberries
½ cup whole wheat pastry flour
¾ cup oat flour
1 teaspoon baking powder
1 egg, slightly beaten
Oil

Cut the apple into wedges and remove the core. Remove the caps from the strawberries. Juice the apple wedges with the strawberries and reserve ¾ cup of the juice and ½ cup of the pulp. If you don't have enough juice, add more apple juice.

In a medium-size bowl, combine the pastry flour, oat flour, and baking powder. Add the egg and mix well. Add the apple-strawberry juice and pulp, and beat until the batter is smooth. (The batter will be thicker than most pancake batters because of the pulp.)

Heat 1 tablespoon of the oil in a skillet over medium-high heat. When the oil is hot, drop ¼ cup of the batter into the skillet, using a spatula to spread out the batter to the desired thickness. Add as many pancakes to the skillet as will easily fit. Cook the pancakes until they are brown on the bottom, about 3 minutes, then flip them and cook them briefly on the other side, about 2 minutes. Repeat with the remaining batter.

Serve the pancakes immediately with fresh strawberries and either the Strawberry Sauce on page 218 or fruit-sweetened strawberry jam.

Yield: *8 pancakes*
Preparation time: *15 minutes*
Cooking time: *15 minutes*

Orange-Cinnamon Pancakes With Apricot-Orange Sauce

These oh-so-light pancakes smell and taste delicately orange.

Apricot-Orange Sauce (page 127)
Fruit Topping (page 128)
1 large orange
1 cup whole wheat pastry flour
1 teaspoon baking soda
½ teaspoon cinnamon
1 egg, beaten
½ cup low-fat dairy yogurt or soy yogurt
2 tablespoons canola oil
Water (optional)
Oil

Prepare the Apricot-Orange Sauce and Fruit Topping.

Peel the orange and cut it into wedges. Juice the orange wedges and reserve all of the juice. Reserve 1 tablespoon of the pulp, with the stringy membranes removed.

In a medium-size bowl, combine the flour, soda, and cinnamon.

In a small bowl, whisk together the egg, orange juice and pulp, yogurt, and oil.

Add the liquid ingredients to the dry ingredients and stir them just until combined. (If you prefer very thin pancakes, add a little bit of water to the liquids before mixing them with the dry ingredients.)

Brush a griddle with 1 tablespoon of oil and place it over medium-high heat. When the oil is hot, drop ¼ cup of the batter onto the griddle, using a spatula to spread out the batter. Add as many pancakes to the griddle as will easily fit. Cook the pancakes until they start to bubble, about 5 minutes, then flip them and cook the other side for about 2–3 minutes. Repeat with the remaining batter.

Serve the pancakes immediately, with Fruit Topping on each pancake and Apricot-Orange Sauce over the Fruit Topping.

Yield: *8 pancakes*
Preparation time: *15 minutes*
Cooking time: *20 minutes*

Apricot-Orange Sauce

3 medium oranges
12 dried apricot halves
¼ cup water
1 teaspoon brown rice syrup
¼ teaspoon cinnamon

Peel the oranges and cut them into wedges. Juice the wedges and reserve 1½ cups of the juice.

In a medium-size saucepan, bring the orange juice and dried apricot halves to a boil. Reduce the heat and add the water, brown rice syrup, and cinnamon. Cover the saucepan and simmer until the apricots are soft, about 10 minutes.

While the sauce is cooking, prepare the Fruit Topping.

When the apricots are soft, pour the sauce mixture into a blender and process until smooth. If it's still too thick, add a little water. Return the mixture to the saucepan and reheat it.

Set the sauce aside until the pancakes are done.

Yield: *4 cups*
Preparation time: *35 minutes*
Cooking time: *10 minutes*

Fruit Topping

1 tablespoon butter or safflower oil
2 teaspoons honey or brown rice syrup
½ teaspoon vanilla extract
2 tablespoons pecans, chopped
2 apples, thinly sliced

In a medium-size skillet, melt the butter or heat the oil over low heat. Add the honey or brown rice syrup, and vanilla extract; blend. Add the pecans and apples, and increase the heat to high. Toss and heat the pecans and apples until the apple slices are warm and tender, about 2 minutes.

Remove the skillet from the heat and set it aside until the pancakes and sauce are prepared.

Yield: *1 cup*
Preparation time: *10 minutes*

Breads, Muffins, and Chapati

Fresh-baked whole grain breads are made even more delicious and nutritious with the addition of juice and pulp. By using juice instead of water or milk in both yeast breads and quick breads, you can add vitamins and minerals to your family's diet without adding fat and cholesterol. Juice also adds flavor, color, and sweetness to baked goods, and pulp adds moistness and fiber.

If you wish, you can substitute juice for equal quantities of water or milk in your own recipes. Be careful, though, when you add pulp. Too much can make baked goods gooey.

Dill Bread

Light in texture but very nutritious.

1 bunch (¼ pound) spinach
4 large stalks celery
¼ cup lukewarm water
1 tablespoon dry active yeast
Drop of honey
2 tablespoons oil
2 tablespoons honey
½ cup gluten flour
1 teaspoon salt
2 cups whole wheat bread flour
⅓ cup finely chopped fresh dill leaves

Separately juice the spinach and celery. Add enough of the celery juice to the spinach juice to get 1 cup of combined juice.

In a small bowl, combine the water, yeast, and drop of honey. Let the mixture sit for 10 minutes to dissolve and proof the yeast. (Proofing verifies that the yeast is active and will work properly, causing the bread to rise. Active yeast will have begun to foam up and bubble by 10 minutes. Inactive yeast will not. If the yeast is inactive, discard it and try again.)

Meanwhile, in a small saucepan, gently heat the spinach-celery juice to lukewarm; do not let it get too hot.

Transfer the warm juice to a large bowl and add the oil, honey, yeast mixture, gluten flour, and salt; mix well. Add 1 cup of the bread flour along with the dill and mix again. Add as much of the remaining bread flour as necessary to make a kneadable dough, mixing after each addition. (The dough is kneadable when it's too stiff to stir and begins to pull away from the sides of the bowl.)

Turn the dough out onto a floured surface and knead in

additional flour to make the dough smooth and not too sticky. (When the dough no longer sticks to the kneading surface and you no longer need to sprinkle the surface with flour, you have added enough flour.) Knead the dough for at least 10 minutes.

Oil the bowl in which you mixed the dough. Place the kneaded dough in the oiled bowl and turn the dough over to oil its top. Cover the bowl with a clean, damp cloth and let the dough rise in a warm place until it has doubled in bulk, about 1 hour.

Punch down the dough. If desired, let it rise again and punch it down again. Shape the dough into a loaf and place it in a well-oiled and lightly floured 8½-by-4½-by-2½-inch loaf pan. Drape a damp cloth over the loaf pan and let the dough rise in a warm place until it has doubled in bulk, about 1 hour. As the loaf rises, pick up the cloth occasionally to make sure it does not stick to the loaf.

When the dough has doubled, remove the cloth and place the loaf in a cold oven. Set the oven at 350°F and bake the loaf until done, about 45 minutes. Remove the bread from the pan and allow the loaf to cool on a wire rack for 15–20 minutes before slicing it. Let it cool completely before wrapping it in plastic or heavy-duty foil.

Yield:	*1 large loaf*
Preparation time:	*20–30 minutes*
Rising time:	*2–3 hours*
Baking time:	*45 minutes*
Cooling time:	*15–20 minutes*

Tomato Focaccia

This bread is great for a party.

2 large tomatoes
1 tablespoon yeast
Drop of honey
⅓ cup gluten flour
¼ teaspoon sea salt
1½ cups whole wheat pastry flour
12 cloves garlic, pressed
2 tablespoons olive oil
1 tablespoon minced fresh rosemary leaves
½ teaspoon sea salt

Cut the tomatoes into wedges, juice the wedges, and reserve 1 cup of the juice.

In a small saucepan, heat the tomato juice to lukewarm; do not let the juice get hot. Transfer the warm juice to a large bowl and add the yeast and honey. Let the mixture sit for 5–10 minutes to dissolve and proof the yeast.

Add the gluten flour and ¼ teaspoon salt to the yeast mixture, then add as much of the pastry flour as necessary to make a kneadable dough. (The dough is kneadable when it's too stiff to stir and begins to pull away from the sides of the bowl.) Turn the dough out onto a floured surface and knead in the remaining pastry flour. The dough should be slightly softer and stickier than a regular yeast bread. Knead the dough for 5 minutes, adding as much additional flour as necessary to keep the dough from sticking to the kneading surface.

Oil the bowl in which you mixed the dough. Place the kneaded dough in the oiled bowl and turn the dough over to oil its top. Cover the bowl with a clean, damp cloth and let the dough rise in a warm place until it has doubled in bulk, about 1 hour.

Meanwhile, in a small bowl, mix together the pressed garlic, olive oil, rosemary, and ½ teaspoon salt. Let the mixture sit undisturbed until you are ready to use it.

When the dough has doubled in bulk, punch it down. If desired, let it rise again and punch it down again. To shape the dough into a loaf, turn it out onto a well-oiled cookie sheet and, using your hands, spread it out and pat it into a ½-inch-thick circle. Using your finger, poke little holes about ¼ inch deep all over the top of the dough at 1-inch intervals. Spread the garlic mixture over the dough, letting it drip into the finger holes. Let the dough rise in a warm place until it has doubled in bulk, about 45–60 minutes.

Preheat the oven to 350°F. When the dough has risen, place it on a rack in the middle of the oven and bake it until the bottom is a light, crispy brown, about 20–25 minutes. Remove the bread from the oven, cut it into wedges, and serve it warm.

Yield: *One 9-inch round loaf*
Preparation time: *20 minutes*
Rising time: *1¾–3 hours*
Baking time: *20–25 minutes*

Carrot Bread

This beautiful golden loaf is the latest winner of our personal "favorite yeast bread" contest.

8–11 medium carrots
2 tablespoons oil
1 tablespoon honey
1 tablespoon dry active yeast
1 cup gluten flour
1 teaspoon sea salt
1½–2 cups whole wheat flour

Cut the greens off the carrots. Juice the carrots and reserve 1½ cups of the juice and 1 cup of the pulp.

In a small saucepan, gently heat the carrot juice until it's warm but not hot. Transfer the warm juice to a large ceramic bowl and add the oil, honey, and yeast; mix. Let the mixture sit undisturbed for 10 minutes to dissolve and proof the yeast.

Add the gluten flour, salt, and carrot pulp to the yeast mixture, and mix. Add as much of the whole wheat flour as necessary to make a kneadable dough, mixing after each addition. (The dough is kneadable when it's too stiff to stir and begins to pull away from the sides of the bowl.)

Turn the dough out onto a floured surface and knead in as much of the remaining whole wheat flour as necessary to make the dough smooth, firm, and not too sticky. Knead the dough for at least 10 minutes.

Oil the bowl in which you mixed the dough. Place the kneaded dough in the oiled bowl and turn the dough over to oil the top. Cover the bowl with a clean, damp cloth and let the dough rise in a warm place until it has doubled in bulk, about 1 hour.

Punch down the dough. If desired, let it rise again and punch it down again. Shape the dough into a loaf, place it in a well-oiled and lightly floured 8½-by-4½-by-2½-inch loaf pan, and cover it lightly with a damp cloth. Let the dough rise in a warm place until it has doubled in bulk, about 1 hour. As the loaf rises, pick up the cloth occasionally to make sure it does not stick to the loaf.

When the dough has doubled, remove the cloth and place the loaf in a cold oven. Set the oven at 350°F and bake the loaf until done, about 45 minutes. Remove the loaf from the pan and allow the bread to cool 10–15 minutes before slicing it. Let it cool completely before wrapping it in plastic or heavy-duty foil.

Yield: 1 large loaf *Preparation time: 20–30 minutes*
Rising time: 2–3 hours *Baking time: 45 minutes*
Cooling time: 10–15 minutes

Carrot Cornbread

This quick cornbread is light and moist
with a beautiful bright color.

5–7 medium carrots
1 cup cornmeal
½ cup barley flour
1 tablespoon baking powder
½ teaspoon sea salt
1 cup sweet corn kernels fresh off the cob
1 egg
¼ cup oil
1 tablespoon honey

Preheat the oven to 375°F.

Cut the greens off the carrots. Juice the carrots and reserve 1 cup of the juice.

In a medium-size bowl, combine the cornmeal, barley flour, baking powder, and salt. Add the corn and mix well.

In a large bowl, beat together the egg, oil, and honey. Add the carrot juice and mix well.

Add the dry ingredients to the liquid ingredients and beat just until combined. Turn the batter into a well-oiled 8-by-8-inch baking dish.

Bake the cornbread until a toothpick inserted into the center of the bread comes out clean, about 25 minutes. Let the bread cool in the pan for 10 minutes before slicing it.

Yield: *One 8-inch square loaf*
Preparation time: *20 minutes*
Baking time: *25 minutes*
Cooling time: *10 minutes*

Three-Grain Spicy Vegetable Muffins

These are really a change from the usual sweet muffins.

5–7 medium carrots
1 cup barley flour
¾ cup cornmeal
½ cup oat flour
1 tablespoon baking powder
1 teaspoon cumin
½ teaspoon sea salt
½ cup soy milk
3 tablespoons dry onion flakes
10 sun-dried tomato halves, cut into small pieces
1 jalapeño pepper, seeded and finely minced
1 egg

Preheat the oven to 350°F.

Cut the greens off the carrots. Juice the carrots and reserve 1 cup of the juice and ½ cup of the pulp.

In a medium-size bowl, sift together the barley flour, cornmeal, oat flour, baking powder, cumin, and sea salt. Set the bowl aside.

In a large bowl, combine the soy milk, onion flakes, sun-dried tomato pieces, jalapeño pepper, egg, and carrot pulp; beat well. Add the carrot juice and beat again.

Add the flour mixture to the pulp mixture, beating with a wooden spoon until just combined; do not overmix. Spoon the batter into 12 oiled and floured muffin cups, filling each cup about ¾ full.

Bake the muffins until a toothpick inserted into the center of a muffin comes out clean, about 15–20 minutes. Remove from the oven and allow the muffins to cool on a wire rack, about 10 minutes.

Serve the muffins in place of bread with soups, salads, or just about anything. Leftover muffins are delicious cut in half and toasted.

Yield: *12 muffins*
Preparation time: *20 minutes*
Baking time: *15–20 minutes*
Cooling time: *10 minutes*

Carob Chip–Orange Bread

This deliciously sweet bread with a hint of orange uses very little sweetener.

½ medium orange
2 large apples
1 cup whole wheat flour
1 cup whole wheat pastry flour
½ tablespoon baking powder
½ tablespoon baking soda
½ tablespoon cinnamon
¼ teaspoon cardamom
¾ cup soy milk
¼ cup low-fat dairy yogurt or soy yogurt
1 egg
1 tablespoon canola oil
1 tablespoon honey or brown rice syrup
2 teaspoons vanilla extract
¼ teaspoon maple or almond extract
½ cup unsweetened carob chips

Preheat the oven to 350°F.

Peel the orange and cut it into wedges. Cut the apple into wedges and remove the seeds. Juice the orange wedges and reserve 1/4 cup of the juice. Juice the apple wedges and reserve 3/4 cup of the juice.

In a large bowl, combine the whole wheat flour, pastry flour, baking powder, baking soda, cinnamon, and cardamom.

In a medium-size bowl, combine the orange juice, apple juice, soy milk, yogurt, egg, oil, honey or brown rice syrup, vanilla extract, and maple or almond extract.

Add the liquid ingredients to the dry ingredients and mix just until a batter is formed; do not beat. Pour the batter into two 8 1/2-by-4 1/2-by-2 1/2-inch loaf pans or four 5 1/4-by-2 1/2-by-2-inch loaf pans. Fill the loaf pans 2/3 full. Sprinkle the carob chips on top of the batter.

Bake the breads until they spring back when lightly touched, about 30 minutes for the large loaves and 20 minutes for the small loaves. Let the loaves cool in the pans until they're firm enough to slice, about 20–25 minutes.

Yield: *2 large loaves or 4 small loaves*
Preparation time: *20 minutes*
Baking time: *20–30 minutes*
Cooling time: *20–25 minutes*

Green Cornbread

4 stalks celery
3 leaves kale
½ bunch parsley
1 cup cornmeal
½ cup barley flour
1 tablespoon baking powder
½ teaspoon sea salt
1 cup sweet corn kernels fresh off the cob
¼ cup oil
1 egg

Preheat the oven to 375°F.

Juice the celery with the kale leaves and parsley, and reserve ¾ cup plus 1 tablespoon of the combined juice.

In a medium-size bowl, combine the cornmeal, barley flour, baking powder, and salt. Add the corn and mix well.

In a large bowl, beat together the oil and egg. Add the combined juice and mix well.

Add the dry ingredients to the liquid ingredients and beat just until combined. Turn the batter into a well-oiled 8-by-8-inch baking dish or 9-inch cast-iron skillet.

Bake the cornbread until a toothpick inserted into the center of the bread comes out clean, about 25 minutes. Let the bread cool in the pan for 10 minutes before slicing it.

Serve the bread with the Quick Carrot Soup on page 159, Garden Gazpacho on page 173, or just about anything else you like.

Yield: *One 8-inch square loaf*
Preparation time: *20 minutes*
Baking time: *25 minutes*
Cooling time: *10 minutes*

Carrot-Bran Muffins

3 medium apples
1½–2 medium carrots
¼ cup oil
⅓ cup pure maple syrup
2 eggs
1½ cups whole wheat pastry flour
1 cup barley flour
½ cup wheat bran flakes
2 teaspoons baking powder
1 teaspoon cinnamon
1 teaspoon pumpkin pie spice
¾ cup chopped pecans (optional)
½ cup raisins

Preheat the oven to 350°F.

Cut the apples into wedges and remove the seeds. Cut the greens off the carrots. Juice the apple wedges and reserve 1 cup of the juice. Juice the carrots and reserve ½ cup of the pulp.

In a small bowl, combine the apple juice, carrot pulp, oil, maple syrup, and eggs; mix well.

In a large bowl, combine the pastry flour, barley flour, wheat bran flakes, baking powder, cinnamon, pumpkin pie spice, pecans, and raisins; mix well.

Add the liquid ingredients to the dry ingredients and stir just until moistened. Spoon the mixture into 12 oiled and floured muffin cups, filling each cup about ¾ full.

Bake the muffins until a toothpick inserted into the center of a muffin comes out clean, about 20–25 minutes. Remove from the oven and allow the muffins to cool on a wire rack, about 10 minutes.

Yield: 12 muffins Preparation time: 15 minutes
Baking time: 20–25 minutes Cooling time: 10 minutes

Carrot Muffins

5–7 medium carrots
1 cup barley flour
1 cup oat flour
1 tablespoon baking powder
1 egg
¼ cup dehydrated cane juice
½ cup raisins

Preheat the oven to 350°F.

Cut the greens off the carrots. Juice the carrots and reserve 1 cup of the juice and ½ cup of the pulp.

In a medium-size bowl, sift together the barley flour, oat flour, and baking powder.

In a large bowl, beat together the egg, dehydrated cane juice, and carrot pulp. Add the raisins and carrot juice, and mix well.

Add the dry ingredients to the liquid ingredients and beat just until combined. Spoon the mixture into 12 oiled and floured muffin cups, filling each cup about ¾ full.

Bake on a rack in the middle of the oven until a toothpick inserted into the center of a muffin comes out clean, about 20 minutes. Remove from the oven and allow the muffins to cool on a wire rack, about 5 minutes.

Variations:

Add 1 teaspoon cinnamon, ½ teaspoon powdered ginger, ¼ teaspoon nutmeg, and/or ¼ teaspoon cloves or allspice along with the dry ingredients.

Add ½ cup chopped walnuts or pecans along with the raisins.

Yield: 12 muffins *Preparation time: 15 minutes*
Baking time: 20 minutes *Cooling time: 5 minutes*

Savory Rosemary-Onion Muffins

These aromatic muffins transform a soup or salad into a richly satisfying meal.

5–7 medium carrots
½–¾ cup minced fresh onion
1 tablespoon safflower oil
1 egg
¼ cup low-fat dairy yogurt or soy yogurt
1 cup coarsely chopped dairy cheddar or soy cheddar cheese, tightly packed
2 tablespoons finely minced fresh parsley
1 cup whole wheat pastry flour
½ cup barley flour
½ cup rolled oats
2 teaspoons baking powder
1–2 teaspoons rosemary
1 teaspoon sea salt
½ teaspoon baking soda
½ teaspoon dry mustard

Preheat the oven to 375°F.

Cut the greens off the carrots. Juice the carrots and reserve 1 cup of the juice.

In a small skillet over low heat, sauté the minced onion in the oil until translucent. Set the skillet aside and allow the onion to cool.

In a small bowl, whisk together the egg, yogurt, and carrot juice. Stir in the cheese and minced parsley. Add the cooled sautéed onion.

In a large bowl, sift together the pastry flour and barley flour. Stir in the oats, baking powder, rosemary, salt, soda, and dry mustard.

Fold the liquid ingredients into the dry ingredients just until mixed. Spoon the mixture into 12 oiled and floured muffin cups, filling each cup about 3/4 full.

Bake the muffins until they're pale golden on the top and a toothpick inserted into the center of a muffin comes out clean, about 20–25 minutes. Remove from the oven and allow the muffins to cool on a wire rack, about 10 minutes.

Yield: *12 muffins*
Preparation time: *15 minutes*
Baking time: *20–25 minutes*
Cooling time: *10 minutes*

Blue Cornmeal Muffins

Serve these with Thanksgiving dinner for a special tribute to Native Americans.

2 large tomatoes
1 cup blue cornmeal
1 cup barley flour
4 teaspoons baking powder
1 teaspoon sea salt
1 egg, slightly beaten
¼ cup brown rice syrup
¼ cup canola oil

Preheat the oven to 425°F.

Cut the tomatoes into wedges. Juice the tomato wedges and reserve 1 cup of the juice.

In a large bowl, sift together the cornmeal, barley flour, baking powder, and sea salt.

In a small bowl, whisk together the egg, brown rice syrup, oil, and tomato juice.

Add the liquid ingredients to the dry ingredients, stirring just until moistened. Pour the batter into 12 oiled and floured muffin cups, filling each cup about 3/4 full.

Bake the muffins until a toothpick inserted into the center of a muffin comes out clean, about 20–25 minutes. Remove from the oven and allow to cool on a wire rack, about 10 minutes.

Yield: 12 muffins *Preparation time: 15 minutes*
Baking time: 20–25 minutes *Cooling time: 10 minutes*

Apple-Cinnamon Muffins

These fat-free muffins are moist and spicy but not too sweet.

3 medium apples
1 cup barley flour
1 cup oat flour
¼ cup whole wheat pastry flour
1 tablespoon baking powder
1 tablespoon cinnamon
1 egg
¼ cup dehydrated cane juice
1 teaspoon vanilla extract
½ cup soy milk
½ cup raisins

Preheat the oven to 350°F.

Cut the apples into wedges and remove the cores. Juice the apple wedges and reserve 1 cup of the juice and ½ cup of the pulp.

In a medium-size bowl, sift together the barley flour, oat flour, pastry flour, baking powder, and cinnamon.

In a large bowl, beat together the egg, dehydrated cane juice, vanilla extract, and apple pulp. Add the apple juice and soy milk, and mix well.

Add the dry ingredients to the liquid ingredients and beat with a wooden spoon just until combined. Stir in the raisins. Spoon the batter into 12 oiled and floured muffin cups, filling each cup about 3/4 full.

Bake the muffins until a toothpick inserted into the center of a muffin comes out clean, about 18–20 minutes.

Serve the muffins warm or at room temperature, plain or with apple butter.

Variation:

Add 1/2 cup chopped walnuts or pecans with the raisins.

Yield: 12 muffins   Preparation time: 15 minutes
Baking time: 18–20 minutes

Tomato-Basil Muffins

2 large tomatoes
10 sun-dried tomato halves, cut into small pieces
1/4 cup soy milk
1 egg
2 tablespoons oil
2 tablespoons fruit concentrate
2 tablespoons minced fresh basil
1/2 teaspoon sea salt
1 cup barley flour
1 cup whole wheat pastry flour
1 tablespoon baking powder
1/4 cup cornmeal

Preheat the oven to 350°F.

Cut the tomatoes into wedges, juice the wedges, and reserve 1 cup of the juice and 1/4 cup of the pulp.

In a large bowl, combine the tomato juice, tomato pulp, and sun-dried tomato halves. Let the mixture sit for at least 15 minutes.

Add the soy milk, egg, oil, fruit concentrate, basil, and salt to the tomato mixture. Beat the mixture with a wire whisk until well blended.

In a medium-size bowl, sift together the barley flour, pastry flour, and baking powder. Add the cornmeal and mix.

Add the flour mixture to the tomato mixture and beat with a wooden spoon until blended; do not overmix. Spoon the batter into 12 oiled and floured muffin cups, filling each cup about 3/4 full.

Bake the muffins until a toothpick inserted into the center of a muffin comes out clean, about 15–20 minutes.

Serve the muffins warm or at room temperature in place of bread.

Yield: 12 muffins Preparation time: 30 minutes
Baking time: 15–20 minutes

Real Peachy Muffins

Vicki's next-door neighbors love these.

1 1/3 pounds peaches
1/2 cup dried peaches, cut into small pieces
1/3 cup soy milk
1/4 cup fruit concentrate
2 tablespoons oil
1 teaspoon vanilla extract
1 egg
1 1/4 cups barley flour
1 cup whole wheat pastry flour
1 tablespoon baking powder
1/4 teaspoon allspice

Preheat the oven to 350°F.

Remove the stones from the peaches and cut the flesh into wedges. Juice the wedges and reserve 1 cup of the juice and ⅓ cup of the pulp.

In a large bowl, combine the peach juice and dried peaches. Let the peach pieces soak undisturbed for about 15–20 minutes.

Add the peach pulp, soy milk, fruit concentrate, oil, vanilla extract, and egg to the peach mixture. Beat the ingredients well.

In a small bowl, sift together the barley flour, whole wheat pastry flour, baking powder, and allspice. Add the flour mixture to the peach mixture and beat the batter just until mixed; do not overmix. Spoon the batter into 12 oiled and floured muffin cups, filling each cup about ¾ full.

Bake the muffins until a toothpick inserted into the center of a muffin comes out clean, about 15–20 minutes. Remove from the oven and allow the muffins to cool on a wire rack, about 10 minutes.

Yield: 12 muffins Preparation time: 30 minutes
Baking time: 15–20 minutes Cooling time: 10 minutes

Chapati

A new version of the traditional East Indian flatbread, these chapati are versatile and easy to make. They also keep well.

5–7 medium carrots
¾ cup gluten flour
½ teaspoon sea salt
1½ cups whole wheat bread flour (approximately)

Cut the greens off the carrots, juice the carrots, and reserve 1 cup of the juice.

In a large bowl, combine the carrot juice, carrot pulp, gluten flour, and salt. Gradually stir in enough of the bread flour to make a kneadable dough. (The dough is kneadable when it's too stiff to stir and begins to pull away from the sides of the bowl.)

Turn the mixture out onto a well-floured surface and knead in enough of the remaining bread flour to make a dough that will not stick to the kneading surface or your hands. Continue to knead the dough until it's smooth and elastic, about 5–10 minutes.

Leave the dough on the kneading surface, cover it with an inverted bowl or damp cloth, and let it rest for about 15 minutes. (This is not absolutely necessary, but it will make the dough easier to roll out.)

Cut the rested dough into 12 equal pieces. Shape each piece into a ball, then press the balls between your hands to flatten them out. Place each flattened ball of dough on a floured surface and sprinkle the top with a little additional flour. Using a rolling pin, roll out each piece of dough until it's very thin, about 1/16 inch thick. As you roll the chapati, try to keep them as round as possible.

Heat an unoiled skillet (preferably cast iron) over medium-high heat. One by one, cook the chapati for about 1 minute on each side. As the chapati cook, use a clean dishtowel to press them firmly down against the bottom of the skillet. This will make them puff up. The chapati are done when they are lightly flecked with dark brown. Stack the cooked chapati on a plate and cover them with a clean towel to keep them warm.

Serve the chapati as bread with soup, curry, or vegetable dishes. Use them in place of flour tortillas for burritos or roll them with any kind of sandwich filling. To reheat leftover chapati, place them briefly in a hot unoiled skillet over medium-high heat, turning them once.

Yield: *10–12 chapati*
Preparation time: *25 minutes*
Cooking time: *25 minutes*

Spreads and Pâtés

A juice extractor is the perfect tool for making vegetarian spreads and pâtés. Both juice and pulp help you create numerous rich-tasting spreads for breads and crackers. Use these delicious spreads to fashion hors d'oeuvres or to make hearty sandwiches with lettuce, sprouts, tomato, and mustard.

Except for Tofu Spread on page 155, these recipes will stay fresh in the refrigerator for about one week. Tofu Spread will keep for only about two days. For a quick, easy, yet truly wonderful meal, make a soup using fresh juice and serve it along with whole grain bread and a healthy pâté.

Mushroom-Onion Pâté

¾ pound potatoes (approximately 2 small)
2 tablespoons olive oil
1 large Spanish onion, chopped
2 cups sliced mushrooms
4 cloves garlic, minced
1 teaspoon tarragon
1 teaspoon thyme
¼ cup tamari
Pinch cayenne pepper

Preheat the oven to 350°F.

Cut the potatoes into chunks, juice the chunks, and reserve all of the juice.

Heat the oil in a skillet over low heat. Add the chopped onion and sauté until it just begins to get tender, about 10 minutes. Add the mushrooms, garlic, tarragon, and thyme, and sauté until the onion and mushrooms are tender, about 10 minutes more.

Transfer the sautéed mixture to a blender or food processor and process just until coarsely ground, about 3 seconds. (If you use a blender, you will probably need to do this in at least two batches.) Add the tamari, cayenne pepper, and potato juice. (If the starch in the potato juice has settled to the bottom of the container, stir the juice before adding it to the food processor.) Process just until combined. (It isn't necessary to make the ingredients smooth.)

Transfer the mixture to an oiled 8-by-8-inch baking dish. Bake, uncovered, for 30 minutes. The pâté will firm as it cools.

Serve the pâté warm, at room temperature, or chilled. Accompany it with whole grain bread or crackers.

Yield: 10–12 appetizer servings or 4–6 sandwich servings
Preparation time: 25 minutes   Baking time: 30 minutes

Veggie Pâté

A truly delicious vitamin-packed pâté to spread on bread or crackers.

1 pound potatoes (approximately 3 small)
4 medium carrots
1 bunch (¼ pound) spinach
3 large leaves kale
1 cup sunflower seeds
¼ cup whole wheat pastry flour
¼ cup nutritional yeast
¼ cup tamari
½ teaspoon sage
½ teaspoon marjoram
5 cloves garlic, pressed
Pinch cayenne pepper

Preheat the oven to 350°F.

Cut the potatoes into chunks. Cut the greens off the carrots. Bunch up the spinach and kale leaves, and juice them with the potato chunks. Combine all of the spinach, kale, and potato juices and pulps in a large bowl. Separately juice just enough of the carrots to make ½ cup of juice; add the ½ cup of juice and all of the pulp to the bowl.

In a blender, grind the sunflower seeds to a powder. Add them to the combined juice and pulp in the bowl, along with the pastry flour, nutritional yeast, tamari, sage, majoram, garlic, and cayenne pepper; mix well.

Transfer the mixture to a well-oiled 8-by-8-inch baking dish. Bake, uncovered, until a toothpick inserted into the center of the mixture comes out clean, about 50 minutes. Let the pâté cool for at least 2 hours before serving it.

To serve the pâté, cut it into squares. Accompany it with whole grain bread or crackers. For a delicious sandwich, spread a generous portion of pâté on one slice of whole grain bread, spread mustard on the other slice of bread, and garnish the sandwich with tomato and lettuce.

Yield: *10–12 appetizer servings or 4–6 sandwich servings*
Preparation time: *30 minutes*
Baking time: *50 minutes*
Cooling time: *2 hours*

Carrot Sandwich Spread

Both children and adults love the sandwiches we make with this spread.

4–5 medium carrots
⅓ cup raw tahini
1 tablespoon celery seeds
1 clove garlic, pressed
Pinch cayenne pepper (optional)

Cut the greens off the carrots. Juice the carrots and reserve ⅔ cup of the juice and 1 cup of the pulp.

In a medium-size bowl, whisk together the carrot juice and tahini until well blended. Add the carrot pulp, celery seeds, garlic, and cayenne pepper, and mix well.

Transfer the spread to a serving bowl and serve it with whole grain bread or crackers. For a delicious sandwich, spread it on whole grain toast and garnish it with lettuce.

Yield: *10–12 appetizer servings or 4–5 sandwich servings*
Preparation time: *15 minutes*

Butternut Pâté

A healthy spread with a rich and buttery flavor.

½ medium butternut squash
1 cup raw pecans
½ cup tomato sauce
2 tablespoons whole wheat pastry flour
2 tablespoons tamari
3 cloves garlic, pressed
1 teaspoon basil

Preheat the oven to 350°F.

Cut the squash into strips and remove the seeds. Juice the squash strips and reserve 1 cup of the juice and 2 cups of the pulp.

Grind the pecans in a blender. Transfer the ground pecans to a medium-size bowl. Add the squash juice to the pecans and mix. Add the squash pulp and mix. Add the tomato sauce, flour, tamari, garlic, and basil; mix well.

Spread the mixture in an oiled 8-by-8-inch baking dish. Bake, uncovered, until firm, about 45 minutes. Let the pâté cool at least 2 hours before cutting and serving it. To make slicing easier, chill the pâté.

To serve, cut the pâté into small squares. Accompany it with whole grain bread or crackers. Butternut Pâté is delicious served with the Carrot Bread on page 133.

Yield: *10–12 appetizer servings or 4–6 sandwich servings*
Preparation time: *20 minutes*
Baking time: *45 minutes*
Cooling/chilling time: *2 hours*

Tofu-Banana-Nut Spread

Sneak tofu into your family's diet
with this delicious bread spread.

½–¾ lemon
1 package (10½ ounces) firm silken tofu
1 large banana, mashed
½ cup nut butter (cashew or sunflower is good)
1 tablespoon fruit sweetener or brown rice syrup
2 teaspoons mellow red or white miso

Cut the lemon into wedges. Juice the lemon wedges and reserve 2–3 tablespoons of the juice.

In a blender or food processor, combine the lemon juice with the silken tofu, mashed banana, nut butter, fruit sweetener or brown rice syrup, and miso; process until smooth and creamy. Refrigerate the spread until chilled, about 45 minutes.

Transfer the spread to a serving bowl. Serve it with crackers, pita bread, or almost any nut bread.

Yield: *10–12 appetizer servings or 4–6 sandwich servings*
Preparation time: *15 minutes*
Chilling time: *45 minutes*

Tofu Spread

A high-protein spread with a wonderful nutty flavor.

3–4 medium carrots
1 cup mashed firm tofu
1 stalk celery, finely chopped
¼ cup finely minced red bell pepper
¼ cup peanut butter or tahini
2 tablespoons tamari
1 tablespoon Dijon-style mustard
¼ teaspoon celery seeds
1–2 cloves garlic, pressed

Cut the greens off the carrots. Juice the carrots and reserve 1 cup of the pulp.

In a medium-size bowl, combine the carrot pulp with the tofu, celery, red bell pepper, peanut butter or tahini, tamari, mustard, celery seeds, and garlic; mix well.

Transfer the spread to a serving bowl lined with lettuce, if desired. Garnish it with sprouts. Accompany the spread with whole grain bread or toast to make sandwiches.

Yield: *4–5 sandwich servings*
Preparation time: *15 minutes*

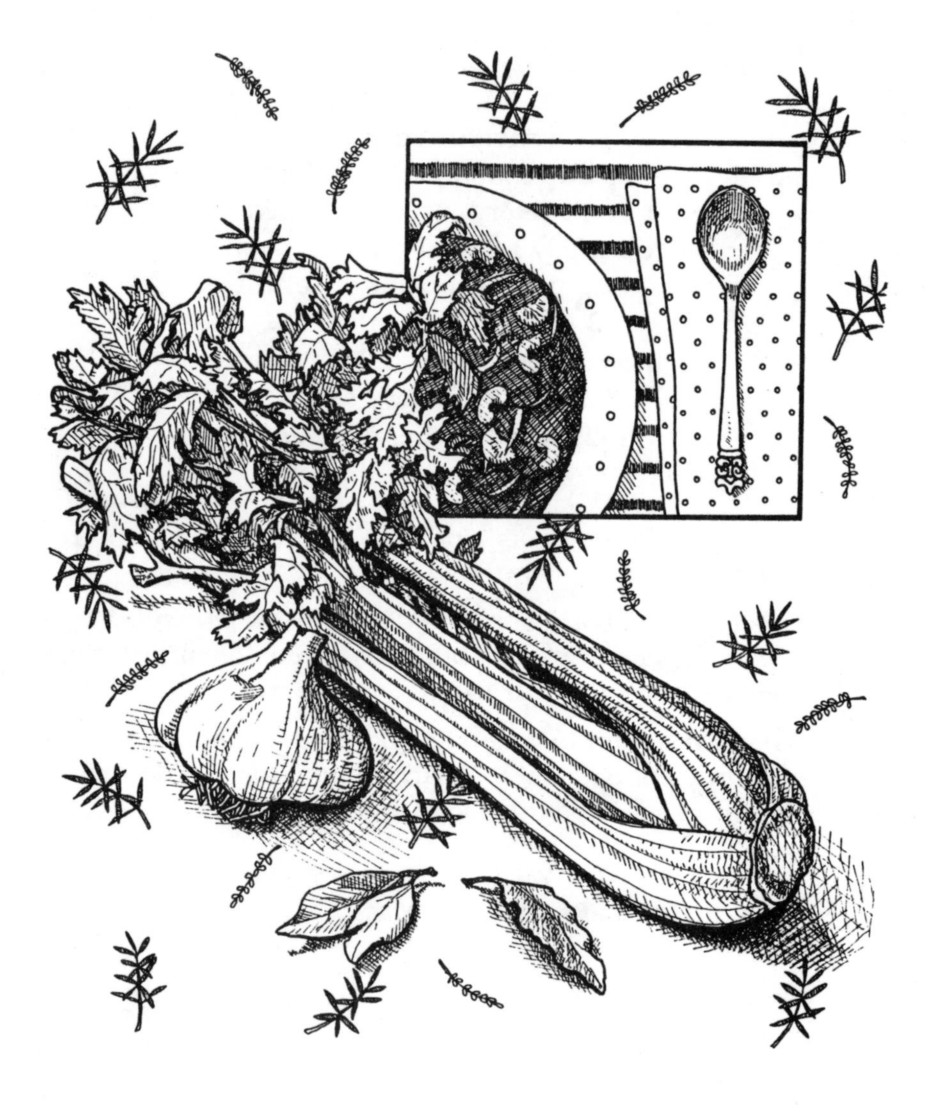

Soups

These soups are really special. Not only are they made with nutritious fresh juice, but the juice is added at the end of cooking to allow its precious vitamins and enzymes to be preserved whenever possible. This cooking method results in soups that are both extraordinarily rich in flavor, and fresh and light in consistency. The soups are also exceptionally colorful because of the vibrant pigments in the juices. Hot or cold, a soup made with fresh juice will be a smash at any luncheon or dinner party.

Miso Soup

Fresh raw juice, cooked greens, sea vegetables, and miso make this light soup very nourishing.

1 head bok choy
3 cups water
¼ cup quick-cooking dry wakame
½ cup frozen peas
2 scallions, chopped
¼ cup barley miso
1 tablespoon balsamic vinegar or lemon juice

Thinly slice the green part from about 3 large leaves of the bok choy and reserve 1 cup. Cut the remainder of the bok choy into pieces. Juice the bok choy pieces and reserve 2 cups of the juice.

In a large kettle, combine the chopped green bok choy and the water. Cover the kettle and bring the water to a boil, then reduce the heat and simmer the bok choy until it's tender.

Wash the wakame and add it to the soup. Simmer the soup until the wakame is just tender, about 5–10 minutes. Add the frozen peas and scallions, and simmer for 1 minute more.

Turn off the heat and add the bok choy juice to the kettle; stir. Using a cup or ladle, scoop up approximately ¼ cup of broth from the soup and transfer it to a larger cup or small bowl. Add the miso to this broth and stir until the miso is dissolved. Add the dissolved miso to the kettle along with the vinegar or lemon juice. Mix the soup well and serve it immediately.

To reheat the soup, bring it to just below a boil; do not allow it to reach a boil.

Yield: *6 servings*
Preparation time: *30 minutes*

Quick Carrot Soup

If you have 20 minutes and a green salad,
you'll have a quick and colorful dinner.

8–11 medium carrots
1½ pounds potatoes (approximately 4 medium)
1 cup water
1 cup chopped onion
1 teaspoon basil
2 tablespoons white or yellow miso
Dash cayenne pepper

Cut the greens off the carrots, juice the carrots, and reserve 1½ cups of the juice.

Scrub the potatoes and dice them. Place them in a pressure cooker with the water, onion, and basil. Cook the mixture over high heat until the pressure cooker starts to gently rock. Remove the pressure cooker from the heat and let it sit for 1–2 minutes, then cool it off in the sink under running water until the pressure comes down.

Immediately transfer about half of the cooked potato mixture to a blender or food processor. Add ½ cup of the carrot juice and blend. Add the miso and blend until smooth and creamy.

Transfer the blended mixture to the pressure cooker with the remaining cooked potato mixture; stir. Add the remaining carrot juice and the cayenne pepper, and mix well. If necessary, reheat the soup over medium heat, stirring constantly; do not boil. Serve the soup immediately.

Note:

To make this soup without a pressure cooker, just boil the diced potatoes in the water in a covered saucepan until tender, about 20–25 minutes; stir occasionally. If necessary, add a little more water to keep the potatoes from sticking.

Yield: *4 servings*
Preparation time: *20 minutes*

Easy Tomato-Vegetable Soup

Busy day? Try this quick soup for a warming lunch.

1 large tomato
1 medium leaf kale
1 stalk celery
1 clove garlic
1 leaf collard greens, chopped
1 teaspoon tamari
Dash sea salt
Croutons, as garnish

Cut the tomato into wedges. Bunch up the kale leaf and juice it with the tomato wedges, celery, and garlic. Reserve all of the combined juice.

In a saucepan, mix together the combined juice, chopped collard greens, and tamari; heat gently. Add the salt and stir. Taste the soup and adjust the seasonings.

Serve the soup hot, garnished with the croutons.

Yield: *1 serving*
Preparation time: *10 minutes*

Tomato Cream Supreme

A truly luscious soup that's quick to make.

1 tablespoon olive oil
1 cup chopped Spanish onion
1 green bell pepper, diced
5 large ripe tomatoes
3 stalks celery
½ cup raw cashews
1 teaspoon sea salt
2 tablespoons fresh basil

Heat the oil in a large, heavy kettle over low heat. Add the chopped onion and sauté until it starts to become tender, about 10 minutes. Add the diced green pepper and sauté until the pepper is tender yet still crisp.

Meanwhile, cut the tomatoes into wedges. Juice the tomato wedges and reserve all of the juice and 1 cup of the pulp. Juice the celery and combine all of the juice with the tomato juice.

In a blender or food processor, combine the tomato pulp, 1 cup of the tomato-celery juice, and the cashews; blend on high until the cashews are no longer gritty and the mixture is very smooth and creamy. Pour the mixture into the kettle with the sautéed vegetables.

Add the remaining combined juice to the kettle along with the salt. Simmer over medium-low heat for 3–4 minutes, then add the basil. Mix the soup well and serve it immediately

Yield: *6 servings*
Preparation time: *25 minutes*

Saint Patrick's Soup

A beautiful and tasty bright green soup that uses up some leftover broccoli stems.

1½ pounds potatoes (approximately 4 medium)
1 cup chopped onion
1 cup water
5 ounces fresh spinach
3 stalks celery
4 stalks broccoli, florets removed
¼ cup white miso
1 teaspoon basil
Pinch cayenne pepper

Scrub the potatoes and cut them into chunks. Place them in a large, heavy saucepan with the onions and water. Cover the saucepan and bring the water to a boil, then reduce the heat and simmer, stirring occasionally, until the potatoes and onions are tender, about 20–25 minutes.

Meanwhile, bunch up the spinach, juice it with the celery and broccoli, and reserve 1½ cups of the combined juice. If you don't have enough juice, add more celery or broccoli.

Transfer the cooked potatoes and onions to a blender or food processor. Add the leftover cooking water, if any, and some of the combined juice; blend. Add the miso and blend until smooth and creamy. (This may need to be done in two batches.)

Pour the blended mixture into a large saucepan and add the remaining combined juice; stir. Add the basil and cayenne pepper, and mix well. If necessary, reheat the soup over medium heat, stirring constantly; do not boil. Serve the soup immediately, accompanied with the Carrot Cornbread on page 135.

Yield: *6 servings*
Preparation time: *20 minutes*

Vegetable Cream Soup

This soup takes just 35 minutes to make but tastes like it simmered for hours.

1 large tomato
4 large carrots
4 stalks celery
1 tablespoon olive oil
2 cups chopped onion
1 teaspoon savory
4–6 cloves garlic, minced
10–15 sun-dried tomato halves, cut into small pieces
2 cups soy milk
½ cup brown rice flour
½ teaspoon sea salt

Cut the tomato into wedges. Cut the greens off the carrots. Juice the tomato wedges and carrots with the celery and reserve 2¼ cups of the combined juice. If you don't have enough juice, add more carrots or celery.

Heat the oil in a large, heavy kettle over low heat. Add the onions, savory, and garlic, and sauté, stirring occasionally, until the onions are tender.

In a medium-size, heavy saucepan, combine the sun-dried tomato halves, soy milk, and brown rice flour. Bring the mixture to a boil, stirring constantly. Then reduce the heat, cover the saucepan, and simmer, stirring occasionally, until the mixture is very thick and the tomato pieces are tender, about 10 minutes.

Add the sun-dried-tomato mixture to the sautéed onions in the kettle and stir. Slowly add the combined juice to the kettle, stirring vigorously with a wire whisk to keep the rice mixture from lumping. (If the rice mixture is still very hot when the juice is added, it will not lump.) Add the salt and stir. Either serve the soup immediately or bring it to a boil, reduce the heat, and simmer for 2–3 minutes before serving.

Yield: 6 servings
Preparation time: 35 minutes

Quick Vegetable Soup for One

Dinner for one doesn't have to be boring.

½ medium cucumber
½ cup spinach
2 stalks celery
1 clove garlic
2 tablespoons finely chopped turnip tops, beet tops, or collard greens
Pinch sea salt or dash tamari
1 tablespoon finely minced chives, as garnish

Cut the cucumber into spears. Bunch up the spinach and juice it with the cucumber spears, celery, and garlic. Reserve all of the combined juice.

In a saucepan, mix together the combined juice, chopped greens, and sea salt or tamari; stir. Warm the mixture gently.

Pour the soup into a mug and serve it garnished with the chives.

Yield: 1 serving
Preparation time: 10 minutes

Tomato-Vegetable-Rice Soup

Canned soup can't hold a candle to this.

½–⅔ pound cabbage
3–6 large tomatoes
5–7 medium carrots
2 tablespoons olive oil
1 cup chopped onion
1 green bell pepper, diced
1 cup cooked brown rice
¼ cup finely minced fresh basil
1 teaspoon sea salt

Cut the cabbage into pieces. Cut the tomatoes into wedges. Cut the greens off the carrots. Juice the cabbage pieces and reserve ½ cup of the juice. Juice just enough of the tomato wedges to make 3 cups of juice; reserve the 3 cups of juice and all of the pulp. Juice the carrots and reserve 1 cup of the juice.

Heat the oil in a large, heavy kettle over low heat. Add the chopped onion and sauté for about 5 minutes. Add the diced green pepper and continue to sauté until the onion and green pepper are tender.

In a blender or food processor, process the tomato pulp with 1 cup of the tomato juice just until blended. Transfer the blended pulp to the kettle with the sautéed vegetables. Turn off the heat below the kettle and add the remaining tomato juice as well as the carrot juice, cabbage juice, rice, basil, and salt; mix well.

If the soup is not hot enough, heat it on medium-high, stirring constantly; do not boil. Leftover soup can be served either heated or chilled.

Yield: *6 servings*
Preparation time: *20 minutes*

Black Bean Chili

Everyone has a favorite chili recipe. This will become yours.

4 large tomatoes
5–7 medium carrots
1 tablespoon olive oil
2 cups chopped onion
1 small red bell pepper, diced
1 small green bell pepper, diced
1 teaspoon cumin
1 teaspoon chili powder
1 teaspoon basil
Kernels from 1 large ear sweet corn
2 cups cooked and drained black beans
1 tablespoon balsamic vinegar
1 teaspoon sea salt
Cayenne pepper, to taste (optional)
Chopped onion, as garnish
Shredded dairy or soy cheddar, as garnish

Cut the tomatoes into wedges. Cut the greens off the carrots. Juice the tomato wedges and reserve 2 cups of the juice and all of the pulp. Juice the carrots and reserve 1 cup of the juice.

Heat the oil in a large, heavy kettle over low heat. Add the chopped onion and sauté until it begins to become translucent. Add the diced green and red bell peppers, cumin, chili powder, and basil, and sauté until the bell peppers and onions are just tender.

Add the corn kernels to the kettle along with the tomato juice, tomato pulp, and carrot juice; stir. Add the black beans, vinegar, and salt, and stir again. Bring the mixture to a boil, reduce the heat, and simmer until the vegetables are tender, about 3 minutes. Add the cayenne pepper and stir.

Ladle the chili into four bowls and serve it garnished with the chopped onion and shredded cheddar.

Variation:

Substitute cooked and drained red kidney beans for the black beans.

Yield: *4 servings*
Preparation time: *35 minutes*

Red Lentil Soup

One of Cherie's favorites, this rosy soup is rich and flavorful.

1 tablespoon olive oil
1 cup diced onion
1 cup diced leeks
2–3 cloves garlic, minced
1 cup dry red lentils
7 cups water
1 can (6 ounces) Italian-style tomato paste
1 vegetable bouillon cube
1 large tomato
¼ lemon
4 cups chopped spinach
Sea salt and pepper, to taste

Heat the oil in a small skillet over low heat. Add the onion, leeks, and garlic, and sauté until the onion is translucent.

Place the lentils in a fine-mesh wire strainer and rinse them; drain well.

In a soup kettle, combine the lentils and the 7 cups of water.

Bring the water to a boil, then skim off any foam that forms on top of the lentils. Add the tomato paste, bouillon cube, and sautéed onions, leeks, and garlic. Reduce the heat and simmer for about 15 minutes.

Meanwhile, cut the tomato into wedges, juice the wedges, and reserve ½ cup of the juice. Juice the lemon and reserve 1 tablespoon of the juice.

Add the chopped spinach to the kettle along with the lemon and tomato juices, salt, and pepper; simmer the soup for an additional 10 minutes. Serve the soup immediately.

Note:

Green lentils can be substituted for the red but take much longer to cook.

Yield: *6 servings*
Preparation time: *40 minutes*

Creamy Potato Soup

This soup makes an excellent nondairy, creamy base for any cream soup. If you want a thicker soup, just reduce the amount of water.

1 tablespoon olive oil
1 cup chopped onion
1 cup chopped leeks
5 cups water
2 vegetable bouillon cubes
1 teaspoon sea salt
5 cups peeled and diced potatoes
2 medium potatoes
3 large stalks celery
Minced chives or parsley, as garnish

Heat the oil in a large, heavy kettle over low heat. Add the chopped onion and leeks, and sauté until the onion is translucent.

Add the water, bouillon cubes, salt, and diced potatoes to the kettle. Bring the mixture to a boil, reduce the heat, and simmer until the potato pieces are tender, about 20–25 minutes.

Meanwhile, cut the 2 medium potatoes into chunks, juice the chunks, and reserve 1 cup of the juice. Juice the celery and reserve ½ cup of the juice.

Transfer as much of the cooked potato mixture as possible to a blender or food processor and process until creamy. (If the mixture is too thick, add some potato or celery juice while processing.) Set the processed mixture aside. Repeat until all of the soup is processed.

Return all of the mixture to the kettle, add the potato and celery juices, and reheat the soup over low heat. Serve the soup garnished with the minced chives or parsley.

Variation:

Add chopped collard greens, corn, or any other vegetable, fresh or frozen, along with the potato and celery juices. Continue heating the soup until the vegetable is cooked.

Yield: *6 servings*
Preparation time: *45 minutes*

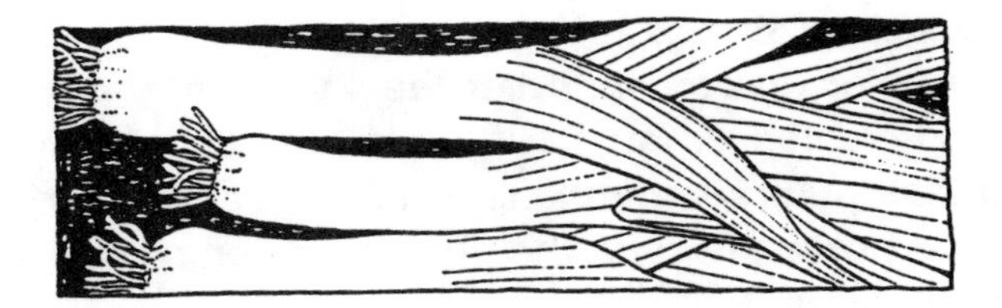

Acorn Squash–Apple Soup

A soup rich with the bounty of the fall harvest.

3 medium apples
¼ lemon
2 medium acorn squashes (approximately 2 pounds), halved and seeded
3 cups vegetable stock (or 3 cups water with 2 vegetable bouillon cubes)
2 tart green apples, cored, peeled, and chopped (approximately 2 cups)
1 onion, chopped
2 teaspoons peeled and grated ginger root
½ teaspoon sea salt
Plain low-fat dairy yogurt or soy yogurt, as garnish
Snipped fresh chives or finely minced fresh basil, as garnish

Cut the apples into wedges and remove the seeds. Juice the apple wedges and reserve 1 cup of the juice. Juice the lemon and reserve 1 tablespoon of the juice.

Position the acorn squash halves cut side down on a wire rack and set the rack in a saucepan over gently simmering water. Do not let the squash touch the water. Cover the saucepan and steam the squash halves until they're tender, about 25 minutes. Cool the squash slightly, then scoop out the pulp from the shells.

In a saucepan, combine ¼ cup of the vegetable stock with the chopped apples and onion; cover the saucepan and cook the apples and onion over low heat for 10 minutes. Add the apple juice, squash pulp, remaining vegetable stock, ginger, and salt; stir. Simmer, covered, until the apples and onion are tender, about 20 minutes.

In a blender or food processor, purée the mixture in batches.

Return it to the saucepan and reheat it gently. Add the lemon juice and stir. Taste the soup and adjust the seasonings.

To serve, ladle the soup into bowls. Serve it garnished with a dollop of the yogurt and some of the chives or basil.

Yield: *4–6 servings*
Preparation time: *60 minutes*

Carrot-Avocado Soup

This elegant and beautiful soup tastes fabulous!

10–14 medium carrots
2 ripe avocados
1 teaspoon cumin
Dash sea salt
2 tablespoons chopped avocado, as garnish
2 tablespoons finely chopped fresh cilantro, as garnish

Cut the greens off the carrots, juice the carrots, and reserve 2 cups of the juice.

Peel the avocados, remove the seeds, and cut the flesh into pieces.

In a blender or food processor, combine the carrot juice, avocado pieces, and cumin; blend until creamy. Add the salt and blend until mixed.

To serve, ladle the soup into 2 bowls and top it with the chopped avocado and cilantro. Accompany it with whole grain rolls or crackers.

Yield: *2 servings*
Preparation time: *10 minutes*

Cold Cucumber Cream

Creamy and refreshing.

1¼ large cucumbers
½ key lime or ¼ lemon
9 stalks celery
1 package (10½ ounces) extra firm silken tofu
2 tablespoons white miso
¼ teaspoon sea salt
1 cucumber, grated
3 scallions, chopped
2 tablespoons finely chopped fresh dill

Refrigerate the cucumbers, key lime or lemon, and celery until well chilled. Cut the cucumbers into spears and the lime or lemon into wedges. Juice the lime or lemon wedges and reserve all of the juice. Juice the cucumber spears and reserve 1¼ cups of the juice. Juice the celery and reserve 1½ cups of the juice. Combine the juices in a large bowl and place the bowl in the refrigerator until you're ready to use the juices.

In a blender or food processor, combine the silken tofu, miso, salt, and 1 cup of the mixed juices; blend until the mixture is very smooth and creamy.

Transfer the blended mixture to the large bowl containing the remainder of the juices. Add the grated cucumber, chopped scallions, and chopped dill; mix well. Serve the soup immediately.

Yield: 4 servings
Preparation time: 15–20 minutes

Garden Gazpacho

*The key to this soup is the refrigerator—
make sure all your ingredients are chilled before you start juicing.*

2½–3 large tomatoes
½ lemon
10–14 medium carrots
3 large stalks celery
2 tablespoons white or yellow miso
1 cucumber, grated
2 scallions, finely chopped
½ green bell pepper, finely chopped
¼ cup whole basil leaves (lightly packed), finely chopped
2 tablespoons finely chopped fresh dill

Refrigerate the tomatoes, lemon, carrots, and celery until well chilled. Cut the tomatoes and lemon into wedges. Cut the greens off the carrots. Juice the tomato wedges and reserve 1½ cups of the juice and all of the pulp. Juice the lemon wedges and reserve all of the juice. Juice the carrots and reserve 2 cups of the juice. Juice the celery and reserve ½ cup of the juice. Place the juices in the refrigerator until you're ready to use them.

In a blender or food processor, combine the tomato juice, tomato pulp, and miso; blend until smooth.

Transfer the blended mixture to a large bowl. Add the lemon, carrot, and celery juices, grated cucumber, scallions, green pepper, basil, and dill; mix well.

Serve the soup as soon as possible for the best flavor.

Yield: *6 servings*
Preparation time: *20 minutes*

Borscht

5–7 medium carrots
1 medium potato
1-inch slice onion
6 large stalks celery
½–⅔ pound cabbage
3 cups grated beets
2 cups water
1 teaspoon tarragon
1 teaspoon sea salt
3 bay leaves
1½ tablespoons balsamic vinegar
1 tablespoon honey
Cashew Sour Cream (page 205), or plain low-fat dairy yogurt or soy yogurt, as garnish

Cut the greens off the carrots. Cut the potato into chunks. Juice the carrots and reserve 1 cup of the juice. Juice the potato chunks and reserve ½ cup of the juice. Juice the onion and reserve ¼ cup of the juice. Juice the celery and reserve 1 cup of the juice. Juice the cabbage and reserve ½ cup of the juice.

In a large kettle, combine the potato juice, onion juice, beets, water, tarragon, salt, and bay leaves. Cover the kettle and bring the mixture to a boil. Reduce the heat and simmer, stirring occasionally, until the beets are tender, about 25 minutes.

Take the kettle off the heat and remove the bay leaves. Add the carrot juice, celery juice, cabbage juice, vinegar, and honey, and mix well. Chill the soup for 2–3 hours.

Serve the soup cold, garnished with a dollop of Cashew Sour Cream or plain low-fat dairy yogurt or soy yogurt.

Yield: 6–8 servings *Preparation time: 40 minutes*
Chilling time: 2–3 hours

Vichyssoise

Two friends from France told Vicki that they like this version better than traditional vichyssoise, which is made with heavy cream.

2 cucumbers
5 stalks celery
2 pounds potatoes (approximately 6 small)
1 cup water
1 teaspoon savory
1 teaspoon sea salt
1 cup soy milk
2 scallions, chopped
¼ cup finely chopped parsley

Cut the cucumbers into spears. Juice the cucumber spears with the celery and reserve all of the combined juice.

Scrub the potatoes and cut them into chunks. Place the potato chunks in a saucepan with the water, savory, and salt. Cover the saucepan and bring the water to a boil. Stir the potatoes, reduce the heat, and simmer, stirring occasionally, until tender, about 20–25 minutes. If necessary, to keep the potatoes from sticking to the saucepan while cooking, add a little more water.

Place about half of the cooked potatoes along with the leftover cooking liquid, if any, in a blender or food processor. Add half of the combined juice and blend until smooth and creamy. If the mixture is too thick to blend, add some of the soy milk. Transfer the puréed potato mixture to a large bowl. Process the remaining potatoes with the rest of the juice and add the second batch to the first batch in the bowl.

Add any remaining soy milk to the potato purée. If the soup is too thick, add even more soy milk. Add the chopped scallions and parsley, and stir.

Place the purée in the refrigerator and chill for 1–2 hours. Serve the soup cold.

Yield:	*6 servings*
Preparation time:	*30 minutes*
Chilling time:	*1–2 hours*

Salads

Gelled vegetable salads add a gourmet touch to any dinner or luncheon. Our recipes are easy, light, and, like other foods made with juice, very nourishing. Fresh juice gives our gelled salads an unexpectedly rich flavor, too. Cut our gelled salads into squares, place them on crisp leaves of lettuce, top them with the suggested sauce, and garnish them with fresh herbs. A colorful aspic or terrine will awaken even the most jaded palate.

When working with agar-agar and raw juices, it's best to juice the vegetables when they're at room temperature. However, when the juice in the recipe is to be cooked, as in Tomato Aspic With Avocado Dressing on page 180, the temperature of the vegetables doesn't matter.

Green Tabouli on page 183 is wonderful. It's the kind of recipe that invites you to be creative. Try it as written the first time, then see if you can make it even better by adding other vegetables, such as cherry tomatoes or scallions, or maybe some chick peas or green peas.

A number of our green salads use juice in their dressing as a delicious addition. Try tossing in some pulp as well for a surprisingly delightful change. For example, Carrot-Cabbage Salad With Pink Yogurt Dressing on page 190 is creamy because of the carrot pulp. And Carrot Salad With Carrot Pulp and Creamy Carrot Juice–Yogurt Dressing on page 181 is an exceptional treat.

Cucumber Aspic

Try this refreshing aspic either at the beginning of your meal (as an appetizer) or near the end of your meal (between the main course and dessert).

2 large cucumbers
1 small lemon
1 large stalk celery
1 cup water
1 tablespoon vegetable broth powder
2 heaping tablespoons agar flakes
½ teaspoon sea salt
1 cucumber, grated
2 scallions, chopped
1½ tablespoons finely chopped fresh dill weed

Cut the cucumbers into spears and the lemon into wedges. Juice the cucumber spears and reserve 2 cups of the juice. Juice the lemon wedges and reserve all of the juice. Juice the celery and reserve ⅓ cup of the juice. Combine the juices in a large bowl and set them aside.

In a medium-size saucepan, combine the water, vegetable broth powder, agar flakes, and salt. Bring the mixture to a boil, then cover the saucepan, reduce the heat, and simmer, stirring occasionally, until the agar flakes are completely dissolved, about 5–10 minutes.

Add the agar mixture to the combined juice and stir. Add the grated cucumber, chopped scallions, and chopped dill, and stir quickly. Immediately pour the mixture into a lightly oiled 8-by-8-inch dish and refrigerate until firm, about 3 hours.

To serve, cut the aspic into 9 squares. Garnish the squares with a dollop of Curry Cream Sauce on page 204 and a sprig of fresh dill.

Yield: 9 servings   Preparation time: 25 minutes   Chilling time: 3 hours

Beet Aspic

The beets make this aspic a bright wine red.

1 large cucumber
1–2 stalks celery
2 cups grated beets
1 cup water
1 teaspoon tarragon
½ teaspoon sea salt
3 bay leaves
2 level tablespoons agar flakes
1 tablespoon balsamic vinegar

Cut the cucumber into spears, juice the spears, and pour all of the juice into a 1-cup measure. Juice the celery and add enough of the juice to the cucumber juice to make 1 cup. Set the combined juice aside.

In a large saucepan, combine the grated beets, water, tarragon, salt, and bay leaves. Cover the saucepan and bring the mixture to a boil, then reduce the heat and simmer for about 10 minutes.

Add the agar flakes to the beet mixture and continue simmering, stirring occasionally, until the beets are tender and the agar flakes are completely dissolved, about 10 minutes more.

Add the vinegar and combined juice to the saucepan; mix well. Remove and discard the bay leaves. Pour the mixture into a lightly oiled 8-by-8-inch pan and refrigerate until firm, about 3 hours.

To serve, cut the aspic into 6 squares. Place a square on a lettuce leaf and garnish it with a dollop of Cashew Sour Cream on page 205 and chives or fresh dill.

Yield: 6 servings   Preparation time: 30 minutes   Chilling time: 3 hours

Tomato Aspic With Avocado Dressing

Tomato salad never tasted better!

4 large tomatoes
2 level tablespoons agar flakes
½ teaspoon celery seeds
½ teaspoon sea salt
¼ teaspoon oregano
1 tablespoon balsamic vinegar
1 cucumber, grated

Dressing
1 small lemon
2 small avocados
¼ teaspoon sea salt

To make the aspic:

Cut the tomatoes into wedges, juice the wedges, and reserve 2½ cups of the juice.

In a large saucepan, combine the tomato juice, agar flakes, celery seeds, salt, and oregano. Bring the mixture to a boil, then cover the saucepan, reduce the heat, and simmer, stirring occasionally, until the agar flakes are completely dissolved, about 5–10 minutes. Remove the mixture from the heat and let it sit, uncovered, for about 10 minutes.

Add the vinegar and cucumber to the saucepan and mix. Pour the mixture into a lightly oiled 8-by-8-inch pan and refrigerate until firm, about 2–3 hours.

To make the dressing:

Cut the lemon into wedges, juice the wedges, and reserve all of the juice.

Peel the avocados, remove the seeds, and cut the flesh into large chunks.

In a blender or food processor, combine the lemon juice, avocado chunks, and salt; blend until smooth and creamy.

To assemble:

Cut the aspic into 6 squares. Place a square on a lettuce leaf and garnish it with a dollop of dressing either next to it or on top of it. For an especially good appetizer or a light lunch, accompany the aspic with the Green Tabouli on page 183.

Yield: *6 servings*
Preparation time: *20 minutes*
Chilling time: *2–3 hours*

Carrot Salad With Carrot Pulp and Creamy Carrot Juice–Yogurt Dressing

*You won't believe this salad has carrot pulp in it—
all you'll notice is the wonderful flavor and rich creamy taste.*

3–4 medium carrots
1 cup grated carrot
Salad bowl lettuce

Dressing
½ lemon
2 tablespoons low-fat mayonnaise
2 tablespoons low-fat dairy yogurt or soy yogurt
1 teaspoon brown rice syrup

To make the salad:

Cut the greens off the carrots, juice the carrots, and reserve 1 cup of the pulp. Set aside 3 tablespoons of the juice for later use in the dressing.

In a medium-size bowl, combine the grated carrot with the carrot pulp. Toss the mixture well.

To make the dressing:

Cut the lemon into wedges, juice the wedges, and reserve 2 tablespoons of the juice.

In a small bowl, combine the lemon juice, 3 tablespoons of carrot juice, mayonnaise, yogurt, and brown rice syrup. Whisk the mixture until creamy.

To assemble:

Mix the salad with the dressing. Line two salad bowls with the lettuce and top with the carrot salad. Serve the salads garnished with a dollop of yogurt.

Yield: 2 servings
Preparation time: 15 minutes

Green Tabouli

This oil-free, ultra-high-chlorophyll version of the traditional Mideastern salad tastes better than the original.

1 small lemon
1 bunch (1/4 pound) spinach
5 large stalks celery
1 1/2 cups whole wheat couscous
1 1/4 cups water
1 teaspoon salt
2 cups finely chopped parsley
2 tablespoons finely chopped fresh mint
2 cloves garlic, pressed

Cut the lemon into wedges, juice the wedges, and reserve 3 tablespoons of the juice. Juice the spinach and pour all of the juice into a 1-cup measure. Juice the celery and add enough of the juice to the spinach juice to make 1 cup.

Put the couscous in a large bowl. In a small bowl, mix the combined juice, water, and salt. Pour the liquid mixture over the couscous, cover the bowl, and let the couscous sit until all of the liquid has been absorbed, about 1 hour.

Fluff the couscous with a fork. Add the lemon juice, parsley, mint, and garlic; mix well. Place the bowl in the refrigerator and chill the tabouli for 1 hour. Serve the tabouli cold.

Yield: *8–10 servings*
Preparation time: *1 1/3 hours*
Chilling time: *1 hour*

Gazpacho Salad With Tomato and Lime Juice Marinade

An excellent accompaniment for any Southwestern or Mexican dish.

2 medium tomatoes, chopped
½ cup finely chopped purple onion
1 medium cucumber, chopped
½ cup chopped green bell pepper
½ cup chopped red bell pepper
½ cup minced fresh cilantro
2 medium cloves garlic, finely minced

Marinade

½–1 large tomato
1½ medium limes
3 tablespoons olive oil
2 tablespoons tarragon vinegar
1 teaspoon thyme
1 teaspoon oregano
Sea salt and pepper, to taste

To make the salad:

In a medium-size bowl, combine the chopped tomatoes, onion, cucumber, green bell pepper, and red bell pepper with the minced cilantro and garlic. Set the bowl aside.

To make the marinade:

Cut the tomato and lime into wedges. Juice the tomato wedges and reserve ¼ cup of the juice. Juice the lime wedges and reserve 3 tablespoons of the juice.

In a small bowl, whisk together the tomato and lime juices, olive oil, and vinegar. Add the thyme, oregano, salt, and pepper, and whisk again.

To assemble:

Pour the marinade over the salad, cover the bowl, and chill the mixture thoroughly, at least 2–3 hours. Serve the salad on a bed of dark leafy greens.

Yield: *4 servings*
Preparation time: *15 minutes*
Chilling time: *2–3 hours*

Vegetable Terrine

This dish was inspired by an appetizer that is served in France in many of the finer restaurants.

1 pound asparagus
1 pound carrots
1 cup water
2 heaping tablespoons agar flakes
½ teaspoon sea salt
1 cucumber
1 medium lime
3 large stalks celery

Snap off the tough bottom end from each stalk of asparagus and set aside for later juicing. Place the upper parts of the asparagus stalks in a vegetable steamer and put the steamer in a saucepan containing about 1 inch of boiling water. Cover the saucepan, leave the heat on medium-high, and steam the asparagus tops until they're just tender, about 3 minutes. Set the steamed asparagus aside.

Cut the greens off the carrots and cut the carrots into strips. Steam the carrot strips until they're just tender, then set them aside.

In a large saucepan, combine the water, agar flakes, and

salt. Bring the mixture to a boil, then cover the saucepan, reduce the heat, and simmer until the agar flakes are completely dissolved, about 10 minutes.

While the agar mixture is cooking, cut the cucumber into spears and the lime into wedges. Juice the cucumber spears and lime wedges with the asparagus ends and celery, and reserve 1½ cups of the combined juice.

Add the combined juice to the simmering agar mixture, then immediately remove the saucepan from the heat; do not cook the combined juice.

Arrange the steamed asparagus and carrot strips in a lightly oiled 8½-by-4½-by-2½-inch loaf pan. Carefully pour the liquid mixture into the loaf pan over the vegetables. Place the loaf in the refrigerator and chill until firm, about 3–4 hours.

To serve, carefully run a knife around the edges of the pan to loosen the loaf. Then invert the pan over a plate and tap it on the bottom to unmold the loaf; be careful not to break the loaf. Cut the loaf into 6 thick slices (thin slices will crumble). Serve the slices with the Sweet and Hot Pepper Sauce on page 206.

Yield: 6 servings
Preparation time: 40 minutes
Chilling time: 3–4 hours

Orange-Almond-Green Salad With Orange-Herb Dressing

One of the Calbom family's favorites.

5–6 cups greens (for example, a combination of salad bowl, romaine, and red leaf lettuce), torn into bite-size pieces
1 orange, peeled and sliced into bite-size pieces
¼ cup finely minced green onions
¼ cup Stilton or bleu cheese, crumbled
½ cup almond slivers, toasted, as garnish

Dressing
½ medium orange
3 tablespoons olive oil
½ teaspoon marjoram
½ teaspoon thyme
½ teaspoon chervil
½ teaspoon tarragon
¼ teaspoon sea salt
1 clove garlic, finely minced or crushed

To make the salad:

In a large bowl, mix the salad greens with the orange pieces, green onion, and crumbled cheese. Set the bowl aside.

To make the dressing:

Peel the orange and cut it into wedges. Juice the orange wedges and reserve ¼ cup of the juice.

In a small bowl, combine the orange juice with the olive oil, marjoram, thyme, chervil, tarragon, salt, and garlic. Whisk the ingredients until well blended.

To assemble:

Pour the dressing onto the greens and toss until well coated. Place the salad in the refrigerator until chilled, at least 30 minutes. Serve the salad garnished with the toasted almond slivers.

Yield: 4 servings
Preparation time: 25 minutes
Chilling time: 30 minutes

Waldorf Salad

This recipe makes lots of dressing—
store it in the refrigerator for up to 2 weeks.

2–3 apples, cored and chopped
2–3 pears, cored and chopped
4 stalks celery, diced
½–¾ cup walnuts, chopped
Raisins or currants, as garnish

Dressing
1 orange
½ lemon
1 package (10½ ounces) firm silken tofu
½ cup low-fat dairy yogurt or soy yogurt
3 tablespoons fruit concentrate or brown rice syrup
1 teaspoon mellow red or white miso
½ teaspoon grated ginger root
¼ teaspoon vanilla extract
Dash each of cloves, cinnamon, nutmeg, and cardamom

To make the salad:

In a medium-size bowl, mix together the apples, pears, celery, and walnuts. Set the bowl aside.

To make the dressing:

Peel the orange and cut it into wedges. Cut the lemon into wedges. Juice the orange wedges and reserve all of the juice. Juice the lemon wedges and reserve 2 tablespoons of the juice.

In a blender or food processor, combine the orange and lemon juices, silken tofu, yogurt, fruit concentrate or brown rice syrup, miso, ginger root, vanilla extract, cloves, cinnamon, nutmeg, and cardamom; process until smooth and creamy.

To assemble:

Add just enough of the dressing to coat the salad; mix well. Place the salad in the refrigerator to chill, at least 30 minutes.

Arrange any dark green lettuce, such as red leaf or salad bowl lettuce, on 4 salad plates. Place 1/4 of the salad on each plate. Garnish each salad with the raisins or currants. Place the salads in the refrigerator to chill until serving time.

Yield: *4 servings of salad*
2 cups of dressing
Preparation time: *20–25 minutes*
Chilling time: *30 minutes*

Carrot-Cabbage Salad With Pink Yogurt Dressing

This salad is as beautiful as it is delicious. Its many colors make it appealing to the eye, and the carrot pulp gives it a creamy texture.

3–4 medium carrots
3 cups coarsely shredded green cabbage
1 cup coarsely shredded purple cabbage
1 cup minced purple onion
2 teaspoons dill weed

Dressing
½ lemon
1 very small piece beet, for color
1½ cups low-fat dairy yogurt or soy yogurt
½ cup low-fat mayonnaise
1 tablespoon honey or brown rice syrup

To make the salad:

Cut the greens off the carrots, then juice the carrots and reserve 1 cup of the pulp.

In a large bowl, mix together the carrot pulp, green and purple cabbages, purple onion, and dill weed. Set the bowl aside.

To make the dressing:

Cut the lemon into wedges, juice the wedges, and reserve 1 tablespoon plus 1 teaspoon of the juice. Juice the beet and add the juice to the lemon juice.

In a small bowl, mix the lemon-beet juice with the yogurt, mayonnaise, and honey or brown rice syrup until well blended.

To assemble:

Add the yogurt dressing to the salad and mix well. Place the salad in the refrigerator until chilled, about 15–30 minutes. Serve the salad cold.

For a spectacular presentation, line a glass salad bowl with the washed outer leaves from the purple cabbage. Pour the salad on top of the cabbage leaves and garnish it with several pansies or other edible flowers.

Note:

This dressing also tastes wonderful with fruit salad.

Yield: *6 servings*
Preparation time: *25–30 minutes*
Chilling time: *15–30 minutes*

Summer Sun Fruit Salad

Throw the sunflower seeds into the water as soon as you get up in the morning and you'll have a wonderful lunch.

½ cup sunflower seeds
1 cup water
1 pound peaches
½ lemon
1 teaspoon vanilla extract
½ teaspoon cinnamon
2 Medjool dates or 4 regular soft dates, pitted
4 small peaches
1 cup strawberries
1 cup blackberries
1 banana
Extra berries, as garnish

In a small bowl, combine the sunflower seeds and water. Let the sunflower seeds soak undisturbed for 6–8 hours.

Remove the stones from the 1 pound of peaches and cut the flesh into wedges. Cut the lemon into wedges. Juice just enough of the peach wedges to make ½ cup plus 2 tablespoons of juice; reserve the ½ cup plus 2 tablespoons of juice and all of the pulp. Juice the lemon wedges and reserve 1½ tablespoons of the juice.

Drain the sunflower seeds in a wire strainer and place them in a blender or food processor. Add the peach juice and lemon juice, and blend until smooth and creamy. Add the peach pulp, vanilla extract, cinnamon, and dates, and blend again until smooth. Refrigerate the dressing until needed.

Peel the 4 small peaches, remove the stones, and cut the flesh into bite-size pieces. Remove the caps from the strawberries.

In a large salad bowl, combine the peach pieces, strawberries, and blackberries. When you are ready to serve the salad, peel and slice the banana and add it to the bowl. Stir the dressing and pour it over the fruit, mixing gently. Serve the salad garnished with the extra berries.

Note:

The dressing will darken if it is not served immediately after being made. This does not affect the taste or quality of the salad. However, the dressing should be served the same day it's made.

Yield: *4–6 servings*
Soaking time: *6–8 hours*
Preparation time: *20 minutes*

Potato Salad

A creamy potato salad without mayonnaise.

2 pounds potatoes (approximately 6 small)
1¼ cups water
1 small lemon
1-inch slice sweet onion
1 package (10½ ounces) extra firm silken tofu
2 tablespoons white or yellow miso
2 stalks celery, finely chopped
½ green bell pepper, chopped
1 can (6 ounces) pitted black olives, drained and sliced
¼ cup finely chopped parsley

Scrub the potatoes, dice them, and place them in a medium-size, heavy saucepan with the water. Cover the saucepan and bring the water to a boil, then reduce the heat and simmer, stirring occasionally, until the potatoes are tender, about 20–25 minutes.

Meanwhile, cut the lemon into wedges, juice the wedges, and reserve all of the juice. Juice the onion and reserve ¼ cup of the juice.

In a blender or food processor, combine the onion juice, lemon juice, silken tofu, and miso; blend until smooth and creamy. Transfer the mixture to a large bowl.

Drain the cooked potatoes and add them to the dressing mixture in the bowl. Add the celery, green pepper, olives, and parsley, and mix well. Place the salad in the refrigerator to chill, about 1 hour.

Serve the salad on a bed of crisp lettuce.

Yield: *6–8 servings*
Preparation time: *30 minutes*
Chilling time: *1 hour*

Cucumber Salad

This is Vicki's version of a classic.

1 small lemon
4–5 large stalks celery
1 package (10½ ounces) extra firm silken tofu
1 tablespoon white or yellow miso
¼ teaspoon sea salt
3–4 medium cucumbers, thinly sliced
6 radishes, thinly sliced
3–4 scallions, finely chopped
¼ cup finely chopped fresh mint

Cut the lemon into wedges, juice the wedges, and reserve all of the juice. Juice the celery and reserve ¾ cup of the juice.

In a blender or food processor, combine the lemon juice, celery juice, silken tofu, miso, and salt; blend until smooth and creamy. Transfer the mixture to a large salad bowl. Add the cucumbers, radishes, scallions, and mint, and mix well. Either serve the salad immediately or, preferably, place it in the refrigerator until chilled, about 1 hour.

Note:

This recipe produces a rather large salad and can be cut in half if desired.

Yield: 8 servings
Preparation time: 20 minutes

Apple-Walnut-Cabbage Salad With Creamy Apple Juice Dressing

If you have 30 minutes, you'll have a wonderful salad.

½ medium head red cabbage, shredded
½ medium head green cabbage, shredded
1 large red apple, cored and chopped
¼ cup minced purple onion
½ cup chopped walnuts, toasted
2 tablespoons bleu cheese or Stilton cheese, crumbled

Dressing
1 medium apple
½ lemon
4 teaspoons low-fat mayonnaise
4 teaspoons low-fat dairy yogurt or soy yogurt
2 teaspoons brown rice syrup

To make the salad:

In a large bowl, combine the red and green cabbage, apple, purple onion, walnuts, and cheese. Set the bowl aside.

To make the dressing:

Cut the apple into wedges and remove the seeds. Cut the lemon into wedges. Juice the apple wedges and reserve ⅓ cup of the juice. Juice the lemon wedges and reserve 2 tablespoons of the juice.

In a small bowl, combine the apple and lemon juices with the mayonnaise, yogurt, and brown rice syrup. Whisk the ingredients until well blended.

To assemble:

Pour the dressing onto the cabbage mixture and toss until well coated. Place the salad in the refrigerator until chilled, about 15–30 minutes. Serve the salad cold.

Yield: 4 servings
Preparation time: 30 minutes
Chilling time: 15–30 minutes

Spinach and Romaine With Ginger-Peach Vinaigrette

A real gourmet treat, this salad will get rave reviews from your company.

3 cups spinach leaves, torn into bite-size pieces
2 cups romaine inner leaves, torn into bite-size pieces
2 green onions, finely minced
½ peach, peeled, pitted, and cut into 12 thin slices, as garnish
½ cup pine nuts, toasted, as garnish

Vinaigrette
1 peach
½ lemon
⅛-inch or smaller slice ginger root
¼ cup walnut or safflower oil
2 tablespoons rice vinegar

To make the salad:

In a large bowl, combine the spinach and romaine with the green onions. Set the bowl aside.

To make the vinaigrette:

Remove the stone from the peach and cut the flesh into wedges. Cut the lemon into wedges. Juice the peach wedges with the ginger root and reserve all of the combined juice. Juice the lemon wedges and reserve 2 tablespoons of the juice.

In a small bowl, combine the peach-ginger juice, lemon juice, walnut oil, and vinegar; whisk until mixed.

To assemble:

Pour the vinaigrette onto the salad greens and toss the greens until coated. Place 1/4 of the mixture on each of 4 salad plates and garnish each salad with three of the peach slices and 1/8 cup of the toasted pine nuts. Place the plates in the refrigerator until the salad is chilled, at least 30 minutes. Serve the salads cold.

Yield: *4 servings*
Preparation time: *20 minutes*
Chilling time: *30 minutes*

Dressings and Sauces

In addition to the various salad dressings we give you in the Salads section of *Cooking for Life*, we also wanted you to have the recipes for these additional basic dressings, all of which are easy to prepare, are low in fat, and include fresh juice among their ingredients. You'll discover, as we have, that fresh juice adds not only extra nutrients but delightful flavors.

Sauces made with fresh fruit or vegetable juice will add vitamins, minerals, and a gourmet touch to any meal. When you think of sauces, don't you usually think of "lots of calories"? Well, here's a surprise! Our sauces are relatively low in calories. They're also low in fat and cholesterol, and can be enjoyed with the knowledge that you are doing something good for yourself. You won't find butter, cream, or milk in these delicious, healthy sauces—just fresh juices, seasonings, small amounts of raw cashews or tahini for a creamy texture, and other healthy ingredients.

The sauces in this section of our cookbook are also so easy to prepare. Some, such as Lemon-Curry Sauce on page 211 (yummy over asparagus or broccoli!), are made completely in a blender or food processor. The vegetable sauces are superb over rice or other grains, pastas, or vegetables, and are wonderful served with veggie burgers or loaves. The fruit sauces gently sweeten pancakes, fresh fruit salads, and sherbets.

Garlic-Orange Dressing

A real pleaser!

½ medium orange
4 teaspoons canola oil
1 tablespoon minced scallion
1 teaspoon freshly grated orange zest
¼ teaspoon minced garlic
Sea salt and pepper, to taste

Peel the orange and cut it into wedges. Juice the wedges and reserve ¼ cup of the juice.

In a small bowl, whisk together the orange juice, oil, scallion, orange zest, garlic, salt, and pepper. Pour the mixture into a salad dressing carafe or a jar and refrigerate until chilled, at least 30 minutes. Shake the dressing before serving it.

Variation:

Combine ¼ cup freshly extracted orange juice with ¼ cup commercially prepared Italian dressing. Cherie tried this out with dinner guests on a very rushed evening, and it was a hit!

Yield: *⅓ cup*
Preparation time: *10–15 minutes*
Chilling time: *30 minutes*

Creamy Basil Dressing

Creamy but low in fat.

½ lemon
1½ large stalks celery
½ package (5¼ ounces) extra firm silken tofu
¼ cup fresh basil leaves
1½ tablespoons white or yellow miso
1 scallion

Cut the lemon into wedges, juice the wedges, and reserve all of the juice. Juice the celery and reserve ¼ cup of the juice.

In a blender or food processor, combine the lemon juice, celery juice, silken tofu, basil, miso, and scallion; blend until smooth and creamy. Serve the sauce either at room temperature or chilled over a green salad, tomatoes, or steamed vegetables.

Yield: *1½ cups*
Preparation time: *10 minutes*

Orange-Tahini Dressing

This dressing will bring you raves!

1 small orange
⅓ cup tahini
1 tablespoon tamari
1 tablespoon lemon juice or balsamic vinegar
1 clove garlic, pressed

Peel the orange and cut it into wedges. Juice the wedges and reserve 1/3 cup of the juice.

In a small bowl, combine the orange juice and tahini; stir until well blended. Add the tamari, lemon juice or vinegar, and garlic, and mix well. Serve the dressing either at room temperature or chilled over any raw-vegetable salad. It is also good over cooked vegetables or tofu.

Yield: 3/4 cup
Preparation time: 10 minutes

Avocado-Pepper Dressing

This dressing is delicious over almost any vegetable.

½ medium green bell pepper
1 small lemon
2 cloves garlic
1-inch slice sweet onion
¾ cup mashed ripe avocado (approximately 1 small)
½ teaspoon sea salt

Cut the bell pepper into pieces and remove the seeds. Cut the lemon into wedges. Juice the bell pepper pieces with the garlic and reserve all of the combined juice. Juice the lemon wedges and reserve all of the juice. Juice the onion and reserve 1/4 cup of the juice.

In a blender or food processor, combine the pepper-garlic juice, onion juice, lemon juice, mashed avocado, and salt; blend until smooth. Serve the dressing either at room temperature or chilled over a vegetable salad or steamed vegetable.

Yield: 1 1/3 cups
Preparation time: 15 minutes

Potato Sauce

Potato juice thickens incredibly when it's cooked. Just add liquid and seasonings, and you have a delicious nonfat gravy.

1 pound potatoes (approximately 3 small)
1–2 medium carrots or ½–⅔ large tomato
3 cups water
3 tablespoons tamari
1 clove garlic, pressed
Pinch cayenne pepper

Cut the potatoes into chunks. Trim the greens from the carrots or cut the tomato into wedges. Juice the potato chunks and reserve all of the juice. Juice the carrots or tomato wedges and reserve ¼ cup of the juice.

Stir the potato juice to mix the starch back in, then pour the potato juice into a large saucepan. Add the carrot or tomato juice, water, tamari, garlic, and cayenne pepper, and bring the mixture to a boil, stirring with a wire whisk. Reduce the heat and simmer for about 3 minutes. If the sauce gets too thick, add more water.

Serve the sauce with the Carrot-Potato Patties on page 242 or with any veggie burger or meatless loaf. It is also delicious with vegetables in a stew.

Note:

This recipe makes a lot of sauce, but since the sauce contains no fat, you can serve it generously. Leftover sauce can be stored in the refrigerator for up to one week and can be reheated. If desired, cut the recipe in half.

Yield: *4 cups*
Preparation time: *10 minutes*

Curry Cream Sauce

This rich and slightly piquant sauce contrasts wonderfully with cool and light Cucumber Aspic.

3–4 medium carrots
½ cup raw cashews
½ teaspoon sea salt
½ teaspoon dry mustard
½ teaspoon curry powder
¼ teaspoon turmeric

Cut the greens off the carrots, juice the carrots, and reserve ½ cup of the juice.

In a blender or food processor, combine the carrot juice, cashews, salt, dry mustard, curry powder, and turmeric; blend on high until the cashews are no longer gritty and the mixture is very smooth and creamy. Serve the sauce with the Cucumber Aspic on page 178 or as a dip for raw vegetables.

Yield: *¾ cup*
Preparation time: *10 minutes*

Green Sauce

Rich and nutritious.

3 stalks celery
1 bunch (¼ pound) spinach
⅓ cup soy milk
⅓ cup cashews
1 tablespoon white or yellow miso

Juice the celery with the spinach and reserve ⅔ cup of the combined juice. If you don't have enough juice, add more celery.

In a blender or food processor, combine the celery-spinach juice, soy milk, cashews, and miso; blend on high until the cashews are no longer gritty and the mixture is very smooth and creamy.

Pour the mixture into a medium-size saucepan and bring it to a boil, stirring constantly. Reduce the heat and simmer, stirring occasionally, for 2–3 minutes. If the sauce becomes too thick, add a little more soy milk to achieve the desired consistency. Serve the sauce immediately.

Yield: *1¼ cups*
Preparation time: *15 minutes*

Cashew Sour Cream

Exceptionally rich and creamy.

½ lemon
½ cup soy milk
½ cup raw cashews
¼ teaspoon sea salt

Cut the lemon into wedges, juice the wedges, and reserve 2 tablespoons of the juice.

In a blender or food processor, combine the lemon juice, soy milk, cashews, and salt; blend on high until the cashews are no longer gritty and the mixture is very smooth and creamy. If the mixture is not thick enough, add more cashews.

Yield: *1 cup*
Preparation time: *5–10 minutes*

Sweet and Hot Pepper Sauce

A subtly sweet and creamy sauce that you can spice to your taste.

2 medium red bell peppers
½ cup cashews
1 tablespoon white or yellow miso
1 tablespoon balsamic vinegar
Pinch cayenne pepper

Cut the red bell peppers into quarters and remove the seeds. Juice the red bell pepper quarters and reserve ½ cup of the juice.

In a blender or food processor, combine the red bell pepper juice, cashews, miso, vinegar, and cayenne pepper; blend on high until the cashews are no longer gritty and the mixture is very smooth and creamy. Serve the sauce with the Vegetable Terrine on page 185, a green salad, or other vegetables, such as cauliflower or broccoli.

Note:

Remember that cayenne pepper is very piquant. Approximately 1/16 teaspoon will spice this sauce nicely.

Yield: *¾ cup*
Preparation time: *10 minutes*

Vegetable Cream Sauce

For the best flavor, serve this quick sauce as soon as it's made.

3 medium tomatoes
5–7 medium carrots
⅓ cup raw cashews
½ teaspoon tarragon
¼ teaspoon sea salt

Cut the tomatoes into wedges. Cut the greens off the carrots. Juice the tomato wedges and reserve ½ cup of the pulp. Juice the carrots and reserve 1 cup of the juice.

In a blender or food processor, combine the tomato pulp, carrot juice, cashews, tarragon, and salt; blend on high until the cashews are no longer gritty and the mixture is very smooth and creamy. Either serve the sauce immediately, at room temperature, or warm it first in a saucepan over medium heat (do not boil).

Yield: *1 cup*
Preparation time: *10 minutes*

Fat-Free Mushroom Sauce

This rich sauce is free of fat but overflowing with flavor and nutrition.

1 small or ½ medium potato
5–7 medium carrots
2 bunches (½ pound) spinach
2 cups sliced mushrooms
2 tablespoons tamari

Cut the potato into chunks. Cut the greens off the carrots. Juice the potato chunks and reserve 1/4 cup of the juice. Juice the carrots and reserve 1 cup of the juice. Juice the spinach and reserve 1/3 cup of the juice.

In a medium-size saucepan, combine the mushrooms with the carrot, potato, and spinach juices. Bring the mixture to a boil, stirring constantly, then reduce the heat and simmer, stirring occasionally, until the mushrooms are tender and the juice has thickened. Add the tamari to the mixture and stir. Serve the sauce over veggie loaves or burgers, or over any grain dish.

Yield: 2 cups Preparation time: 15 minutes

Tomato-Herb Vinaigrette

1 large tomato
1/4 cup red wine vinegar
1 tablespoon finely chopped fresh chives or scallions
1/2 teaspoon sea salt
1/4 teaspoon honey
1 clove garlic, crushed
Pinch savory or oregano
Pinch cayenne pepper

Cut the tomato into wedges, juice the wedges, and reserve 3/4 cup of the juice.

In a small bowl, whisk together the tomato juice, vinegar, chives or scallions, salt, honey, garlic, savory or oregano, and cayenne pepper. Refrigerate the dressing until chilled, at least 30 minutes. Pour the mixture into a salad dressing carafe or a jar and shake before serving.

Yield: 1 cup Preparation time: 10–15 minutes
Chilling time: 30 minutes

Quick Tomato Sauce

Use up some tomato pulp with this easy sauce.
Its fragrant flavor comes from using fresh rosemary.

8 large tomatoes
1 medium tomato, coarsely chopped
2 branches fresh rosemary, stems removed
(approximately 2 teaspoons)
½ teaspoon oregano
½ teaspoon sea salt
1 clove garlic, pressed

Cut the tomatoes into wedges, juice the wedges, and reserve 2½ cups of the pulp.

In a blender or food processor, blend the tomato pulp and chopped tomato for a few seconds. Transfer the mixture to a medium-size saucepan. Add the rosemary, oregano, salt, and garlic, and stir. Bring the mixture to a boil, then reduce the heat and simmer, stirring occasionally, for 5–10 minutes. Either serve the sauce immediately or store it in an airtight container in the refrigerator for up to 7 days.

Yield: 2½ cups
Preparation time: 15 minutes

Dominique's Tomato Sauce

An outstanding tomato sauce that requires hardly any cooking.

5 large tomatoes
1 tablespoon arrowroot
1 tablespoon olive oil
1 cup chopped onions
1 teaspoon oregano
1 teaspoon basil
⅛ teaspoon powdered cloves
2 cloves garlic, pressed
3 bay leaves
½ teaspoon sea salt

Cut the tomatoes into wedges and juice them. Reserve 2 cups of the juice and 1½ cups of the pulp.

In a large bowl, combine the tomato juice, tomato pulp, and arrowroot; mix well.

In a large skillet, heat the oil over low heat. Add the onions, oregano, basil, cloves, garlic, and bay leaves; sauté until the onions are tender, about 5 minutes.

Add the tomato mixture to the skillet and bring the sauce to a boil. Reduce the heat and simmer for about 5 minutes, stirring occasionally. Add the salt and remove the bay leaves.

Serve the sauce over pasta, polenta, or veggie loaves or burgers. Leftover sauce can be stored in an airtight container in the refrigerator for up to 7 days.

Yield: *3 cups*
Preparation time: *25 minutes*

Lemon-Curry Sauce

Delicious over steamed vegetables, baked potatoes, pasta, broiled fish, or fish cakes.

1 small lemon
¾ cup low-fat dairy yogurt or soy yogurt
½ cup firm silken tofu, mashed
1 tablespoon tahini
½ teaspoon tamari
½ teaspoon curry powder
¼ teaspoon sea salt

Cut the lemon into wedges, juice the wedges, and reserve 3 tablespoons of the juice.

In a blender or food processor, blend the yogurt and silken tofu. Add the lemon juice, tahini, tamari, curry powder, and salt; blend until just combined. Serve the sauce over steamed vegetables or another hot dish. Serve it at room temperature; it's better not to heat it.

Yield: 1¼ cups
Preparation time: 15 minutes

Ruby Red Sauce

This sauce is so delicious, you'll have to watch yourself. Cherie even eats it all by itself! But if you can manage to save some, it's great over fish.

8 medium beets
1½ limes
2 teaspoons finely minced fresh chives
1 teaspoon butter (optional)
Sea salt, to taste

Cut the beets into chunks and the limes into wedges. Juice the beet chunks and reserve 2 cups of the juice. Juice the lime wedges and reserve 3 tablespoons of the juice. Be careful to keep the juices separated.

In a small saucepan, bring the beet juice to a boil, then lower the heat and simmer until the juice is reduced by half and thickened, about 20 minutes.

Add the lime juice and butter to the reduced beet juice, and whisk. Bring the mixture to a boil, then remove it from the heat. Add the chives and salt, and stir.

Serve the sauce over a vegetable aspic or any white fish.

Yield: *1 cup*
Preparation time: *35–40 minutes*

Tahini-Carrot Sauce

Some things are meant to go together.
This sauce shows that carrots and tahini are two of them.

1 lemon
3–4 medium carrots
2–3 cloves garlic
⅔ cup tahini
1 teaspoon tarragon
1 teaspoon paprika
½ teaspoon sea salt

Cut the lemon into wedges. Cut the greens off the carrots. Juice the lemon wedges with the garlic and reserve all of the combined juice. Juice the carrots and reserve ½ cup of the juice.

Place the tahini in a small bowl. Slowly stir in the lemon-garlic juice and carrot juice. Add the tarragon, paprika, and salt, and stir until creamy and well blended. Serve the sauce at room temperature with grains, pasta, or steamed or raw vegetables. It's excellent over lightly steamed asparagus and snow peas served on a bed of quinoa.

Yield: *1¼ cups*
Preparation time: *10 minutes*

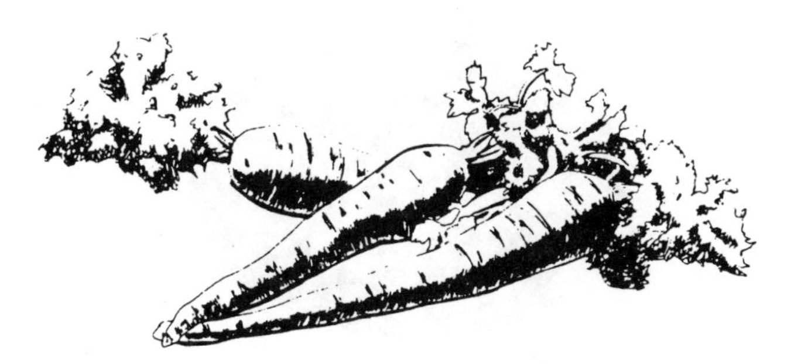

Salsa

Spice up some leftover tomato pulp and turn it into salsa!

6 medium tomatoes
1 jalapeño pepper, seeded and finely minced
¼ cup finely chopped green bell pepper
¼ cup finely chopped sweet onion
3 tablespoons minced fresh cilantro
1 tablespoon balsamic vinegar
1 teaspoon fruit concentrate
¼ teaspoon sea salt

Cut the tomatoes into wedges, juice the wedges, and reserve 1 cup of the pulp.

In a blender or food processor, buzz the tomato pulp; it does not have to be blended until smooth. Transfer the pulp to a small bowl. Add the jalapeño pepper, bell pepper, onion, cilantro, vinegar, fruit concentrate, and salt; mix well. Either serve the salsa immediately or, preferably, let it sit for at least 2 hours in or out of the refrigerator. Store it in a covered container in the refrigerator.

Yield: *1½ cups*
Preparation time: *10 minutes*

Green and Red Pasta Sauce

Use this sauce to make a fresh and healthy meal in 20 minutes (and use up some broccoli stems at the same time!).

2–3 stalks broccoli, florets removed
1 package (10½ ounces) extra firm silken tofu
2 tablespoons white or yellow miso
2 small scallions, green part included
1 clove garlic
2 medium tomatoes, coarsely chopped
2 tablespoons finely chopped fresh basil
2 tablespoons finely chopped fresh parsley
2 tablespoons finely chopped chives

Juice the broccoli and reserve ½ cup of the juice.

In a blender or food processor, combine the broccoli juice, silken tofu, miso, scallions, and garlic; blend until smooth and creamy. If necessary, use a rubber spatula to scrape the sides of the blender or food processor to make sure that all of the ingredients are well blended. Transfer the mixture to a medium-size bowl and add the tomatoes, basil, parsley, and chives; mix well. If desired, pour the sauce into a saucepan and heat it gently; do not boil it. Serve the sauce over hot whole grain pasta. (If the pasta is hot, the sauce is wonderful at room temperature, especially in the summer.)

Variations:

Add steamed broccoli florets or other steamed vegetables to the sauce along with the tomatoes and herbs.

Yield: *4 cups*
Preparation time: *20 minutes*

Pineapple Chutney

An easy way to add an exotic touch to curries or grain dishes.

1 pineapple
½ cup raisins
2 tablespoons balsamic vinegar
1 tablespoon grated fresh ginger
1 tablespoon fruit concentrate
Pinch cayenne pepper

Peel and core the pineapple and cut it into strips. Juice the strips and reserve all of the pulp.

In a blender or food processor, combine the pineapple pulp, raisins, vinegar, ginger, fruit concentrate, and cayenne pepper; blend until the raisins are coarsely ground.

The chutney can be served immediately, but it will taste better if it's refrigerated first for 30 minutes. Leftover chutney can be stored in a covered container in the refrigerator for at least a week.

Yield: 1½ *cups*
Preparation time: *10 minutes*
Chilling time: *30 minutes*

Orange Sauce

With breakfast or dessert, this sauce makes any dish a treat.

3 medium oranges
2 tablespoons fruit concentrate
1½ tablespoons arrowroot

Peel the oranges and cut them into wedges. Juice the orange wedges and reserve 1½ cups of the juice.

In a small saucepan, combine the orange juice, fruit concentrate, and arrowroot. Bring the mixture to a boil, stirring constantly, then remove it from the heat. Serve the sauce over pancakes, cake, or sherbet. If serving it over sherbet, let it first cool to room temperature, about 1 hour, but do not chill it.

Yield: *1½ cups*
Preparation time: *10 minutes*
Cooling time: *1 hour*

Pear and Fresh Mint Sauce

Easy but so elegant!

2½ medium pears
½ cup fresh mint, lightly packed
1½ tablespoons arrowroot
1 tablespoon fruit concentrate

Cut the pears into wedges, juice the wedges, and reserve 1½ cups of the juice. Juice the mint and reserve all of the juice.

In a medium-size saucepan, combine the pear juice, mint juice, arrowroot, and fruit concentrate. Bring the mixture to a boil, stirring constantly, then remove it from the heat. Serve the sauce warm over plain, chocolate, or carob cake, or at room temperature over fresh fruit. Garnish the cake or fruit with a sprig of mint, if desired.

Yield: *1½ cups*
Preparation time: *15 minutes*

Strawberry Sauce

Not only for strawberry lovers.

1 pint strawberries
2 tablespoons fruit concentrate
1 tablespoon arrowroot

Juice the strawberries and reserve all of the juice.

In a small saucepan, combine the strawberry juice, fruit concentrate, and arrowroot; mix well. Bring the sauce to a boil, then remove it from the heat and allow it to cool to room temperature, about 1 hour.

Serve the sauce with strawberry sherbet. Spoon a pool of sauce onto a small plate and place a scoop of sherbet on top of the sauce. Garnish the sherbet with a fresh strawberry, if desired. The sauce can also be served with plain cake, crêpes, or pancakes.

Variation:

To make Strawberry Patch Fruit Salad, combine 1 pint strawberries, sliced, caps removed; 1 cup blueberries; and 2 kiwis, peeled and sliced. Add 1 recipe cooled Strawberry Sauce and mix gently. Serve the salad at room temperature, garnished with fresh mint.

Yield: *1 cup*
Preparation time: *15 minutes*
Cooling time: *1 hour*

Vegetable and Grain Side Dishes

No more ho-hum vegetable or grain dishes. With the addition of juice or pulp, vegetable and grain dishes become spectacular. One of Vicki's latest delectable discoveries is whole wheat couscous soaked in vegetable juice. It makes a beautiful, fluffy-textured bed for a stew or stir-fry—without cooking! See the recipes for Tomato Couscous on page 231 and Brightly Colored Couscous on page 232.

Surprise and delight your company or family with the Orange Potatoes on page 228, Pink Potatoes on page 229, or Green Potatoes With Herbs on page 230. And don't forget to try the Green Polenta on page 233; you've never tasted grits this delicious before! When you cook with juice and pulp, your vegetable and grain dishes will no longer be mere accompaniments to your entrées; they'll be multicolored stars in your meals.

Orange-Ginger Carrots

Cherie served Orange-Ginger Carrots to a dinner guest who hated cooked carrots. Now this man thinks they're spectacular!

1½ medium oranges
3 cups carrots, cut into 1½-inch pieces
2 tablespoons finely chopped fresh ginger root
1 tablespoon honey
¼ cup water

Peel the orange and cut it into wedges. Juice the orange wedges and reserve ¾ cup of the juice.

In a medium-size saucepan, combine the carrot pieces with the orange juice. Add the ginger root and honey, and stir. Add just as much water as necessary and stir again. Bring the mixture to a boil, then reduce the heat. Simmer until the carrots are tender but still crunchy, adding the remainder of the water as needed. Pour the carrots into a serving bowl and serve immediately.

Yield: *4 servings*
Preparation time: *10–15 minutes*

Broccoli in Cream Sauce

1 pound broccoli
1 tablespoon olive oil
½ Spanish onion, chopped
1 teaspoon basil
2 cloves garlic, minced
3–5 tablespoons water
1 package (10½ ounces) extra firm silken tofu
3 tablespoons white or yellow miso
Pinch cayenne pepper

Cut the florets off the broccoli stems, chop them, and set them aside for later use. Juice the stems and reserve all of the juice (approximately ½ cup).

In a large, heavy skillet, heat the oil over low heat. Add the onion, basil, and garlic, and sauté until the onion starts to become tender, about 5 minutes. Add the chopped broccoli florets and stir. Add about 3 tablespoons of the water and bring the mixture to a boil. Cover the skillet, reduce the heat, and simmer, stirring occasionally, until the broccoli is tender, about 8 minutes. If the vegetables stick to the skillet before becoming tender, add 1–2 more tablespoons of water.

Meanwhile, in a blender or food processor, combine the broccoli juice, silken tofu, miso, and cayenne pepper; blend until smooth and creamy. If necessary, use a rubber spatula to scrape the sides of the blender or food processor to make sure that all of the ingredients are blended.

When the broccoli is tender, pour the tofu sauce into the skillet over the broccoli; stir. If the mixture needs to be reheated, just stir it over medium-high heat until hot; do not boil. Serve the broccoli immediately, as a side dish or over rice, couscous, millet, or pasta.

Yield: 4–6 servings *Preparation time: 20 minutes*

Apple–Spice–Sweet Potato Bake

This is the nutritious answer to those holiday candied sweet potatoes. Once you taste these healthy but delicious sweet potatoes, you'll never want those gooey marshmallow sweet potatoes again.

3 medium apples
5 medium sweet potatoes, peeled and thinly sliced
2 teaspoons pumpkin pie spice
½ cup chopped pecans

Preheat the oven to 375°F.

Cut the apples into wedges and remove the seeds. Juice the apple wedges and reserve 1 cup of the juice.

In the bottom of an oiled 8-by-8-inch baking dish, arrange about one-quarter of the sweet potato slices in a layer. Pour ¼ cup of the apple juice over the sweet potatoes, and sprinkle ½ teaspoon of the pumpkin pie spice over the juice. Repeat the layers three more times.

Bake until the sweet potatoes are tender, about 35–40 minutes. Sprinkle the pecans over the potatoes, then return the potatoes to the oven for an additional 5–10 minutes. Serve the sweet potatoes immediately.

Yield: *6–8 servings*
Preparation time: *10 minutes*
Baking time: *40–50 minutes*

Creamy and Spicy Corn

You'll find a hint of Mexico in this creamy but dairy-free side dish.

½ medium potato
¾-inch slice sweet onion
3 cups sweet corn kernels fresh off the cob
½ cup soy milk
½ medium red bell pepper, diced
1 jalapeño pepper, minced
1 teaspoon cumin
¼ teaspoon sea salt

Cut the potato into chunks, juice the chunks, and reserve 3 tablespoons of the juice. Juice the onion and reserve 3 tablespoons of the juice.

In a large, heavy saucepan, combine the onion juice, corn, soy milk, bell pepper, jalapeño pepper, cumin, and salt. Bring the mixture to a boil, stirring constantly. Then cover the saucepan, reduce the heat, and simmer gently, stirring occasionally, until the corn is just tender, about 3–5 minutes.

Stir the potato juice and add it to the saucepan. Cook and stir the corn over medium heat until the sauce thickens, about 1–2 minutes.

Serve the corn with millet and beans, accompanied by sliced tomatoes.

Yield: 4 servings
Preparation time: 15–20 minutes

Oriental Broccoli

The broccoli in this dish simmers in its own juice.

1 pound broccoli
½ medium potato
1-inch slice onion
½- to 1-inch slice fresh ginger root
1½ tablespoons tamari
1 teaspoon toasted sesame oil

Cut the florets off the broccoli stems, cut them into smaller florets, and set them aside for later use. Juice the stems and reserve all of the juice (approximately ½ cup). Cut the potato into chunks, juice the chunks, and reserve ¼ cup of the juice. Juice the onion and reserve ¼ cup of the juice. Juice the ginger root and reserve 1 tablespoon of the juice.

In a large, heavy saucepan, combine the broccoli juice, onion juice, ginger juice, tamari, and toasted sesame oil. Add the broccoli florets, cover the saucepan, and bring the mixture to a boil. Reduce the heat and simmer until the broccoli is tender but still crisp, about 6 minutes.

Stir the potato juice and add it to the saucepan. Bring the mixture to a second boil, stirring gently.

Serve the broccoli warm over brown rice, millet, or quinoa. It is delicious as an accompaniment to a tofu, tempeh, or seitan dish.

Yield: *2 servings*
Preparation time: *15–20 minutes*

Winter Squash Casserole

This is a quick and simple side dish for a busy fall day.

5–7 medium carrots
1 medium or large butternut squash
½ cup cashews
1 teaspoon tarragon
½ teaspoon sea salt
3–4 cloves garlic, minced

Preheat the oven to 350°F.

Cut the greens off the carrots, juice the carrots, and reserve 1 cup of the juice.

Peel the squash, cut it in half, and remove the seeds. Cut the squash into ½-inch cubes and distribute the cubes in the bottom of an oiled 2-quart casserole.

In a blender or food processor, combine the carrot juice, cashews, tarragon, salt, and garlic; blend on high until the cashews are no longer gritty and the mixture is very smooth and creamy.

Pour the blended mixture over the squash in the baking dish. Bake, uncovered, until the squash is tender, about 45 minutes. Stir the sauce 2 or 3 times during baking. Test the squash for doneness by piercing it with a fork or knife.

Serve the squash as a side dish to a grain, bean, tofu, or tempeh dish.

Yield: 6 servings
Preparation time: 20 minutes
Baking time: 45 minutes

Savory Baked Rice

The fresh juice and herbs give the rice extra flavor, and baking makes it nice and fluffy.

2 medium green bell peppers
1½ large stalks celery
1-inch slice sweet onion
1½ cups long-grain brown rice or brown basmati rice
½ teaspoon thyme
½ teaspoon tarragon
3 bay leaves
¼ teaspoon sea salt
2 cups boiling water

Preheat the oven to 350°F.

Cut the bell peppers into quarters and remove the seeds. Juice the pepper quarters and reserve ½ cup of the juice. Juice the celery and reserve ¼ cup of the juice. Juice the onion and reserve ¼ cup of the juice.

In a medium-size bowl, combine the rice with water to cover. Using your hand, swish the rice around in the water, then drain the rice through a fine wire strainer. Place the rice in a lightly oiled 2-quart casserole.

Add the pepper juice, celery juice, onion juice, thyme, tarragon, and bay leaves to the rice in the baking dish; mix well. Add the salt to the boiling water, and pour the salted water over the rice mixture. Stir the rice mixture and cover the casserole.

Bake the rice, without stirring it again, until all the liquid is absorbed, about 1 hour. Remove the casserole from the oven and fluff the rice with a fork. Find and remove the bay leaves.

Serve the rice as a side dish or as a bed for a vegetable, tofu, tempeh, or bean dish.

Yield: 4–6 servings
Preparation time: 15 minutes
Baking time: 1 hour

Yellow Squash With Tomatoes

This easy-to-make dish is delicious.

2 large tomatoes
2 cloves garlic, pressed
4 medium yellow squash, sliced
1½ tablespoons white or yellow miso

Cut the tomatoes into wedges, juice the wedges, and reserve ½ cup of the juice and ¾ cup of the pulp.

In a medium-size, heavy saucepan, combine the tomato juice and garlic; mix well. Add the squash slices, cover the saucepan, and bring the juice to a boil. Reduce the heat and simmer, stirring occasionally, until the squash is tender, about 3–5 minutes.

In a blender or food processor, briefly blend the tomato pulp and miso. Add the blended mixture to the squash in the saucepan and stir. Heat gently and serve.

Yield: 4 servings
Preparation time: 20 minutes

Orange Potatoes

Vicki hardly ever peels the nutritious skin from potatoes. However, the following recipes are just for fun and would not have the same delightful appearance with the skin left on. Indulge; not only are these dishes not fattening, but they're full of vitamins and minerals!

2–3 medium carrots
2 pounds potatoes (approximately 6 small), peeled and cut into chunks
1 teaspoon paprika
1 teaspoon sea salt

Cut the greens off the carrots, juice the carrots, and reserve 1/3 cup of the juice.

In a medium-size saucepan, cover the potato chunks with water. Bring the water to a boil, then cover the saucepan, reduce the heat, and simmer until the potatoes are tender, about 20–25 minutes.

Drain the potatoes and mash them. Mash in as much of the carrot juice as necessary to achieve the desired consistency and to tint the potatoes a lovely pale orange color. Mash in the paprika and salt.

Serve the potatoes immediately. For a delicious meal, serve them with the Fat-Free Mushroom Sauce on page 207 and accompany them with the Spinach Loaf on page 246.

Yield: *6 servings*
Preparation time: *30–40 minutes*

Pink Potatoes

Children and the young at heart will love these fanciful pink potatoes, especially with green gravy!

1 small beet
2 pounds potatoes (approximately 6 small), peeled and cut into chunks
¼ cup soy milk
1 teaspoon tarragon
1 teaspoon sea salt

Cut the beet into chunks, juice the chunks, and reserve 3 tablespoons of the juice.

In a medium-size saucepan, cover the potato chunks with water. Bring the water to a boil, then cover the saucepan, reduce the heat, and simmer until the potatoes are tender, about 20–25 minutes.

Drain the potatoes and mash them. Mash in the beet juice and as much of the soy milk as necessary to achieve the desired consistency and to tint the potatoes the desired pink color. Mash in the tarragon and salt.

Serve the potatoes immediately. For a delicious combination, serve them with the Green Sauce on page 204.

Yield: *6 servings*
Preparation time: *30–40 minutes*

Green Potatoes With Herbs

One way to get children to eat spinach.

2 bunches (½ pound) spinach
2 pounds potatoes (approximately 6 small), peeled and cut into chunks
2 tablespoons minced fresh chives
2 tablespoons minced parsley
2 tablespoons minced fresh dill
1 teaspoon sea salt

Juice the spinach and reserve ⅓ cup of the juice.

In a medium-size saucepan, cover the potato chunks with water. Bring the water to a boil, then cover the saucepan, reduce the heat, and simmer until the potatoes are tender, about 20–25 minutes.

Drain the potatoes and mash them. Mash in as much of the spinach juice as necessary to achieve the desired consistency and to tint the potatoes a vibrant green color. Mash in the chives, parsley, dill, and salt.

Serve the potatoes immediately. For an especially delicious dish, serve them with the Vegetable Cream Sauce on page 207.

Note:

For a child's party, make orange, pink, and green potatoes and swirl them together in one large serving bowl!

Yield: 6 servings
Preparation time: 30–40 minutes

Tomato Couscous

Tasty and so easy.

4 large tomatoes
1 cup whole wheat couscous
10–12 sun-dried tomato halves, cut into pieces
2 tablespoons finely chopped fresh basil
½ teaspoon sea salt
1 clove garlic, pressed
½ cup water

Cut the tomatoes into wedges, juice the wedges, and reserve 2 cups of the juice.

In a medium-size bowl, combine the couscous, sun-dried tomatoes, basil, salt, and garlic; mix well. Add the tomato juice and water, and mix again. Let the mixture sit undisturbed until the liquid has been absorbed, about 45–60 minutes. Fluff the couscous with a fork and serve it as a side dish to a vegetable, bean, or tofu dish.

Variation:

Add ½ cup pitted and chopped black olives along with the tomato pieces.

Yield: 4 servings
Preparation time: 15 minutes
Soaking time: 45–60 minutes

Brightly Colored Couscous

Two colors of couscous, bright orange and bright green, make a stunning contrast when served together. The flavors are mild and subtle. But you don't need to make both colors—a single or double portion of one color is fine, too.

Orange Couscous
5–7 medium carrots
1 cup whole wheat couscous
½ cup water
Pinch salt

Green Couscous
4 bunches (1 pound) spinach
1 cup whole wheat couscous
½ cup water
Pinch salt

Cut the greens off the carrots, juice the carrots, and reserve 1 cup of the juice. Juice the spinach and reserve 1 cup of the juice. Be careful to keep the juices separated.

Place each 1-cup portion of couscous in a separate medium-size bowl. Add the carrot juice, water, and salt to one bowl and the spinach juice, water, and salt to the other bowl. Mix the ingredients in each bowl well and let them sit undisturbed until the liquid has been absorbed, about 45–60 minutes. Fluff the couscous in each bowl with a fork.

Serve the couscous as a bed for a vegetable, tofu, tempeh, or bean dish, or for the Moroccan Stew on page 263. You can also use the two colors to make a creative tabouli-type salad.

Note:

Vicki serves this couscous at room temperature. However, if you prefer it warm, you can heat this couscous by steaming it briefly. To steam, place the prepared couscous in a wire strainer, and put the strainer inside a large kettle containing about 1 inch of water. Don't let the strainer touch the water. Cover the kettle, bring the water to a boil, and let the couscous sit above the boiling water until warm, about 2–3 minutes. Remove the strainer from the kettle and fluff the couscous with a fork.

Yield: *6 servings*
Preparation time: *15 minutes*
Soaking time: *45–60 minutes*

Green Polenta

1 bunch (¼ pound) spinach
3 stalks celery
2 cups water
1 cup cornmeal
½ teaspoon sea salt

Juice the spinach and pour all of the juice into a 1-cup measure. Juice the celery and add enough of the juice to the spinach juice to make 1 cup. If you don't have enough combined juice, add more celery.

In a medium-size, heavy saucepan, combine the spinach-celery juice, water, cornmeal, and salt. Bring the mixture to a boil, stirring constantly. Then cover the saucepan, reduce the heat, and simmer, stirring occasionally, until the mixture is very thick, about 20 minutes. Serve the polenta with Dominique's Tomato Sauce on page 210 or as a bed for a vegetable or bean stew.

Yield: *4 servings*
Preparation time: *30 minutes*

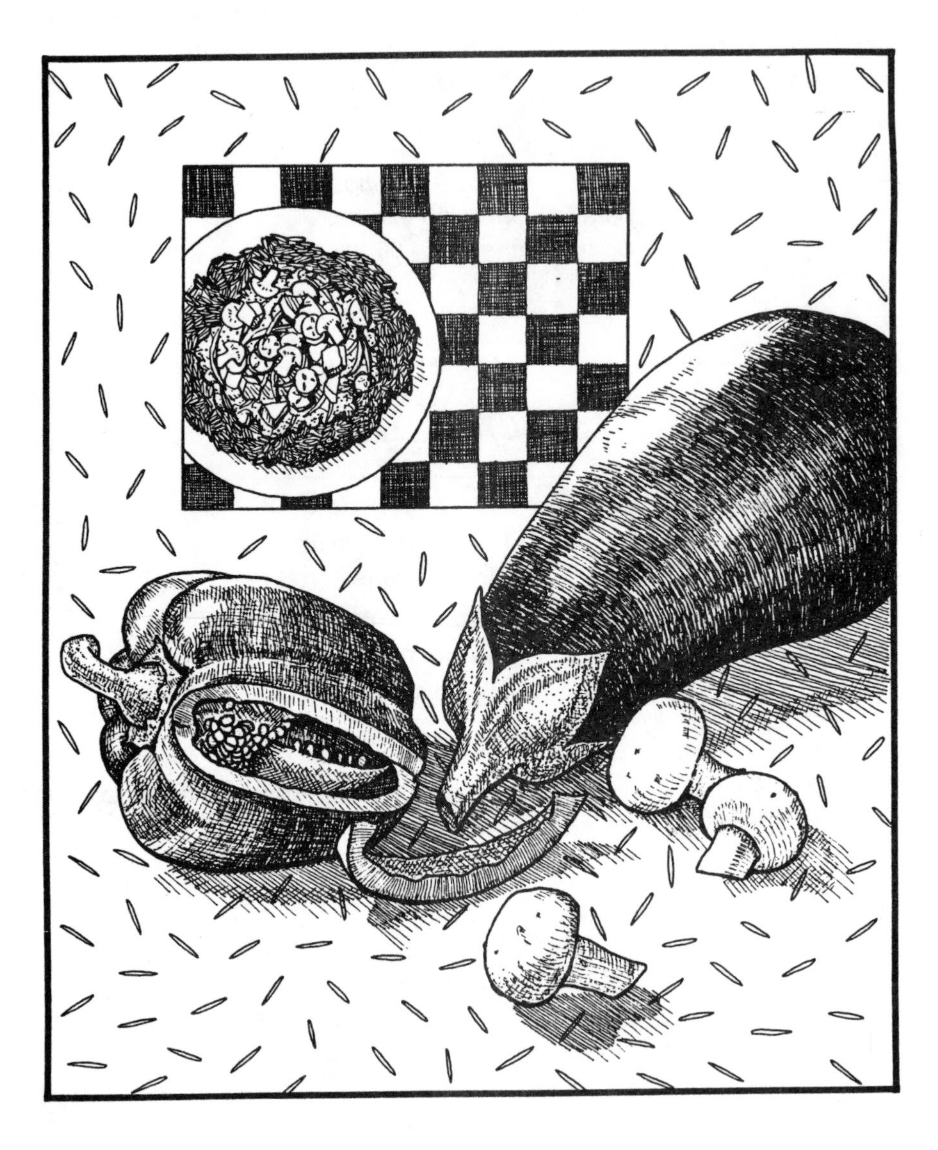

Main Dishes

Juice and pulp can enhance vegetarian main dishes. Once you discover how well carrot pulp works in veggie burgers and meatless loaves, you'll find yourself making carrot juice as much for the pulp as for the juice. This section of *Cooking for Life* offers you many easy new recipes incorporating juice and pulp to markedly improve your old favorite dinner loaves, croquettes, and burgers.

For a quick meal, try one of our pasta dishes. In less than thirty minutes, you can have a dinner that is visually appealing, delicious, and very healthy, too. If you have a little more time, try a hearty stew slowly simmered in vegetable juice. You will agree that the flavor is beyond compare. Or how about a creamy yet egg-free quiche in a whole wheat crust?

Fresh juice and pulp will add a new dimension both tastewise and healthwise to your main dishes just as they do to your side dishes and other recipes. But please don't take our word for it. Try these richly satisfying recipes yourself. You'll be glad you did!

Spaghetti With Tomato Sauce

You'll enjoy this variation of a classic dish.

2 large tomatoes
2 tablespoons olive oil
2 large yellow onions, chopped
1 cup chopped green bell pepper
2 large cloves garlic, minced
8 cups chopped tomatoes
4 teaspoons oregano
2 teaspoons basil
2 teaspoons honey or brown rice syrup
1 teaspoon sea salt
1 box (1 pound) whole wheat spaghetti

In a Dutch oven, put up water to boil the pasta.

Cut the tomatoes into wedges, juice the wedges, and reserve 1 cup of the juice.

In a medium-size, heavy soup kettle, heat the oil over low heat. Add the onions, green pepper, and garlic, and sauté until the onion is translucent, about 5 minutes. Add the tomato juice, chopped tomatoes, oregano, basil, honey or brown rice syrup, and salt, and stir. Cover the kettle, reduce the heat, and simmer for 20 minutes.

Remove the kettle from the heat and pour the mixture into a blender or food processor. Purée the mixture, then return it to the kettle and adjust the seasonings. Bring the mixture to a boil. Reduce the heat and simmer, uncovered, until the sauce is thickened, about 10 minutes.

Meanwhile, add the pasta to the boiling water in the Dutch oven and cook it according to the directions on the package; drain well.

Divide the pasta between 4 individual serving plates and top each portion with 1/4 of the sauce. If necessary, first reheat the sauce over medium-high heat, stirring constantly; do not boil. Serve the spaghetti and sauce with Vegetarian Meatballs (see below).

Variation:

Substitute spaghetti squash for the whole wheat spaghetti.

Yield: 4 servings *Preparation time: 40 minutes*

Vegetarian Meatballs

These "meatballs" are delicious as well as nutritious!

6–8 carrots
1 tablespoon olive oil
1 cup chopped onion
1 cup finely chopped zucchini
1½ cups water
1 vegetable bouillon cube
1 tablespoon tamari
2 teaspoons curry powder
1½ cups TVP (textured vegetable protein)
1½ cups sunflower seeds, finely ground
3 green onions, finely chopped
½ teaspoon sea salt
Olive oil

Cut the greens off the carrots, juice the carrots, and reserve 2 cups of the pulp.

In a large skillet, heat the 1 tablespoon oil over low heat. Add the chopped onion and zucchini, and sauté until the onion is translucent, about 5 minutes.

In a small saucepan over high heat, boil the water. Remove the saucepan from the heat and add the bouillon cube, tamari, and curry powder. When the bouillon cube has dissolved, stir the hot broth.

In a large bowl, combine the hot broth and TVP. Let the mixture sit until the TVP is hydrated, about 10 minutes. Add the carrot pulp and ground sunflower seeds, and mix with a spoon or your hands. Add the sautéed vegetables and green onion, and mix again. Mix in the salt.

Pinch off a small piece of the meatball mixture and form it into a ball about 1 inch in diameter. Repeat until all of the mixture is used.

In a large skillet, pour in just enough of the remaining oil to coat the bottom. Add the meatballs and cook them over low heat, turning them to keep them from sticking, until they're golden brown on all sides, about 10–15 minutes. Remove them from the skillet with a slotted spoon and serve them, if desired, with the Spaghetti With Tomato Sauce on page 236.

Variations:

To make Vegetarian Burgers, shape the meatball mixture into patties and cook the patties until they're golden brown on both sides. Serve the patties on whole wheat hamburger buns with all the trimmings.

Add ¼ cup finely chopped waterchestnuts, green pepper, or celery, sautéeing it with the onion and zucchini.

Note:

If you're in a real hurry, add 1 cup carrot pulp to a meatless burger mix such as Nature's Burger by Fantastic Foods. Follow the directions and enjoy!

Yield: 12–15 small meatballs
Preparation time: 20–30 minutes
Cooking time: 10–15 minutes

Curried Tempeh Croquettes

Try these with Pineapple Chutney.

3–4 medium carrots
½ lemon
1 package (8 ounces) tempeh, unfrozen
½ cup finely chopped onion
⅓ cup tahini
2 tablespoons tamari
½ teaspoon curry powder
¼ teaspoon turmeric
¼ teaspoon dry mustard powder
Oil

Cut the greens off the carrots. Cut the lemon into wedges. Juice the carrots and reserve 1 cup of the pulp. Juice the lemon wedges and reserve 2 tablespoons of the juice.

Cut the tempeh into small (½–1 inch) cubes. Place the tempeh cubes in a vegetable steamer, and put the steamer in a saucepan containing about 1 inch of boiling water. Cover the saucepan, leave the heat on medium-high, and steam the tempeh cubes for about 10 minutes.

In a large bowl, combine the steamed tempeh cubes with the carrot pulp, lemon juice, onion, tahini, tamari, curry powder, turmeric, and dry mustard powder; mix well with a fork, mashing the tempeh cubes. Shape the mixture into approximately 12 small patties.

In a large skillet, pour in just enough of the oil to coat the bottom. Add as many patties as will easily fit into the skillet and cook them over low heat until they're golden brown on the bottom, about 5 minutes. Turn them over and cook them until the other side is golden brown, about 5 minutes. Remove the patties from the skillet and repeat the procedure until all the patties are cooked.

Serve the croquettes with the Pineapple Chutney on page 216. Accompany them with brown basmati rice and a salad or steamed vegetable.

Yield: *12 croquettes*
Preparation time: *20 minutes*
Cooking time: *20 minutes*

Whole Wheat Pie Crust

This is Vicki's basic, all-purpose, never-fail pie crust.

1 cup whole wheat pastry flour
¼ cup oil
3 tablespoons hot water

Put the flour in a medium-size bowl. Put the oil and water in a small bowl but do not mix them. Slowly pour the oil and water over the flour in the medium-size bowl, mixing them with a fork while you pour. Mix the ingredients just enough to form a dough that will hold together; do not overmix.

Place the dough between two sheets of wax paper and roll it out. (To keep the wax paper from slipping on the table or countertop, lightly sprinkle the table or counter with water before laying the paper on it.) Peel off the top piece of paper, then carefully pick up the bottom piece with the dough, turn the dough paper side up into a pie pan, and peel off the remaining paper. Flute the edges of the pie crust and add the desired filling. Bake the filled crust according to the directions in the filling recipe.

Yield: *One 9-inch pie crust*
Preparation time: *15 minutes*
Baking time: *See filling recipe*
Cooling time: *See filling recipe*

Lentil Burgers

Veggie burgers with a meaty flavor and texture.

2 medium tomatoes
2–3 medium carrots
1 cup cooked lentils, well drained
½ cup TVP (textured vegetable protein)
⅓ cup finely chopped onion
2 tablespoons peanut butter
2 tablespoons tamari
½ teaspoon sage
¼ teaspoon celery seeds
1 clove garlic, pressed
Oil

Cut the tomatoes into wedges. Cut the greens off the carrots. Juice the tomato wedges and reserve ⅓ cup of the pulp. Juice the carrots and reserve ⅔ cup of the pulp.

In a large bowl, mash the lentils with a fork. (The lentils do not have to be puréed, just coarsely mashed.) Add the tomato pulp, carrot pulp, TVP, onions, peanut butter, tamari, sage, celery seeds, and garlic; mix well, using your hands if necessary, and let the mixture sit undisturbed until the TVP is hydrated, about 5–10 minutes. Shape the mixture into 8 small patties.

In a large skillet, pour in just enough of the oil to coat the bottom. Add as many patties as will easily fit into the skillet and cook them over low heat until they're golden brown on the bottom, about 5 minutes. Turn them over and cook them until the other side is golden brown, about 5 minutes. Remove the patties from the skillet and repeat the procedure until all the patties are cooked.

Serve the burgers with Dominique's Tomato Sauce on page 210 or on whole grain buns with all the trimmings.

Variation:

To make a Lentil Loaf, pack the mixture into an oiled 8½-by-4½-by-2½-inch loaf pan and bake it at 350°F for 1 hour. Serve the loaf with tomato sauce, a steamed vegetable, and a salad.

Yield: *8 small patties*
Preparation time: *15–20 minutes*
Cooking time: *20 minutes*

Carrot-Potato Patties

Carrots and potatoes combine to make a different but wonderful Salisbury steak substitute.

1 pound potatoes (approximately 3 small)
3–4 medium carrots
1 cup pecans, finely ground
1 cup whole grain bread crumbs
⅔ cup finely chopped celery
½ cup rolled oats
¼ cup finely chopped onion
2 tablespoons peanut butter
2 tablespoons tamari
1 teaspoon thyme
1 teaspoon basil
2 cloves garlic, pressed
Oil

Cut the potatoes into chunks. Cut the greens off the carrots. Juice the potato chunks and reserve all of the pulp. Juice the carrots and reserve ¼ cup of the juice and 1 cup of the pulp.

In a large bowl, mix together the potato pulp, carrot juice, and carrot pulp. Add the pecans and mix. Add the bread crumbs, celery, rolled oats, onion, peanut butter, tamari, thyme, basil, and garlic; mix well, using your hands if necessary. Shape the mixture into 8–9 patties.

In a large skillet, pour in just enough of the oil to coat the bottom. Add as many patties as will easily fit into the skillet and cook them over low heat until they're golden brown on the bottom, about 5 minutes. Turn them over and cook them until the other side is golden brown, about 5 minutes. Remove the patties from the skillet and repeat the procedure until all the patties are cooked.

Serve the patties with the Potato Sauce on page 203.

Yield: *8–9 small patties*
Preparation time: *15 minutes*
Cooking time: *20 minutes*

Fettucini Rosé

A visual delight that's both quick to prepare and delicious to eat.

3–4 medium carrots
1 tablespoon olive oil
½ large Spanish onion, cut into strips
1 large red bell pepper, cut into strips
1 teaspoon basil
½ teaspoon oregano
1 package (10½ ounces) extra firm silken tofu
2 tablespoons yellow miso
Pinch cayenne pepper
1 box (10 ounces) whole grain fettucini

In a Dutch oven, put up water to boil the pasta.

Meanwhile, cut the greens off the carrots, juice the carrots, and reserve ½ cup of the juice.

In a large skillet, heat the olive oil over low heat. Add the onion and sauté until it starts to get tender, about 5 minutes. Add the red bell pepper, basil, and oregano, and continue to sauté until both the pepper and onion are tender, about 5 minutes more.

In a blender or food processor, combine the carrot juice, silken tofu, miso, and cayenne pepper; blend until very smooth and creamy. Add the tofu mixture to the sautéed vegetables in the skillet and mix thoroughly.

Add the pasta to the boiling water in the Dutch oven and cook it according to the directions on the package; drain well. Divide the pasta between 3 individual serving plates and top each portion with ⅓ of the sauce. If necessary, first reheat the sauce over medium-high heat, stirring constantly; do not boil. Serve the pasta immediately.

Yield: *3 servings*
Preparation time: *25 minutes*

Springtime Pasta

After a winter of heavier foods, this dish is a real treat.

8–11 medium carrots
½ cup raw cashews
2 tablespoons white or yellow miso
1 pound fresh asparagus
1 box (10 ounces) whole grain fettucini
½ cup frozen peas
2 scallions, chopped
¼ cup marinated sun-dried tomato halves, thinly sliced
3 tablespoons finely chopped fresh basil
2 cloves garlic, pressed

In a Dutch oven, put up water to boil the pasta.

Meanwhile, cut the greens off the carrots, juice the carrots, and reserve 1½ cups of the juice.

In a blender or food processor, combine the carrot juice, cashews, and miso; blend on high until the cashews are no longer gritty and the mixture is very smooth and creamy.

Snap off the tough bottom end from each stalk of asparagus. Cut the tender upper parts into 1-inch pieces.

In a medium-size saucepan or skillet, combine the cashew mixture and asparagus pieces. Bring the sauce to a boil, then cover the pan, reduce the heat, and simmer, stirring occasionally, for 2–3 minutes.

While the sauce is cooking, add the pasta to the boiling water in the Dutch oven and cook it according to the directions on the package.

Add the peas to the sauce and simmer until the asparagus is just tender, about 2 minutes more. Add the scallions, sun-dried tomatoes, basil, and garlic, and mix well. Remove the sauce from the heat.

Drain the pasta and divide it between 4 individual serving plates. Top each portion with ¼ of the sauce and serve it immediately.

Yield: *4 servings*
Preparation time: *20 minutes*

Spinach Loaf

The mild flavor and light texture of this loaf will remind you of a soufflé.

2 bunches (½ pound) spinach
1 pound firm tofu
½ cup finely chopped onion
2 tablespoons white miso
1 teaspoon basil
½ teaspoon thyme
½ teaspoon sea salt
1 cup cashews, finely ground
1 cup whole grain bread crumbs
1 cup rolled oats

Preheat the oven to 350°F.

Juice the spinach and reserve all of the juice and all of the pulp.

In a large bowl, mash the tofu with a fork. Add the spinach juice, spinach pulp, onion, miso, basil, thyme, and salt; mix well. Add the cashews, bread crumbs, and rolled oats, and mix again, using your hands if necessary.

Pack the mixture into an 8½-by-4½-by-2½-inch loaf pan and bake it for 1 hour. Let it sit for at least 15 minutes before removing it from the pan. Unmold it onto a serving platter and slice it thickly.

Serve the loaf with the Fat-Free Mushroom Sauce on page 207. Accompany it with the Orange Potatoes on page 228.

Yield: *1 large loaf*
Preparation time: *30 minutes*
Baking time: *1 hour*
Cooling time: *15 minutes*

Butternut Squash Loaf

Try this hearty, nutty loaf with Fat-Free Mushroom Sauce.

¼ medium butternut squash
1 pound firm tofu
1 cup pecans, ground
1 cup rolled oats
1 teaspoon sea salt
½ cup whole grain bread crumbs
2 teaspoons olive oil
1 clove garlic, pressed

Preheat the oven to 350°F.

Cut the squash into strips and remove the seeds. Juice the squash strips and reserve ½ cup of the juice and 1 cup of the pulp.

In a large bowl, mash the tofu. Add the pecans and mix well. Add the squash juice, squash pulp, oats, and salt; mix well, using your hands if necessary. Set the bowl aside.

In a small bowl, combine the bread crumbs, oil, and garlic; mix well. Set the bowl aside.

Oil the bottom and sides of an 8½-by-4½-by-2½-inch loaf pan. Sprinkle about 2 tablespoons of the bread-crumb mixture over the sides and bottom of the pan, then pack the squash mixture into the pan. Sprinkle the loaf with the remaining crumb mixture, lightly pressing the crumbs into the top of the loaf.

Bake the loaf until the bread crumbs are brown and the loaf is firm, about 50 minutes. Let the loaf sit for 10–15 minutes before removing it from the pan, then unmold it onto a serving platter and cut it into thick slices. Serve it with a sauce, such as the Fat-Free Mushroom Sauce on page 207. To reheat leftover loaf, brown the slices in a little oil. Leftover loaf is also delicious cold in sandwiches.

Yield:	*1 large loaf*
Preparation time:	*20 minutes*
Cooking time:	*50 minutes*
Cooling time:	*10–15 minutes*

Pasta With Peas and Mushrooms in Cream Sauce

Quick, elegant, and delicious.

6 large stalks celery
½ cup cashews
½ teaspoon sea salt
2½ cups sliced mushrooms
1 teaspoon tarragon
1 cup frozen peas
Pinch cayenne pepper
1 box (10 ounces) whole grain fettucini
2 scallions, finely chopped
2 tablespoons finely minced fresh parsley

In a Dutch oven, put up water to boil the pasta.

Meanwhile, juice the celery and reserve 1 cup of the juice.

In a blender or food processor, combine the celery juice, cashews, and salt; blend on high until the cashews are no longer gritty and the mixture is very smooth and creamy.

In a large skillet or saucepan, combine the cashew mixture, mushrooms, and tarragon. Bring the mixture to a boil, stirring constantly. Then cover the saucepan, reduce the heat, and simmer, stirring occasionally, until the mushrooms are just tender and the sauce starts to thicken, about 3–4 minutes. Add the peas and simmer 1–2 minutes more. Add the cayenne and mix well. Remove the mixture from the heat.

Add the pasta to the boiling water in the Dutch oven and cook it according to the directions on the package; drain well. Divide the pasta between 3 individual serving plates and top each portion with ⅓ of the sauce. Sprinkle the scallions and parsley over the sauce, and serve the pasta immediately.

Yield: *3 servings*
Preparation time: *20 minutes*

Marinated Baked Tempeh With Vegetables

Tempeh adds its own special goodness to this wonderful dish.

4–6 medium carrots
1 bunch (¼ pound) spinach
2 cloves garlic
½-inch slice ginger root
1–2 large stalks celery
½ medium potato
1 package (8 ounces) tempeh, unfrozen
3 tablespoons tamari
1 tablespoon olive oil
1 cup chopped onions
1 medium yellow squash, sliced
1 medium zucchini, sliced
2 cups sliced mushrooms

Preheat the oven to 350°F.

Cut the greens off the carrots, juice the carrots, and pour ¾ cup of the juice into a large measuring cup. Juice the spinach, garlic, and ginger root, and add all of the combined juice to the carrot juice in the measuring cup. Juice the celery and add enough of the juice to the combined juice in the measuring cup to measure 1½ cups.

Cut the potato into chunks, juice the chunks, and reserve ¼ cup of the juice. Be careful to keep the potato juice separated from the combined juice.

Cut the tempeh into 1-inch cubes. In a shallow baking dish, arrange the cubes in a single layer.

Add the tamari to the combined juice in the measuring cup and stir. Pour the juice mixture over the tempeh in the baking dish and let the tempeh marinate for 1 hour.

Using a slotted spoon, remove the tempeh cubes from the marinade and spread them out on a well-oiled cookie sheet. Set aside the marinade for later use. Bake the tempeh for 30 minutes, turning the cubes once.

About 20 minutes before the tempeh should be finished baking, heat the oil in a large, heavy kettle over low heat. Add the onions and sauté until they start to become translucent, about 5 minutes. Add the squash, zucchini, and mushrooms, and stir. Add the marinade and stir again. Cover the kettle and bring the mixture to a boil, then reduce the heat and simmer, stirring occasionally, until the vegetables are almost tender, about 5 minutes.

Stir the potato juice and add it to the kettle. Stir the vegetable mixture and return it to a boil. Remove the tempeh from the oven and add it to the mixture; stir. Reduce the heat and simmer until the vegetables are tender and the sauce has thickened, about 2–3 minutes.

Serve the stew over brown rice, millet, or pasta.

Yield: *4 servings*
Preparation time: *20 minutes*
Marinating time: *1 hour*
Baking time: *30 minutes*

Onion Pie

You won't believe how easy and delicious this onion pie is!

1 recipe Whole Wheat Pie Crust (page 240)
1 medium potato
2 tablespoons olive oil
6 cups chopped Spanish onions
1 teaspoon thyme
½ teaspoon sage
2 tablespoons tamari

Make one 9-inch Whole Wheat Pie Crust but do not bake it. Set the unbaked pie crust aside.

Preheat the oven to 350°F.

Cut the potato into chunks, juice the chunks, and reserve ⅓ cup of the juice.

In a large skillet or heavy kettle, heat the oil over low heat. Add the onions, thyme, and sage, and sauté until the onions are translucent, about 15 minutes.

Stir the potato juice to mix the starch back in, then add the potato juice along with the tamari to the sautéed onions in the skillet. Cook over medium heat, stirring constantly, until the mixture is thickened, about 3 minutes.

Pour the onion mixture into the unbaked pie crust, spreading it out evenly. Bake until the crust is done and the filling is firm, about 50 minutes. Cut the pie into 6 slices and serve.

Yield: *One 9-inch pie*
Preparation time: *25 minutes*
Baking time: *50 minutes*

Vegetable Quiche

You'll never miss the eggs in this creamy, richly flavored quiche.

1 recipe Whole Wheat Pie Crust (page 240)
3–4 medium carrots
3 cups broccoli florets, cut into small pieces
1 pound firm tofu
⅓ cup dry onion flakes
¼ cup marinated sun-dried tomato halves, thinly sliced
1 tablespoon Dijon-style mustard
1 teaspoon basil
1 teaspoon sea salt
¾ cup shredded soy cheese
3–4 marinated sun-dried tomato halves, as garnish

Make one 9-inch Whole Wheat Pie Crust but do not bake it. Set the unbaked pie crust aside.

Cut the greens off the carrots, juice the carrots, and reserve ½ cup of the juice and ½ cup of the pulp.

Place the broccoli florets in a vegetable steamer and put the steamer in a saucepan containing about 1 inch of boiling water. Cover the saucepan, leave the heat on medium-high, and steam until the broccoli is just barely tender, about 5 minutes. Set the steamed broccoli aside.

In a blender or food processor, blend the carrot juice and tofu until smooth and creamy. Pour the mixture into a large bowl and add the carrot pulp, steamed broccoli, onion flakes, sun-dried tomato slices, mustard, basil, and salt; mix well.

Pour the vegetable mixture into the unbaked pie crust, spreading it out evenly. Sprinkle the shredded soy cheese over the vegetable mixture and decorate the top using the sun-dried tomato halves. Bake until the crust is golden brown and the filling is firm, about 35–40 minutes. Let the quiche sit for 10 minutes, then cut it into 6–8 slices and serve it.

Yield:	*One 9-inch pie*
Preparation time:	*40 minutes*
Baking time:	*40 minutes*
Cooling time:	*10 minutes*

Cashew Croquettes

The cashews add a fantastic taste and texture.

5–6 medium carrots
1 cup raw cashews
½ package (5¼ ounces) extra firm silken tofu
2 tablespoons yellow miso
1 clove garlic
⅓ cup finely chopped onion
1 teaspoon basil
Oil

Cut the greens off the carrots, juice the carrots, and reserve 1½ cups of the pulp.

In a blender or food processor, coarsely grind the cashews. Transfer the ground cashews to a large bowl.

In the blender or food processor, combine the silken tofu, miso, and garlic; blend until smooth and creamy. Add the tofu mixture to the ground cashews in the bowl.

Add the chopped onion and basil to the cashew-tofu mixture and mix well, using your hands if necessary. Shape the mixture into 8 small patties.

In a large skillet, pour in just enough of the oil to coat the bottom. Add as many patties as will easily fit into the skillet and cook them over low heat until they're golden brown on the bottom, about 5 minutes. Turn them over and cook them until the other side is golden brown, about 5 minutes. Remove the patties from the skillet and repeat the procedure until all the patties are cooked.

Serve the croquettes plain, with Dominique's Tomato Sauce on page 210, or with your favorite relish.

Yield: *8 croquettes*
Preparation time: *15 minutes*
Cooking time: *20 minutes*

Spinach-Asparagus Quiche

Romeo and Juliet, Antony and Cleopatra . . .
spinach and asparagus!

1 recipe Whole Wheat Pie Crust (page 240)
1 pound asparagus
1 bunch (¼ pound) spinach
1 pound firm tofu
2 tablespoons white miso
1 tablespoon Dijon-style mustard
1 teaspoon thyme
½ teaspoon sea salt
1 tablespoon olive oil
1 cup chopped onion

Make one 9-inch Whole Wheat Pie Crust but do not bake it. Set the unbaked pie crust aside.

Snap off the tough bottom end from each stalk of asparagus and set the more tender upper stalks aside for later use. Juice the bottom ends and reserve all of the juice. Juice the spinach and reserve all of the juice and all of the pulp.

In a blender or food processor, combine the asparagus juice, spinach juice, tofu, miso, mustard, thyme, and salt; blend until smooth and creamy. If necessary, use a rubber spatula to scrape the sides of the blender or food processor to make sure that all of the ingredients are combined. Transfer the mixture to a large bowl.

Setting aside 3–4 stalks for decoration, chop the reserved asparagus into ½-inch pieces and add them to the tofu mixture in the bowl; stir. Add the spinach pulp and stir again.

In a small skillet, heat the oil over low heat. Add the onions and sauté until tender, about 5 minutes. Add the sautéed onions to the tofu mixture and mix well.

Pour the tofu mixture into the unbaked pie crust, spreading it out evenly. Cut in half lengthwise the 3–4 reserved asparagus stalks and position them decoratively on top of the tofu mixture. Bake the quiche until the crust is golden brown and the filling is firm, about 60–70 minutes. Let the quiche sit for about 15 minutes, then cut it into 6 slices and serve it.

Yield:	*One 9-inch quiche*
Preparation time:	*30 minutes*
Baking time:	*60–70 minutes*
Cooling time:	*15 minutes*

Black Bean Stew

A nutritious, low-fat, flavorful dish.
This stew is delicious served over rice or with cornbread.

4 tomatoes
4 large carrots
3 stalks celery
4 cups chopped cabbage
2 cups chopped onions
2 cups sliced carrots
1 red bell pepper, cut into 1-inch strips
1 teaspoon cumin
1 teaspoon chili powder
1 teaspoon basil
1 teaspoon sea salt
½ teaspoon oregano
2 cups cooked and drained black beans

Cut the tomatoes into wedges. Cut the greens off the carrots. Juice the tomato wedges with the carrots and reserve all of the combined juice. Juice the celery and add enough of the juice to the tomato-carrot juice to make 3 cups.

In a large, heavy kettle, mix together the combined juice, cabbage, onion, carrots, red bell pepper, cumin, chili powder, basil, salt, and oregano. Cover the kettle and bring the mixture to a boil, then reduce the heat and simmer, stirring occasionally, until the vegetables are almost tender, about 40 minutes. Add the beans to the kettle and continue simmering until all the vegetables are tender, about 5 more minutes. Serve the stew over rice or with one of the cornbreads from the Breads, Muffins, and Chapati section of this cookbook.

Yield: *4 servings*
Preparation time: *20 minutes*
Cooking time: *45 minutes*

Marinated Baked Tofu With Vegetables

Suitable for company.

2 large tomatoes
5–7 medium carrots
¼-inch slice ginger root
1 pound firm tofu
3 tablespoons tamari
2 cloves garlic, pressed
2 tablespoons olive oil
4 cups chopped cabbage
2 cups chopped onions
2 cups sliced carrots
3 stalks celery, chopped
3 bay leaves

Cut the tomatoes into wedges. Cut the greens off the carrots. Juice the tomato wedges and reserve 1 cup of the juice. Juice the carrots and reserve 1 cup of the juice. Juice the ginger root and reserve all of the juice.

Cut the tofu into ¼-inch slices. Arrange the tofu slices in a single layer in a shallow baking dish.

In a small bowl, combine the tomato, carrot, and ginger root juices. Add the tamari and garlic, and mix well. Pour the marinade over the tofu slices in the baking dish and allow the tofu to sit undisturbed for 1 hour.

Meanwhile, in a large, heavy kettle, heat the oil over low heat. Add the cabbage, onions, carrots, celery, and bay leaves; sauté until the onions are translucent, about 10 minutes. Drain the marinade from the baking dish and add it to the kettle. Cover the kettle and bring the mixture to a boil. Reduce the heat and simmer, stirring occasionally, until the vegetables are tender, about 45 minutes.

Meanwhile, preheat the oven to 375°F.

While the vegetables are simmering, arrange the tofu slices on an oiled cookie sheet. Bake them for 30–45 minutes, turning them once. The longer the tofu bakes, the crispier it becomes, so bake the tofu until the desired crispness is reached.

Add the baked tofu to the stew and simmer for an additional 3–4 minutes. Take the stew off the heat and remove the bay leaves.

Serve the stew over a bed of rice, polenta, millet, couscous, or pasta.

Yield: 4 servings *Marinating time: 1 hour*
Preparation time: 20 minutes *Baking time: 30–45 minutes*

Savory Baked Tofu With Onions

A satisfying main dish that is enjoyed even by people who say they don't like tofu.

6 large stalks celery
½ sweet onion
1-inch slice ginger root
2 pounds firm tofu
¼ cup plus 1 tablespoon tamari
1 teaspoon toasted sesame oil
2–3 cloves garlic, pressed
2 tablespoons oil
2 cups sliced sweet onions
¼ cup whole wheat pastry flour
Water

Juice the celery and reserve 1 cup of the juice. Juice the onion and reserve ½ cup of the juice. Juice the ginger root and reserve all of the juice.

Cut the tofu into ½-inch-thick slices. Place the slices in a shallow baking dish or other container.

In a small bowl, combine the celery juice, onion juice, ginger juice, tamari, toasted sesame oil, and garlic; mix well. Pour the mixture over the tofu in the baking dish or container. Let the tofu marinate for at least 1 hour; the longer it marinates, the more flavor it will have. If you let the tofu marinate for more than 1–2 hours, place it in the refrigerator.

Preheat the oven to 375°F.

Remove the tofu from the baking dish and set aside the marinade for later use. Arrange the tofu on a well-oiled cookie sheet and bake it until it's a crispy golden brown, about 35–40 minutes. Turn the tofu once during baking.

Meanwhile, in a large, heavy kettle, heat the oil over low heat. Add the onions and sauté them, stirring occasionally, until tender. Add the flour and mix well. Raise the heat to medium-high, and cook, while stirring, for 1–2 minutes. Add the marinade and bring the sauce to a boil, stirring vigorously to keep it from lumping.

Add the tofu and stir. If the sauce becomes too thick, add water as necessary (approximately ¼ cup) to achieve the desired consistency.

Serve the baked tofu over rice or millet, accompanied by a steamed vegetable and a salad.

Yield: 4–6 servings
Marinating time: 1 hour or more
Preparation time: 15 minutes
Baking time: 35–40 minutes

Eggplant Lasagna Primavera

Like any lasagna, this one takes a few minutes to prepare, but it can be made in advance and reheated just before serving.

2 medium eggplants (approximately 1 pound each)
Sea salt
2 cups shredded soy cheese or dairy cheese

Sauce
4 large tomatoes
5–7 medium carrots
1 tablespoon olive oil
2 cups sliced carrots
1½ cups chopped onions
1 teaspoon basil
½ teaspoon oregano
4 cloves garlic, minced
⅓ cup TVP (textured vegetable protein)
1 can (6 ounces) tomato paste
½ teaspoon sea salt
Pinch cayenne pepper

Filling
1 bunch (¼ pound) spinach
1 pound firm tofu
1 teaspoon sea salt
2 cloves garlic, pressed

Preheat the oven to 350°F.

Cut the eggplants into round slices that are no more than ½ inch thick. Lightly sprinkle the slices with the salt and place them in a shallow baking dish. Let them sit undisturbed for 1–1½ hours to draw out excess moisture. Meanwhile, make the sauce and filling.

To make the sauce:

Cut the tomatoes into wedges. Cut the greens off the carrots. Juice the tomato wedges and reserve 2 cups of the juice. Juice the carrots and reserve 1 cup of the juice.

In a large, heavy kettle or skillet, heat the oil over low heat. Add the carrots, onions, basil, oregano, and garlic, and sauté, stirring occasionally, until the onions start to become tender, about 5 minutes. Add the tomato juice, carrot juice, and TVP, and simmer until the TVP is hydrated, about 5 minutes. Add the tomato paste, salt, and cayenne pepper, and mix well. Remove the kettle from the heat and set it aside.

To make the filling:

Juice the spinach and reserve all of the juice and all of the pulp.

In a large bowl, crumble the tofu. Add the spinach juice, spinach pulp, salt, and garlic; mix well. Set the bowl aside.

To assemble:

Remove the eggplant slices from the baking dish and briefly rinse them under running water to remove the salt. Pat the eggplant slices dry.

Oil a 9-by-13-by-2-inch baking dish. Spread just enough sauce over the bottom of the dish to lightly cover it. Layer half of the eggplant slices over the sauce, spread half of the filling over the eggplant, and cover the filling with half of the remaining sauce. Sprinkle 1 cup of the grated cheese over the sauce. Repeat the layers, ending with the sauce.

Bake the lasagna for 45 minutes. Sprinkle the remaining shredded cheese over the top and return the lasagna to the oven for an additional 15 minutes. Remove the lasagna from the oven and let it sit for about 15 minutes before slicing it.

Serve the lasagna with whole grain bread and a big green salad.

Yield: 6–8 servings
Preparation time: 1½ hours
Baking time: 1 hour
Cooling time: 15 minutes

Bulgur With Tomatoes and Squash

3–3½ large tomatoes
1 tablespoon olive oil
1 cup chopped onion
1 teaspoon basil
½ teaspoon oregano
3 cloves garlic, minced
1 red bell pepper, diced
1 medium zucchini, sliced
1 medium yellow squash, sliced
1 cup bulgur wheat
¼ cup water
1–2 tablespoons tamari
1 cup cooked and drained beans (chick peas, black beans, great northern beans, or another bean)
½ cup sliced pitted black olives

Cut the tomatoes into wedges, juice the wedges, and reserve 1¾ cups of the juice and all of the pulp.

In a large, heavy skillet, heat the olive oil over low heat. Add the onion, basil, oregano, and garlic, and sauté until the onion starts to become translucent, about 5 minutes. Add the bell pepper, zucchini, and yellow squash, and stir. Add the bulgur wheat and stir again.

In a small bowl, mix together the tomato juice, water, and tamari. Pour the mixture over the vegetables in the skillet. Cover the skillet and bring the mixture to a boil, then reduce the heat and simmer for about 10 minutes. Add the tomato pulp and continue to cook, covered, until most of the liquid has been absorbed and the bulgur is tender, about 10 minutes more.

Add the beans and olives, and mix well. Serve immediately.

Yield: 3–4 servings *Preparation time: 35 minutes*

Moroccan Stew

Looking for an unusually delicious recipe for your next dinner party? Serve this spicy stew with the Brightly Colored Couscous on ***page 232*** ***for an easy yet exotic meal. Let the couscous soak while you prepare the stew.***

2 large tomatoes
1–1⅓ pounds cabbage
2 tablespoons olive oil
1½ cups chopped onions
4 cups chopped white cabbage
2 cups sliced Jerusalem artichokes (sun chokes)
1½ cups chopped celery
1½ cups sliced carrots
1½ teaspoons cumin
3 bay leaves
3 tablespoons tamari
2 cups cooked and drained chick peas
½ teaspoon red pepper flakes
¼ teaspoon sea salt

Cut the tomatoes into wedges and the cabbage into chunks. Juice the tomato wedges and reserve 1 cup of the juice and all of the pulp. Juice the cabbage chunks and reserve 1 cup of the juice.

In a large, heavy kettle, heat the oil over low heat. Add the onions and sauté, stirring constantly, for 1–2 minutes. Add the white cabbage, Jerusalem artichokes, celery, carrots, cumin, and bay leaves; continue to sauté, stirring occasionally, for 3–4 minutes.

Add the tomato juice, cabbage juice, and tamari to the kettle and bring the mixture to a boil. Cover the kettle, reduce the heat, and simmer, stirring occasionally, until the vegetables are almost tender, about 45 minutes. Add the chick peas and simmer until the vegetables are tender, about 5 minutes.

Meanwhile, in a blender or food processor, combine the tomato pulp, red pepper flakes, and salt; blend briefly. Pour the hot sauce into a serving bowl.

Remove the bay leaves from the stew. Serve the stew either on a platter in the center of the table, with couscous and the hot sauce on the side, or on individual dinner plates, on a bed of couscous with the hot sauce on the side. Place a generous portion of couscous on a plate, make a well in the center of the couscous with the back of a spoon, and ladle the stew into the well.

Yield: *6 servings*
Preparation time: *75 minutes*

Double Tomato Pizza

The light, crisp crust of this pizza is made with tomato juice instead of water, and the topping uses the leftover tomato pulp.

Dough

2 large tomatoes
2 tablespoons olive oil
1 tablespoon dry active yeast
½ teaspoon sea salt
⅓ cup gluten flour
2 cups whole wheat pastry flour

Topping

1 tablespoon olive oil
2 cups sliced sweet onion
6–12 cloves garlic, minced
2 cups sliced mushrooms
12 sun-dried tomato halves, cut into small pieces
2 tablespoons tamari
½ teaspoon oregano
¼ cup minced fresh basil

To make the dough:

Cut the tomatoes into wedges, juice the wedges, and reserve 1 cup of the juice. Set aside all of the pulp for later use in the topping.

In a small saucepan, heat the tomato juice to lukewarm, stirring constantly; do not let it get hot. If the juice becomes hot, let it cool to warm before continuing.

In a large bowl, combine the warm juice, olive oil, yeast, and salt. Let the mixture sit undisturbed for 5–10 minutes to dissolve and proof the yeast.

Add the gluten flour to the yeast mixture in the bowl, then add 1 cup of the pastry flour; beat the mixture 100 strokes. Add as much of the remaining pastry flour as necessary to make a kneadable dough. (The dough is kneadable when it's too stiff to stir and begins to pull away from the sides of the bowl.) Knead in the remaining pastry flour to make a soft dough (see illustration on page 266). This dough is softer than a bread dough.

Transfer the kneaded dough to an oiled bowl and turn the dough in the bowl to oil it all around. Cover the bowl with a clean, damp cloth (see illustration) and let the dough rise in a warm place until it has doubled in bulk, about 45–60 minutes.

To make the topping:

In a large skillet, heat the oil over low heat. Add the onion and sauté for 2–3 minutes. Add the garlic and sauté until the onion starts to become tender, about 2–3 minutes more. Add the mushrooms and sun-dried tomato pieces, and sauté until the mushrooms are done, about 2–3 minutes. Add the leftover tomato pulp, tamari, and oregano, and let the mixture simmer for 1–2 minutes. Add the basil and mix well.

Remove the saucepan from the heat and let the topping cool while the dough finishes rising.

1. Combine all the dough ingredients and knead to make a soft dough for the crust.

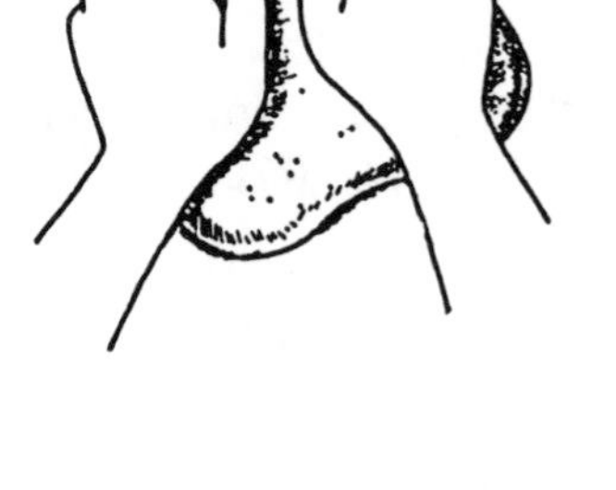

2. Put the kneaded dough in an oiled bowl, cover, and let double in bulk in a warm place.

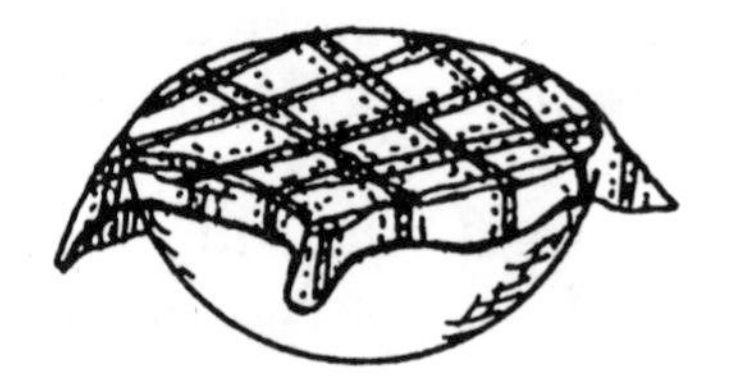

3. Press and stretch the risen dough until it covers the entire pizza sheet.

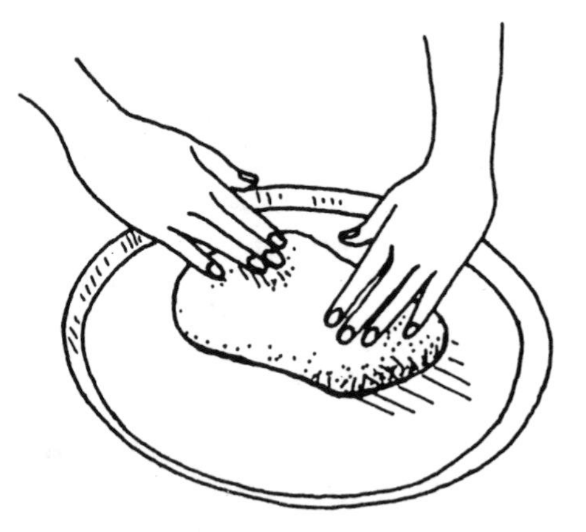

4. Spread the cooled topping over the dough, then bake.

To assemble the pizza:

Preheat the oven to 375°F.

Oil a round pizza sheet or a 15½-by-10½-inch cookie sheet. Place the risen dough on the sheet and, using your hands, press and stretch the dough until it evenly covers the entire surface of the sheet (see illustration).

Spread the partially cooled topping over the dough on the sheet in an even layer. Place the sheet in a warm spot and let the dough rise for 15 minutes.

Bake the pizza for 15 minutes on the bottom rack of the oven. To test the pizza for doneness, lift up a corner of the crust and look at the underside. It should be crispy and golden brown. Remove the pizza from the oven and serve it immediately.

Note:

Vicki has made this pizza with good results using whole wheat bread flour. With bread flour, you will probably need about ¼ cup less flour.

Variation:

Add sliced olives, grated soy cheese or dairy cheese, or just about any other standard pizza topping.

Yield: *4 servings*
Preparation time: *1½–2 hours*
Baking time: *15 minutes*

Almond Loaf

Beef loaf has nothing over this recipe.

3–4 medium carrots
1 pound firm tofu
1 cup raw almonds, coarsely ground
1 cup rolled oats
½ cup chopped onions
¼ cup plus 1 tablespoon tamari
2 tablespoons almond butter
1 tablespoon Dijon-style mustard
1 teaspoon sage
3 cloves garlic, pressed

Preheat the oven to 350°F.

Cut the greens off the carrots, juice the carrots, and reserve 1 cup of the pulp.

In a large bowl, mash the tofu with a fork. Add the carrot pulp, almonds, oats, onions, tamari, almond butter, mustard, sage, and garlic; mix well, using your hands if necessary.

Oil an 8½-by-4½-by-2½-inch loaf pan and sprinkle the sides and bottom with rolled oats. Pack the loaf mixture into the pan and bake it for 50 minutes. Let the loaf sit for a least 10 minutes before removing it from the pan. Unmold it onto a serving platter and slice it.

Serve the loaf with the Vegetable Cream Sauce on page 207 or with Dominique's Tomato Sauce on page 210.

Yield: *1 large loaf*
Preparation time: *20 minutes*
Baking time: *50 minutes*
Cooling time: *10 minutes*

Ratatouille

There are many recipes for ratatouille, but this low-fat version is especially good. The fresh tomato juice adds flavor, and the potato juice thickens the broth into a rich sauce.

2 large tomatoes
1 medium potato
1 tablespoon olive oil
1 cup chopped onion
6 cloves garlic, minced
1 large eggplant, diced
2 medium zucchini, sliced
3 cups sliced mushrooms
3 tablespoons tamari
1 teaspoon thyme
4 bay leaves

Cut the tomatoes into wedges and the potato into chunks. Juice the tomato wedges and reserve 1 cup of the juice and all of the pulp. Juice the potato chunks and reserve 1/3 cup of the juice.

In a large kettle, heat the oil over low heat. Add the onion and sauté for 2–3 minutes. Add the garlic and sauté until the onion starts to get tender, about 2–3 minutes more. Add the tomato juice, tomato pulp, eggplant, zucchini, mushrooms, tamari, thyme, and bay leaves; stir. Bring the mixture to a boil, then cover the kettle, reduce the heat, and simmer, stirring occasionally, until the vegetables are almost tender, about 20 minutes.

Add the potato juice to the kettle, stir, and bring the mixture to another boil. Reduce the heat and simmer until the vegetables are tender, about 3 minutes. Take the kettle off the heat and remove the bay leaves.

Serve the ratatouille over brown rice, millet, quinoa, or pasta. Accompany it with a green salad.

Variation:

Add ½–2 cups cooked and drained chick peas or great northern beans along with the potato juice.

Yield: *4–6 servings*
Preparation time: *1 hour*

Oilless Stir-Fry

This recipe is a variation of one in "Cooking With the Right Side of the Brain," by Vicki Rae Chelf. Fresh juice gives it extra flavor.

½ medium potato
3 stalks broccoli, florets removed
1-inch slice ginger root
3 cloves garlic
2 tablespoons tamari
2 cups broccoli florets
2 cups snow peas
6 ounces (approximately 3 cups) mung bean sprouts
2 scallions, chopped

Cut the potato into chunks, juice the chunks, and reserve ¼ cup of the juice. Juice the broccoli stems and reserve ⅓ cup of the juice. Juice the ginger root and garlic, and reserve all of the combined juice.

In a wok or large pan with a cover, combine the broccoli juice, ginger-garlic juice, and tamari. Add the broccoli florets and bring the juice to a boil, stirring constantly. Boil and stir the mixture over high heat for about 1 minute, then reduce the heat, cover the wok or pan, and simmer for 1–2 minutes. Raise the heat to high again, remove the cover, and add the snow peas; cook and stir for another 1–2 minutes. Then add the bean sprouts, and cook and stir for an additional 1–2 minutes. Cover the wok or pan, reduce the heat, and simmer until the vegetables are cooked but still crisp, about 1–3 minutes.

Stir the potato juice and add it to the wok. Cook and stir until the sauce boils and thickens, just a few seconds. Add the scallions and stir.

Serve the stir-fry over brown rice, millet, or noodles.

Note:

If the liquid evaporates too much during cooking, or if the sauce becomes too thick, add a little water.

Variations:

Either substitute or add other quick-cooking vegetables. Vegetables that work well with this cooking method are thinly sliced carrots, bell peppers, onions, and mushrooms.

Add preseasoned baked tofu, which is sold in most natural food stores. Cut the tofu into thin slices and add the slices along with the scallions.

Yield: *2 servings*
Preparation time: *20 minutes*

Desserts

The desserts in this section of *Cooking for Life* are treats that you can enjoy occasionally without feeling one ounce of guilt. They are made from whole grains, fresh fruits, juices, and other very wholesome ingredients. Both sweeteners (usually fruit concentrate) and fat (vegetable oil or nuts) are kept to a bare minimum, and, whenever possible, the fruits and juices are not cooked.

Have you ever bought a dessert at a health food store or restaurant and thought that it just didn't measure up tastewise to the good old desserts of your past? If so, you may have consoled yourself with the thought that "at least it's healthy."

With these desserts, you won't encounter such disappointment. These desserts are not just good compared to other healthy choices, they are really outstanding! So if you want to convince someone that healthy food can also be delicious, get out your mixing bowls and whip up a dessert made from fresh fruit and juices. If you want to go all out, make one of the cakes or pies in this section and top it off with one of our homemade sherbets. Have fun, and enjoy!

Carrot Cookies

A sweet way to use up some carrot pulp.

3–4 medium carrots
1 cup barley flour
1 cup rolled oats
1 cup raisins
½ cup dehydrated cane juice
¼ teaspoon nutmeg
⅓ cup safflower, sunflower, canola, or other light-flavored oil
1 egg, slightly beaten
2 teaspoons vanilla extract

Preheat the oven to 350°F.

Cut the greens off the carrots, juice the carrots, and reserve 1 cup of the pulp.

In a large bowl, combine the carrot pulp, barley flour, oats, raisins, dehydrated cane juice, and nutmeg; mix well. Add the oil and stir until the oil is blended in well. Add the egg and vanilla extract, and mix until the dough holds together.

Drop the dough by heaping tablespoons onto an oiled cookie sheet. Flatten each dollop with the palm of your hand or a fork dipped in water. Bake on the top rack of the oven until the cookies are golden brown on the bottom, about 8 minutes. Let the cookies cool, then place them in an airtight container for storage.

Yield: 14–18 cookies
Preparation time: 10 minutes
Baking time: 8 minutes

Tropical Squares

For an extra special treat, serve these with Coconut Sherbet. Make the sherbet first and use the leftover coconut pulp for this recipe.

1 coconut or 1 cup finely shredded unsweetened coconut
1 pineapple
1 cup pitted soft dried dates
½ cup fruit-sweetened orange marmalade
1 cup barley flour
1 cup whole grain bread crumbs
½ cup oat flour
¼ cup dehydrated cane juice
¼ cup safflower, sunflower, canola, or other light-flavored oil
1 tablespoon dehydrated cane juice

Preheat the oven to 350°F.

Drain the coconut, break it open, and remove the flesh from the shell. Peel and core the pineapple and cut it into strips. Juice the coconut pieces and reserve 1 cup of the pulp. Juice the pineapple strips with the dates and reserve ½ cup of the combined juice and all of the combined pulp. Be careful to keep the coconut juice and pulp separated from the pineapple-date juice and pulp.

In a large bowl, combine the pineapple-date pulp with the marmalade; mix well.

In another large bowl, combine the coconut pulp or shredded coconut, barley flour, bread crumbs, oat flour, and ¼ cup dehydrated cane juice. Add the oil and mix well. Add the pineapple-date juice and mix again.

Spread half of the dough in the bottom of an oiled 8-by-8-inch pan. Cover the dough with the pineapple-date pulp mixture.

Drop the remaining dough by spoonfuls at even intervals over the top of the pulp mixture and, using a rubber spatula, spread it out evenly to cover the surface. Sprinkle the 1 tablespoon of dehydrated cane juice over the top of the dough.

Bake for 35 minutes. Remove from the oven and let cool for at least 20 minutes. Cut into 8–10 squares and serve plain, with the Pineapple Sherbet on page 290, or with the Coconut Sherbet on page 297.

Yield: *8–10 squares*
Preparation time: *25 minutes*
Baking time: *35 minutes*
Cooling time: *20 minutes*

Piña Colada Cake

Pineapple and lightly toasted coconut are scrumptious in this cake.

1 coconut or ½ cup finely shredded unsweetened coconut
1 pineapple
2 tablespoons safflower, sunflower, canola, or other light-flavored oil
2 tablespoons dehydrated cane juice
1 cup barley flour
½ cup whole wheat pastry flour
½ cup dehydrated cane juice
1 tablespoon baking powder
2 tablespoons safflower, sunflower, canola, or other light-flavored oil
2 teaspoons vanilla extract
1 egg

Preheat the oven to 350°F.

Drain the coconut, break it open, and remove the flesh from the shell. Peel and core the pineapple and cut it into strips. Juice the coconut pieces and reserve ½ cup of the pulp. Juice the pineapple strips and reserve ¾ cup of the juice and all of the pulp.

In a small shallow pan, spread out the coconut pulp or shredded coconut. Place the pan in the oven until the coconut is lightly toasted, about 3–4 minutes. Watch the coconut carefully because it can burn quickly. Remove the pan from the oven and set it aside.

Oil an 8-by-8-inch cake pan with 2 tablespoons of oil, letting any excess oil rest in the bottom of the pan. Sprinkle the 2 tablespoons dehydrated cane juice in the bottom of the pan over the oil, then spread an even layer of the pineapple pulp over the dehydrated cane juice. Set the pan aside.

In a small bowl, sift together the barley flour, pastry flour, ½ cup dehydrated cane juice, and baking powder. Add the toasted coconut and mix well. Set the bowl aside.

In a large bowl, beat together 2 tablespoons of oil, the vanilla extract, and the egg. Add the pineapple juice and beat well. Add the flour mixture and beat just until combined.

Pour the batter into the cake pan over the pineapple pulp. Bake the cake until a toothpick inserted into the center comes out clean, about 25 minutes. Let the cake cool, then serve it plain or with the Pineapple Sherbet on page 290 or the Coconut Sherbet on page 297.

Yield: *One 8-by-8-inch cake*
Preparation time: *25 minutes*
Baking time: *25 minutes*

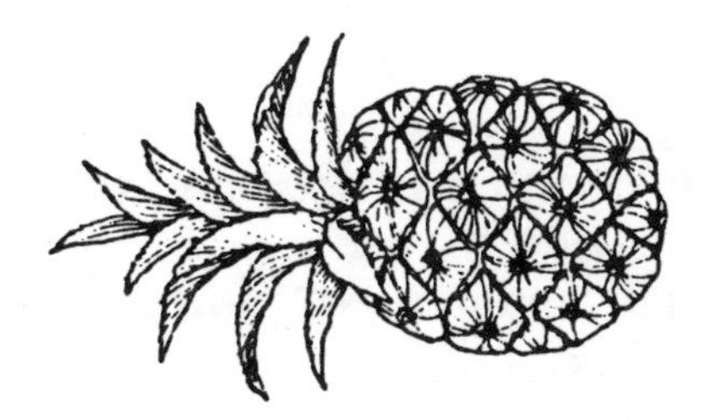

Carrot Cake

Vicki thought it would be easy to develop a recipe for carrot cake using carrot pulp, but it wasn't. It took five tries to get this recipe right, but everyone who samples this exceptional cake agrees that it was worth the trouble!

5–7 medium carrots
1-inch slice ginger root
1 cup barley flour
1 cup oat flour
1 tablespoon baking powder
1 tablespoon cinnamon
1 teaspoon baking soda
¼ teaspoon ground cloves
¼ cup safflower, sunflower, canola, or other light-flavored oil
1 egg
½ cup dehydrated cane juice
½ cup raisins
½ cup walnuts or pecans, chopped
⅓ cup soy milk

Cut the greens off the carrots, juice the carrots, and reserve 1 cup of the juice and 1 cup of the pulp. Juice the ginger root and reserve all of the juice.

In a small bowl, sift together the barley flour, oat flour, baking powder, cinnamon, baking soda, and cloves. Set the bowl aside.

In a large bowl, beat together the oil and egg. Add the dehydrated cane juice and beat again. Add the carrot juice and ginger juice, and stir. Add the carrot pulp, raisins, walnuts or pecans, and soy milk, and mix well. Add the flour mixture and beat just until combined.

Pour the batter into an oiled and floured 10-inch cast-iron skillet. Bake the cake until a toothpick inserted into the center comes out clean, about 35 minutes. Let the cake cool, then frost it with a Carrot Cake Icing from page 280, if desired.

Yield: *One 10-inch round cake*
Preparation time: *20 minutes*
Baking time: *35 minutes*

Pink Raspberry Icing

This elegant icing is a perfect mate for the Beet Cake on page 281.

¼ medium beet
1 cup tofu cream cheese
⅔–1 cup fruit-sweetened seedless raspberry jam

Cut the beet into chunks, juice the chunks, and reserve 1 tablespoon of the juice.

In a blender or food processor, combine the beet juice, tofu cream cheese, and 2/3 cup of the jam; blend until smooth and creamy. Add the remainder of the jam if a sweeter icing is desired. If necessary, use a rubber spatula to scrape the sides of the blender or food processor to make sure that all of the ingredients are well blended.

Spread the icing over a cooled cake.

Yield: *1 2/3–2 cups*
Preparation time: *10 minutes*

Carrot Cake Icing

These fruit-sweetened icings really do taste better than the standard cream cheese icing that is typically spread over carrot cake. Try both variations to see which one you like the best.

Icing #1
1 medium carrot
1 cup tofu cream cheese
1 jar (10 ounces) fruit-sweetened apricot-pineapple jam

Icing #2
1 medium carrot
1 cup tofu cream cheese
⅔ cup fruit-sweetened orange marmalade

For both variations, trim the greens from the carrot. Juice the carrot and reserve 2 tablespoons of the juice for Icing #1 and 1½ tablespoons of the juice for Icing #2.

In a blender or food processor, combine the carrot juice, tofu cream cheese, and jam or marmalade; blend until smooth and creamy. If necessary, use a rubber spatula to scrape the sides of the blender or food processor to make sure that all of the ingredients are blended.

Spread the icing over a cooled carrot cake or other cake.

Note:

The carrot juice adds a beautiful pale orange color to the icing. However, it also gives it a thinner consistency, which Vicki likes. If you prefer an icing that is thicker and more like a standard cream cheese icing, reduce or omit the carrot juice.

Yield: 1⅔ cups
Preparation time: 10 minutes

Beet Cake

Why not? This cake is pretty, pink, and absolutely delicious.

2 medium beets
1 package (10½ ounces) extra firm silken tofu
½ cup fruit concentrate
¼ cup safflower, sunflower, canola, or other light-flavored oil
1 teaspoon vanilla extract
1 cup whole wheat pastry flour
1 cup barley flour
1 tablespoon baking powder
1 teaspoon allspice
1 cup raisins

Preheat the oven to 350°F.

Cut the beets into chunks. Juice the beet chunks and reserve ½ cup of the juice and ½ cup of the pulp.

In a blender or food processor, combine the beet juice, silken tofu, fruit concentrate, oil, and vanilla extract; blend until smooth and creamy. If necessary, use a rubber spatula to scrape the sides of the blender or food processor to make sure that all of the ingredients are well blended. Pour the mixture into a large bowl.

In a medium-size bowl, sift together the pastry flour, barley flour, baking powder, and allspice. Add the flour mixture to the tofu mixture and beat with a wooden spoon until well blended. Fold in the beet pulp and raisins. (The batter will be thick.)

Spread the batter in an oiled and floured 8-by-8-inch baking pan. Bake the cake until a toothpick inserted into the center comes out clean, about 35 minutes. Let the cake sit in the pan for about 10 minutes, then turn it out onto a serving plate. Serve it warm and plain, or cooled and frosted with the Pink Raspberry Icing on page 279.

Yield: One 8-by-8-inch cake
Preparation time: 25 minutes
Baking time: 35 minutes
Cooling time: 10 minutes

Graham Cracker Crust

A crisp yet tender pie crust easy enough for anyone to make.

1 package (1/4 pound) graham crackers, broken into pieces
1/2 cup whole wheat pastry flour
1/2 cup pecans
3 tablespoons safflower, sunflower, canola, or other light-flavored oil
3 tablespoons water

Preheat the oven to 350°F.

In a food processor, grind the graham crackers, flour, and pecans to a powder. Add the oil and process for a few seconds more. Add the water and process again for a few seconds.

Transfer the mixture to a 9-inch pie pan and press it firmly onto the sides and bottom. Bake the pie crust for 20 minutes. Remove the pan from the oven and let the crust cool before filling it, about 1 hour.

Yield: One 9-inch pie crust
Preparation time: 15 minutes
Baking time: 20 minutes
Cooling time: 1 hour

Strawberry Kanten Cake

Though no more complicated than the average recipe, this cake takes a little bit longer to make—but it's well worth the time.

Cake

½ pint strawberries
1 cup barley flour
1 cup oat flour
1 tablespoon baking powder
½ cup fruit concentrate
¼ cup safflower, sunflower, canola, or other light-flavored oil
1 egg
1 teaspoon vanilla extract

Custard

⅓ pint strawberries
⅓ cup fruit concentrate
1 tablespoon agar flakes
1 teaspoon vanilla extract
1 package (10½ ounces) extra firm silken tofu

Topping

3 medium apples
½ pint strawberries
1-inch cube beet, for coloring
¼ cup fruit concentrate
1 tablespoon agar flakes
1½ cups strawberries, sliced, caps removed, as garnish

To make the cake:

Preheat the oven to 350°F.

Juice the ½ pint of strawberries and reserve ½ cup of the juice.

In a medium-size bowl, sift together the barley flour, oat flour, and baking powder. Set the flour mixture aside.

In a large bowl, mix the ½ cup fruit concentrate, oil, egg, and 1 teaspoon vanilla extract. Add the strawberry juice and mix well. Add the flour mixture and beat just until combined.

Pour the batter into a well-oiled and floured 8-by-8-inch baking dish. Bake the cake until a toothpick inserted into the center comes out clean, about 20–25 minutes. Let the cake cool to room temperature in the baking dish, at least 2 hours.

To make the custard:

Juice the ⅓ pint strawberries and reserve ⅓ cup of the juice.

In a small saucepan, combine the strawberry juice, ⅓ cup fruit concentrate, 1 tablespoon agar flakes, and 1 teaspoon vanilla extract. Bring the mixture to a boil, then reduce the heat, cover the saucepan, and simmer, stirring occasionally, until the agar flakes are completely dissolved, about 5–10 minutes.

Meanwhile, in a blender or food processor, blend the silken tofu until smooth and creamy. If necessary, use a rubber spatula to scrape the sides of the blender or food processor to make sure that all of the tofu is processed. Add the agar mixture and blend again.

When the cake has cooled to room temperature, spread the custard over the top and refrigerate the cake until chilled, about 1 hour.

To make the topping:

Cut the apples into wedges and remove the seeds. Juice the apple wedges and reserve ¾ cup of the juice. Juice the ½ pint strawberries and reserve ½ cup of the juice. Juice the beet and reserve all of the juice.

In a small saucepan, combine the apple juice, strawberry juice, and beet juice. Add the ¼ cup fruit concentrate and 1 tablespoon agar flakes, and stir. Bring the mixture to a boil, then cover the saucepan, reduce the heat, and simmer, stirring occasionally, until the agar flakes are completely dissolved, about 5–10 minutes. Let the mixture cool at room temperature for about 15 minutes.

Decorate the top of the chilled cake with the sliced strawberries (use as many berries as necessary to cover the cake). Gently pour the agar mixture over the berries and refrigerate the cake until the topping is firm, about 1 hour.

To serve the cake, cut it into 9 squares.

Yield: *One 8-by-8-inch cake*
Preparation time: *1 hour*
Baking time: *20–25 minutes*
Chilling time: *4 hours*

Apple-Cinnamon Upside-Down Cake

3 medium apples
2 tablespoons safflower, sunflower, canola, or other light-flavored oil
½ cup walnuts or pecans, coarsely ground
2 tablespoons maple syrup
1 large Rome apple, cored and cut into thin wedges
1 cup barley flour
½ cup oat flour
1 tablespoon baking powder
1 tablespoon cinnamon
1 egg, slightly beaten
¼ cup safflower, sunflower, canola, or other light-flavored oil
⅓ cup maple syrup

Preheat the oven to 350°F.

Cut the 3 apples into wedges and remove the cores. Juice the apple wedges and reserve 1 cup of the juice and ½ cup of the pulp.

Oil an 8-by-8-inch baking dish with the 2 tablespoons of oil. Sprinkle the ground nuts in the bottom of the baking dish over the oil, then drizzle the 2 tablespoons maple syrup over the nuts. Arrange the Rome apple wedges over the syrup. Set the baking dish aside.

In a small bowl, sift together the barley flour, oat flour, baking powder, and cinnamon. Set the bowl aside.

In a large bowl, combine the apple pulp, egg, ¼ cup oil, and ⅓ cup maple syrup; beat well. Add half of the apple juice and beat again. Add the flour mixture and mix quickly. Add the remaining apple juice and beat until the batter is well blended; do not overbeat. Pour the batter into the baking dish over the apple wedges.

Bake the cake until it springs back when lightly pressed and a toothpick inserted into the center comes out almost clean, about 40–45 minutes. Let the cake cool for at least 20 minutes, then cut it into 9 squares. For a delightful dessert, serve the cake slightly warm with the Lemon Sherbet on page 296. The tart sherbet contrasts wonderfully, making the cake seem sweeter.

Yield: *One 8-by-8-inch cake*
Preparation time: *30 minutes*
Baking time: *40–45 minutes*

Strawberry-Rhubarb Pie

A perennial favorite.

1 recipe Pecan Pie Crust (page 288)
2 large apples
¼ pint strawberries
2 cups chopped rhubarb
1 heaping tablespoon agar flakes
½ cup honey or fruit concentrate
1 cup strawberries, sliced, caps removed

Make one 9-inch Pecan Pie Crust and let it cool.

Cut the apples into wedges and remove the seeds. Juice the strawberries and pour all of the juice into a 1-cup measure. Juice the apple wedges and add enough of the juice to the strawberry juice to make 1 cup.

In a large, heavy saucepan, combine ⅓ cup of the strawberry-apple juice with the chopped rhubarb and agar flakes. Bring the mixture to a boil, then cover the saucepan and reduce the heat. Simmer, stirring occasionally, until the rhubarb is tender and the agar flakes are dissolved, about 10–12 minutes.

In a large bowl, combine the cooked rhubarb mixture, remaining ⅔ cup of the juice, and honey or fruit concentrate; mix well. Carefully fold in the sliced strawberries. Pour the mixture into the cooled pie crust and chill the pie until the filling is set, about 2 hours.

Yield: One 9-inch pie
Preparation time: 20 minutes
Chilling time: 2 hours

Pecan Pie Crust

A light, crisp, and tender crust.

¾ cup whole wheat pastry flour
¾ cup oat flour
½ cup pecans
¼ cup minus 1 teaspoon safflower, sunflower, canola, or other light flavored oil
2 tablespoons water

Preheat the oven to 350°F.

In a food processor, process the pastry flour, oat flour, and pecans until the nuts are finely ground. Slowly add the oil while the blade is working and blend briefly, just until the oil is mixed in. Transfer the flour mixture to a bowl and stir in just enough of the water to make the dough hold together. Mix the dough only until the water is incorporated; do not overmix.

Place the dough between two sheets of wax paper and roll it out. (To keep the wax paper from slipping on the table or countertop, lightly sprinkle the table or counter with water before laying the paper on it.) Peel off the top piece of paper, then carefully pick up the bottom piece with the dough, turn the dough paper side up into a pie pan, and peel off the remaining paper. Flute the edges of the crust and pierce the sides and bottom with the tines of a fork to prevent the dough from bubbling up during baking. Bake the crust until golden brown, about 20 minutes. For a crispier crust, let the crust cool before filling it, about 1 hour.

Yield: *One 9-inch pie crust*
Preparation time: *10 minutes*
Baking time: *20 minutes*
Cooling time: *1 hour*

Fresh Coconut Cream Pie

Rich and creamy, but not nearly as rich as a traditional coconut cream pie.

1 coconut
1 recipe Coconut Pie Crust (page 294)
Soy milk
½ cup fruit concentrate
1 tablespoon agar flakes
2 teaspoons vanilla extract

Preheat the oven to 350°F.

Drain the coconut and strain the milk through a fine wire sieve to remove any pieces of shell that may have fallen into it. Set aside the strained milk for later use. Break the coconut open and remove the flesh from the shell. Juice the coconut flesh and reserve all of the juice and ½ cup of the pulp.

Make one 9-inch Coconut Pie Crust and let it cool.

Meanwhile, in a shallow baking dish, evenly distribute the coconut pulp in a thin layer. Place the coconut pulp in the oven and bake, stirring occasionally, until the coconut is lightly toasted, about 20 minutes. Remove the toasted coconut from the oven and let it cool.

In a large measuring cup, combine the coconut juice with the coconut milk. Add enough of the soy milk to make 2½ cups.

In a large saucepan, combine the coconut juice mixture with the fruit concentrate, agar flakes, and vanilla extract. Bring the mixture to a boil, stirring constantly, then cover the saucepan, reduce the heat, and simmer, stirring occasionally, until the agar flakes are completely dissolved, about 5–10 minutes.

In a blender or food processor, blend the filling just until combined, no more than a few seconds. Let the filling sit, uncovered, at room temperature for about 15 minutes.

Pour the filling mixture into the baked and cooled pie crust. Sprinkle the toasted coconut over the top of the pie, and refrigerate the pie until the filling is firm, about 3 hours.

Serve the pie plain or with the Pineapple Sherbet, below.

Yield: *One 9-inch pie*
Preparation time: *20 minutes*
Chilling time: *3 hours*

Pineapple Sherbet

1 pineapple
¼ cup fruit concentrate
2 teaspoons vanilla extract

Peel and core the pineapple and cut it into strips. Juice the pineapple strips and reserve 2 cups of the juice and 1 cup of the pulp.

In a medium-size bowl, combine the pineapple juice, pineapple pulp, fruit concentrate, and vanilla extract; mix well. Pour the mixture into a shallow metal or plastic dish and freeze until solid, about 3–4 hours.

Using a metal spatula, break the frozen sherbet into chunks. In a food processor, blend the chunks until smooth and creamy. Stop the food processor occasionally to scrape the sides and stir the sherbet.

Serve the sherbet immediately or return it to the freezer in a covered container for storage.

Yield: *6–8 servings*
Preparation time: *15 minutes*
Freezing time: *3–4 hours*

Strawberry Pie

This has to be the world's best strawberry pie . . . and the healthiest!

1 recipe Graham Cracker Crust (page 282)
2 pints strawberries, chilled, sliced, caps removed
3 medium apples
1-inch cube beet, for coloring
¼ cup fruit concentrate
1 heaping tablespoon agar flakes

Make one 9-inch Graham Cracker Crust and let it cool.

Fill the cooled pie crust with sliced strawberries. Set aside the leftover strawberries for later use and place the filled pie crust in the refrigerator.

Cut the apples into wedges and remove the seeds. Juice the apple wedges and reserve 1 cup of the juice. Juice the leftover strawberries with the beet and reserve all of the combined juice.

In a small bowl, combine the apple juice with the strawberry-beet juice; stir.

In a small saucepan, combine ½ cup of the juice with the fruit concentrate and agar flakes. Bring the mixture to a boil, then cover the saucepan, reduce the heat, and simmer until the agar flakes are dissolved, about 5–10 minutes.

Add the agar mixture to the remaining juice in the small bowl and mix well. Remove the filled pie crust from the refrigerator and pour the mixture over the strawberries. Immediately return the pie to the refrigerator and chill until the filling is firm, about 3 hours.

Serve the pie plain or with the Strawberry Sherbet on page 295.

Yield: *One 9-inch pie*
Preparation time: *30 minutes*
Chilling time: *3 hours*

No-Bake Pineapple Pie With Graham Crust

Fruit-sweetened, fresh, and wonderful.

1 pineapple
1 cup chopped dried dates
1 cup water
1 heaping tablespoon agar flakes
1 teaspoon vanilla extract
1 package (1/4 pound) graham crackers, broken into pieces
1 cup walnuts

Peel and core the pineapple and cut it into strips. Juice the pineapple strips and reserve all of the juice and all of the pulp.

In a medium-size bowl, combine the dates, water, agar flakes, and vanilla extract. Bring the mixture to a boil, then reduce the heat and simmer, stirring occasionally, until the agar flakes are dissolved and the dates have formed a purée.

Meanwhile, in a food processor, combine the graham crackers and walnuts. Process them until the graham crackers are in crumbs and the nuts are ground. Add 1/3 cup of the cooked date mixture to the food processor and process the dough again.

Transfer the dough to a lightly oiled 9-inch pie pan. Using your hands, press the dough onto the sides and bottom of the pan. Set the pan aside.

In a large bowl, combine the pineapple juice and pineapple pulp. Add the remaining cooked date mixture and mix well. Pour the mixture into the pie crust and chill until the filling is set, about 2–3 hours.

Note:

The no-bake pie crust made with this recipe is softer and chewier than a conventional crust. For a crispy crust, substitute either the Graham Cracker Crust on page 282 or Coconut Pie Crust on page 294. The 1/3 cup of date mixture that is added to the no-bake crust can be added to the filling instead.

Yield: One 9-inch pie *Preparation time: 30 minutes*
Chilling time: 2–3 hours

Melon-Mint Sherbet

1 cantaloupe
1 cup fresh mint, tightly packed
2 tablespoons honey

Cut the cantaloupe into strips. Juice the cantaloupe strips with the mint and reserve all of the combined juice.

In a medium-size bowl, combine the cantaloupe-mint juice and honey. (If the honey is too thick to mix with the juice, mix the honey with a little juice in a blender first.) Stir the mixture well, then pour it into a shallow metal or plastic dish and freeze until solid, about 3–4 hours.

Using a metal spatula, break the frozen sherbet into chunks. In a food processor, blend the chunks until smooth and creamy. Stop the food processor occasionally to scrape the sides and stir the sherbet.

Serve the sherbet immediately or return it to the freezer in a covered container for storage.

Yield: 6–8 servings *Preparation time: 15 minutes*
Freezing time: 3–4 hours

Coconut Pie Crust

A tropical base for your pies.

1 coconut or ½ cup finely shredded unsweetened coconut
1 package (¼ pound) graham crackers, broken into pieces
½ cup whole wheat pastry flour
¼ cup safflower, sunflower, canola,
or other light-flavored oil
¼ cup water

Preheat the oven to 350°F.

Drain the coconut, break it open, and remove the flesh from the shell. Juice the coconut flesh and reserve ½ cup of the pulp.

In a food processor, grind the graham crackers into fine crumbs. Transfer the crumbs to a small bowl and add the coconut pulp or shredded coconut. Add the flour and mix well. Add the oil and mix with a fork until the oil is well distributed. Add the water and mix again.

Transfer the mixture to a 9-inch pie pan and press it firmly onto the sides and bottom. Bake the pie crust for 20 minutes. Remove the pan from the oven and let the crust cool before filling it, about 1 hour.

Yield: *One 9-inch pie crust*
Preparation time: *15 minutes*
Baking time: *20 minutes*
Cooling time: *1 hour*

Strawberry Sherbet

Pretty and pink.

1 pint strawberries
2 apples
1 pear
¼ cup fruit concentrate

Remove the caps from the strawberries. Cut the apples and pear into wedges. Juice the strawberries and reserve all of the juice and all of the pulp. Juice the apple wedges with the pear wedges and reserve all of the combined juice.

In a medium-size bowl, combine the strawberry juice, strawberry pulp, and apple-pear juice. Add the fruit concentrate and mix well. Pour the mixture into a shallow metal or plastic dish and freeze until solid, about 4 hours.

Using a metal spatula, break the frozen sherbet into chunks. In a food processor, blend the chunks until smooth and creamy. Stop the food processor occasionally to scrape the sides and stir the sherbet.

Serve the sherbet plain or with the Strawberry Sauce on page 218. Store the sherbet in a covered container in the freezer.

Yield: *6–8 servings*
Preparation time: *15 minutes*
Freezing time: *4 hours*

Lemon Sherbet

Like frozen lemonade, only better.

9 medium apples
2 lemons
5–6 tablespoons honey

Cut the apples into wedges and remove the seeds. Cut the lemons into wedges. Juice the apple wedges and reserve 2¾ cups of the juice. Juice the lemon wedges and reserve ½ cup of the juice.

In a medium-size bowl, combine the apple juice, lemon juice, and honey; mix well. Pour the mixture into a shallow metal or plastic dish and freeze until solid, about 3–4 hours.

Using a metal spatula, break the frozen sherbet into chunks. In a food processor, blend the chunks until smooth and creamy. Stop the food processor occasionally to scrape the sides and stir the sherbet.

Serve the sherbet alone or with the Apple-Cinnamon Upside-Down Cake on page 285. Store the sherbet in a covered container in the freezer.

Yield: *6–8 servings*
Preparation time: *15 minutes*
Freezing time: *3–4 hours*

Coconut Sherbet

This won't stay around long.

1 coconut
1/3 cup fruit concentrate
2 teaspoons vanilla extract
Soy milk

Drain the coconut and strain the milk through a fine wire sieve to remove any pieces of shell that may have fallen into it. Set aside the strained milk for later use. Break the coconut open and remove the flesh from the shell. Juice the coconut flesh and reserve all of the juice and 1 cup of the pulp.

In a large measuring cup, combine the strained coconut milk with the coconut juice. Add the fruit concentrate and vanilla extract, then add enough of the soy milk to make 2 cups. Pour the mixture into a shallow metal or plastic dish and add the coconut pulp; mix well. Freeze the mixture until solid, about 3–4 hours.

Using a metal spatula, break the frozen sherbet into chunks. In a food processor, blend the chunks until smooth and creamy. Stop the food processor occasionally to scrape the sides and stir the sherbet.

Serve the sherbet immediately or return it to the freezer in a covered container for storage.

Yield: *6–8 servings*
Preparation time: *20 minutes*
Freezing time: *3–4 hours*

Orange-Amazake Sherbet

Add an exotic touch to your meal with this exceptional sherbet.

3 medium oranges
½ cup amazake
1 teaspoon vanilla extract

Peel the oranges and cut them into wedges. Juice the orange wedges and reserve 1½ cups of the juice.

In a medium-size bowl, combine the orange juice, amazake, and vanilla extract; mix well. Pour the mixture into a shallow metal or plastic dish and freeze until solid, about 3–4 hours.

Using a metal spatula, break the frozen sherbet into chunks. In a food processor, blend the chunks until smooth and creamy. Stop the food processor occasionally to scrape the sides and stir the sherbet.

Serve the sherbet plain or with the Orange Sauce on page 216. Garnish each serving with a twist of fresh orange, if desired.

Store the sherbet in a covered container in the freezer.

Yield:	*6–8 servings*
Preparation time:	*15 minutes*
Freezing time:	*3–4 hours*

PART THREE

The Plans

Menu Ideas

Cooking with juice and pulp truly enables cooks to expand their culinary repertoires and to create colorful, highly nutritious menus for entertainment as well as everyday meals. Listed below are just a few of our favorite meals using the recipes in this book.

Included in some of the menus for everyday meals is a green salad. This is simply a salad made of fresh leafy lettuce or a mixture of whichever seasonal tender greens (such as lettuce, arugula, watercress, kale, or spinach) are available. Just wash and dry the greens, tear them into bite-size pieces, and serve them with the dressing of your choice.

Menus for Entertaining

When planning a dinner party, be sure to check each recipe for its approximate yield. If necessary, double the recipes.

Some of Vicki's favorite dishes for entertaining are the pretty and refreshing aspics in the Salads section. Serve one of these aspics, with its suggested sauce, as a first course. Homemade breads or savory muffins are always appreciated by Cherie's dinner guests, as are delectable spreads or pâtés served with whole grain crackers.

For a wonderful finale for your special dinner, serve one of our sumptuous desserts. Impress your guests with a pie or cake and some homemade sherbet.

Spring

Ginger Hopper
Spinach and Romaine With Ginger-Peach Vinaigrette
Springtime Pasta
Strawberry-Rhubarb Pie

Summer

Cold Cucumber Cream
Moroccan Stew with Brightly Colored Couscous
Melon-Mint Sherbet

Fall

Vegetable Cream Soup
Green Cornbread
Lentil Burgers with Dominique's Tomato Sauce
Orange-Almond-Green Salad With Orange-Herb Dressing

Winter

Quick Carrot Soup
Savory Baked Tofu With Onions
Apple-Walnut-Cabbage Salad With Creamy Apple Juice Dressing
Beet Cake with Pink Raspberry Icing

Holiday

Carrot Bread
Beet Aspic
Onion Pie
Almond Loaf with Fat-Free Mushroom Sauce
Apple-Cinnamon Upside-Down Cake

Any or all of the following vegetable or grain side dishes:
Winter Squash Casserole
Orange Potatoes and Pink Potatoes with Green Sauce
Broccoli in Cream Sauce

Menus for Every Day

The following menus are for easy family meals. A simple, nutritious lunch can consist of a vegetable juice, a sandwich, and a salad. For sandwiches, use any of the spreads or pâtés, or try leftover veggie burgers or slices of leftover meatless loaf. Add mustard, tomato slices, thin onion slices, sprouts, a slice of soy cheese, or any other garnish you enjoy. For a different kind of sandwich, use chapati instead of sliced bread. Spread the chapati with your choice of filling, top them with finely chopped raw vegetables, and roll them up.

Soups are also perfect for lunch. Enjoy them with a sandwich or just some whole grain bread and a salad. Leftover pasta dishes, stews, grain dishes, salads, and vegetable dishes also make wonderful lunches. And what could be easier?

Some of the menus were created around one-dish meals. By just adding a simple green salad and a vegetable juice, you'll give your family a truly special meal.

Breakfast or Brunch

Australian Surprise
Muesli with low-fat dairy yogurt or soy yogurt
Apple-Cinnamon Muffins
Strawberry Patch Fruit Salad

Luncheon

Tomato-Basil Muffins
Vegetable Tureen with Sweet and Hot Pepper Sauce
Vegetable Quiche
Orange-Amazake Sherbet (or an assortment of sherbets) with Orange Sauce

Lunch

Veggie Combo
Carrot Sandwich Spread with lettuce or sprouts on whole grain bread
Cucumber Salad

Salad in a Glass
Mushroom-Onion Pâté with Dijon-style mustard, soy cheese, and lettuce on whole grain bread
Garden Gazpacho

Tofu Spread with lettuce and/or sprouts on whole grain bread
Green Tabouli

Carrot Cornbread, Green Cornbread, or Three-Grain Spicy Vegetable Muffins
Vegetable Cream Soup
Green salad

Dinner

Southwestern Cocktail
Carrot Cornbread
Black Bean Chili
Green salad

John's Zombie
Fettucini Rosé
Green salad

Carotene Cocktail
Cashew Croquettes with
Quick Tomato Sauce
Baked rice
Oriental Broccoli

Recipes for Common Health Problems

Many nutrients have been scientifically shown to help prevent, relieve, or cure certain ailments. The following is a brief review of the most common ailments along with the nutrients that have been found to benefit them. The recipes in this book that are rich in the recommended nutrients are also listed.

For more extensive descriptions of these common ailments plus an overview of an additional sixty-five conditions, several diet plans, and the references in the scientific literature that support these suggestions, see *Juicing for Life*, by Cherie Calbom and Maureen Keane (Avery Publishing Group, 1992).

Arthritis (Osteoarthritis)

The most beneficial nutrients for the treatment of osteoarthritis include niacinamide, pantothenic acid, vitamin C, vitamin E, methionine, copper, bioflavonoids, and bromelain. Ginger root has also been found to have anti-inflammatory properties.

Suggested recipes:
Pineapple-Ginger Express—vitamin C, bioflavonoids, bromelain, ginger root.
Grape-Pineapple Party—vitamin C, bioflavonoids, bromelain.

Ginger Hopper—ginger root.
Sweet Magnesium Smoothie—niacin, pantothenic acid, bioflavonoids.
Almond Loaf—vitamin E, copper, pantothenic acid.

Cancer

The most beneficial nutrients for both the prevention and treatment of cancer include beta-carotene, vitamin C, vitamin E, selenium, calcium, potassium, and chromium. Also, several foods have been identified as possessing cancer-fighting properties. These include garlic, onions, shiitake mushrooms, ginger root, and cruciferous vegetables (broccoli, Brussels sprouts, cauliflower, cabbage, kale, and turnips).

Suggested recipes:
Gabby Gourmet's Cocktail—beta-carotene, chromium, potassium, selenium.
Veggie Combo—beta-carotene, potassium.
Borscht—beta-carotene, onion, cabbage.
Carrot-Cabbage Salad With Pink Yogurt Dressing—beta-carotene, potassium, cabbage.
Spinach Loaf—vitamin E, chromium.
Onion Pie—onion.
Vegetable Quiche—beta-carotene, onion, broccoli.

Cholesterolemia (High Cholesterol)

Nutrients that have been shown to be helpful in lowering cholesterol include the B vitamins, vitamins C and E, chromium, copper, magnesium, potassium, selenium, and zinc. In addition, several foods have been found to have cholesterol-lowering properties. Cholesterol-lowering foods include carrot, apple, ginger root, orange, strawberry, onion, garlic, and beans.

Suggested Recipes:
Ginger Hopper—zinc, chromium, carrot, apple, ginger root.
Zippy Tomato Express—B vitamins, magnesium, potassium, vitamin C.
Black Bean Stew—beans, onion, carrot.

Diabetes Mellitus

The diet currently recommended as the best for reducing the symptoms and risks associated with diabetes is the modified high-carbohydrate plant-fiber diet (for a more detailed explanation of this diet, see *Juicing for Life*). Nutrients that have been shown to help diabetes include vitamin B_6, vitamin C, vitamin E, chromium, copper, magnesium, manganese, potassium, and zinc. A traditional remedy for diabetes calls for green beans as a restorative for the pancreas. Other foods shown to be helpful include garlic and onions. In general, consuming a large percentage of raw foods is recommended.

Suggested recipes:
Green Garden Cocktail—vitamin B_6, vitamin C, vitamin E, magnesium, manganese, potassium.
Three-Bean Juice—green beans.
Gazpacho Salad With Tomato and Lime Juice Marinade—raw foods.
Bulgur With Tomatoes and Squash—onion and garlic.

Diverticulitis

Current research shows that a high-fiber diet is essential for those suffering from diverticulitis. Oat bran is often recommended. Adding leftover pulp to recipes is an excellent way to get more fiber into your diet. Nutrients known to help diverticulitis include beta-carotene and vitamin K.

Suggested recipes:
Mineral Medley—beta-carotene, vitamin K.
Muesli—oats (add extra oat bran to the recipe for even more fiber).
Carrot Salad With Carrot Pulp and Creamy Carrot Juice–Yogurt Dressing—beta-carotene, fiber.
Spinach Loaf—beta-carotene, fiber.

Hypoglycemia

Nutrients that help prevent or relieve hypoglycemia include chromium and manganese. The diet that is recommended calls for foods high in complex carbohydrates and fiber such as beans, whole grain pasta, lentils, and split peas. In addition, foods containing insulin promoting factor, which improves glucose tolerance, are helpful. These foods include peanut butter, cloves, bay leaves, apple pie spice, cinnamon, and turmeric.

Suggested recipes:
Ginger Tea—glucose tolerance factor.
Black Bean Chili—complex carbohydrates and fiber.
Red Lentil Soup—complex carbohydrates and fiber.
Borscht—glucose tolerance factor.
Curry Cream Sauce—glucose tolerance factor.
Green Potatoes With Herbs—chromium.
Carrot-Potato Patties—glucose tolerance factor.
Almond Loaf—manganese.
Pasta With Peas and Mushrooms in Cream Sauce—complex carbohydrates and fiber.

Insomnia

Nutrients that help you sleep include niacin, vitamin B_6, magnesium, calcium, and folate. Also, celery and lettuce are traditional remedies for insomnia.

Suggested recipes:
Green Suprise—calcium.
Hot Tomato on Ice—niacin.
Jack and the Bean—lettuce.
Popeye's Garden Favorites—celery.
Easy Tomato-Vegetable Soup—magnesium.
Springtime Pasta—vitamin B_6, folate.

Menopausal Symptoms

Nutrients that have been shown to ameliorate menopausal symptoms include vitamin E, magnesium, calcium, and bioflavonoids. The diet designed to reduce menopausal symptoms calls for the consumption of foods from the soybean family, such as tofu, tempeh, soy milk, and soy cheese.

Suggested recipes:
Pink Plum Cooler—bioflavonoids.
Mineral Medley—calcium, magnesium.
Spaghetti With Tomato Sauce and Vegetarian Meatballs—vitamin E, soy products.
Curried Tempeh Croquettes—soy products.
Spinach Loaf—magnesium, soy products.
Vegetable Quiche—soy products.

Osteoporosis

Nutrients that help improve bone density include calcium, magnesium, boron, vitamin K and K_1, and vitamin D. Helpful foods are sesame seeds, which are rich in calcium; dark leafy greens, which are good sources of vitamin K and K_1; and sunflower seeds and mushrooms, which provide lots of vitamin D.

Suggested recipes:
Chlorophyll Cocktail—vitamin K and K_1.
Seven-Vegetable Cocktail—calcium, magnesium, vitamin K.
Green Garden Cocktail—vitamin K and K_1.
Mushroom-Onion Pâté—vitamin D.
Veggie Pâté—vitamin D.
Curried Tempeh Croquettes—calcium.

Premenstrual Syndrome

Nutrients that have been shown to relieve premenstrual syndrome (PMS) include beta-carotene, magnesium, bromelain, vitamin E, vitamin B_6, and riboflavin. Foods especially rich in vitamin E include sunflower seeds, almonds, wheat germ, and peanuts.

Suggested recipes:
Pineapple-Ginger Express—bromelain.
Grape-Pineapple Party—bromelain.
Bunny Hopper—beta-carotene.
Cherie's Spring Tonic—beta-carotene.
Watercress Express—beta-carotene.
Veggie Pâté—magnesium.

Vegetarian Burgers—vitamin E.
Carrot-Potato Patties—vitamin E.
Cashew Croquettes—magnesium.
Lentil Burgers—vitamin E.
Almond Loaf—magnesium, vitamin E.

Suggested Reading List

Calbom, Cherie, and Maureen Keane. *Juicing for Life: A Guide to the Health Benefits of Fresh Fruit and Vegetable Juicing.* Garden City Park, NY: Avery Publishing Group, 1992.

Chelf, Vicki Rae. *Arrowhead Mills Cookbook.* Garden City Park, NY: Avery Publishing Group, 1993.

Chelf, Vicki Rae. *Cooking With the Right Side of the Brain.* Garden City Park, NY: Avery Publishing Group, 1991.

Connor, Sonja, and William Connor. *The New American Diet.* New York: Simon and Schuster, 1989.

Diamond, Harvey, and Marilyn Diamond. *Fit for Life.* New York: Warner Books, 1985.

Katzen, Mollie. *Moosewood Cookbook.* Berkeley, CA: Ten Speed Press, 1977.

Kenton, Leslie, and Susannah Kenton. *Raw Energy.* London: Century Publishing, 1984.

Mitchell, Paulette. *The 15-Minute Vegetarian Gourmet.* New York: Collier Books, 1992.

Morningstar, Amadea. *The Ayurvedic Cookbook.* Wilmot,Wisconsin: Lotus Light Publications, 1990.

Robbins, John. *Diet for a New America.* Walpole, NH: Stillpoint Publishing, 1987.

Szekely, Deborah. *Vegetarian Spa Cuisine From Rancho LaPuerta.* Escondido, CA: Rancho LaPuerta, 1990.

Index

Cherie Calbom received her master's of science in nutrition from Seattle's Bastyr College. She is certified as a nutritionist in Washington State, and is a member of the American Nutritionists Association and the Society for Nutrition Education. In addition to her private practice, she has served as the clinical nutritionist for St. Luke Medical Center in Bellevue, Washington. Cherie is the author of several books and writes a monthly column in *Choices*. She conducts health seminars nationwide and has appeared on numerous television and radio shows. Cherie lives with her husband in Kirkland, Washington.

Vicki Rae Chelf is both an experienced natural food cooking instructor and an accomplished artist. She has owned and managed a health foods store, and has served as head chef in a natural foods restaurant. While living in Montreal, Vicki's natural food cooking classes gained her a great deal of media attention. Her popular cooking program gave rise to four cookbooks that were published in French. Over the years, these titles have become perennial bestsellers. After moving back to the States to pursue her interest in art, Vicki graduated from the Ringling School of Art and Design in Sarasota, Florida. Her work has been shown in galleries throughout the United States and abroad.